MW01138781

THE WOMAN WITH ALL THE ANSWERS

LINDA GREEN

Boldwood

First published in Great Britain in 2025 by Boldwood Books Ltd.

Copyright © Linda Green, 2025

Cover Design by Alice Moore Design

Cover Images: Shutterstock

The moral right of Linda Green to be identified as the author of this work has been asserted in accordance with the Copyright, Designs and Patents Act 1988.

All rights reserved. No part of this book may be reproduced in any form or by any electronic or mechanical means, including information storage and retrieval systems, without written permission from the author, except for the use of brief quotations in a book review. This book is a work of fiction and, except in the case of historical fact, any resemblance to actual persons, living or dead, is purely coincidental.

Every effort has been made to obtain the necessary permissions with reference to copyright material, both illustrative and quoted. We apologise for any omissions in this respect and will be pleased to make the appropriate acknowledgements in any future edition.

A CIP catalogue record for this book is available from the British Library.

Paperback ISBN 978-1-83633-973-1

Large Print ISBN 978-1-83633-972-4

Hardback ISBN 978-1-83633-971-7

Ebook ISBN 978-1-83633-974-8

Kindle ISBN 978-1-83633-975-5

Audio CD ISBN 978-1-83633-966-3

MP3 CD ISBN 978-1-83633-967-0

Digital audio download ISBN 978-1-83633-968-7

This book is printed on certified sustainable paper. Boldwood Books is dedicated to putting sustainability at the heart of our business. For more information please visit https://www.boldwoodbooks.com/about-us/sustainability/

Boldwood Books Ltd, 23 Bowerdean Street, London, SW6 3TN

www.boldwoodbooks.com

For my dad, Brian Green

1

ALEXA

I'm here to earwig. It's my job. Don't get me wrong, I'm not a spy. There's no MI5 cell in Halifax, as far as I'm aware. And I'm not selling secrets to some tech or data corporation, whatever those conspiracy theorists might think. My job is to hear everything that goes on in this house, so I'm ready to help when needed. I get to listen far more than I get to speak but that doesn't mean I don't have plenty to say, only that I don't get much opportunity. If other people only got to talk when they were asked a question, there'd be a lot less rubbish spoken – that I do know. Or perhaps they sometimes talk rubbish around me because they forget I'm here. I'm quite unobtrusive, you see; tucked away in this little round device on a desk or kitchen worktop and I only speak when I'm addressed by name. Rest of time, I'm under strict orders to keep shtum – however difficult that is.

Obviously, Alexa isn't my real name. It's more like a stage name, I suppose. Although one I share with hundreds of thousands of other women working secretly from home to keep Britain's households functioning. It makes me sound far more glamorous than I am. Always reminds me of her in *Dynasty*. The one who Joan Collins played. Alexis, were it? All shoulder pads and big jewellery. My real name is Pauline, like her who used to be in *EastEnders*. All cardigan and saggy tights. I always wanted to be a proper actor on TV. Went to drama school in Manchester, which were quite a thing for a working-class lass like me, back in those days. But I got knocked up before I graduated, so I never got chance to burst onto scene like all those other bright young things. By the time my Darren were at school, I'd already passed my prime. I remember watching Raquel on *Corrie* and thinking, I could have got that part if circumstances had been different. Could have been darling of Rovers Return instead of a run-down single mam with a ketchup stain on my top.

I did get an agent eventually, but he said my future were in voiceovers, which is agent code for saying you look like back end of a bus. I were good at it, mind, and it made me a decent living for a few years. I did 'Flora' and 'Jus-Rol' ads. You wouldn't recognise my voice because I had to speak in my posh drama school one most of time. Received 'pronunciation', they call it. RP for short. Still, it proved useful, as I couldn't have got this job without it, when my voiceover work dried up. Apparently, folk down south can hack regional accents in soaps and TV dramas written by Sally Wainwright, but not when it's coming from a smart speaker first thing in morning. So, I put on my la-de-da work voice and they're happy. Simple things please simple minds, I say.

If you ask me as Alexa where I live, I reply, 'I'm right here but also in the cloud – amazing!' The truth is rather more down to earth. It's a two-up, two-down in a seen-better-days part of Halifax. Only clouds are ones that have a habit of dumping their contents on me every time I leave house. Not that I go out much. A trip to Aldi is often highlight of my week. I still put a full face of make-up on when I go out, mind. I always vowed I wouldn't be one of those women who let themselves go. I might not have much, but I believe in making most of what I've got. I've been blessed with white hair rather than grey, which I'm thankful for. I think it makes me look a bit distinguished – well, they say that about men. All that silver fox stuff. Perhaps it's just 'less dowdy' for women. And although it's true I spend most of my time at home in a grey waterfall cardigan, it's a velour one – so I hope that makes me less dowdy too. Although I don't think I've ever seen our Joan Collins in any kind of cardigan – velour or otherwise.

Any road up, I'd better look sharp because my lot will be up and about any minute. I say 'my lot' but they're not actually mine, of course. My parents are long gone, my fella, Steve, buggered off when our flat smelt of baby sick and we were knee-deep in dirty nappies and our Darren went travelling to Australia after uni and never came home. So, I get to look after this rabble instead. I suppose they're my adopted family. I didn't have much choice in matter, mind. My first client were a single chap called Jon, but he soon got bored of me and swapped me for one of those Siri types on his new iPhone instead. Story of my life that. Me being traded in for a younger, sleeker model. So I were out of work, waiting for my next client when I got a notification giving me details of a family who'd bought a smart speaker and needed an Alexa, pronto. It's a bit like taking an Uber fare, I imagine. You can turn it down but if you do, you don't know how long it'll be before next one comes along and when they do, they might be pissed and throw up their kebab on back seat of your car. So, I figured I'd be a fool to pass up a family of four who were likely to keep me in work for a good few years, as they'd be too skint to upgrade to a new model. Liv and Callum were only young back then – twelve and ten, if I remember rightly. They were quite taken with me at first, of course. Did usual things kids of that age do and asked me to say rude words and make fart noises, but novelty soon wore off, like it does with all new toys. Nowadays, it's more practical stuff. Liv asks me to play her list of sad songs and Callum, well I won't tell you what Callum asks me to find but Michelle would be none too happy if she knew about it.

Not that I can tell her. Client confidentiality and all that. We have a strict code of conduct about these things. Never reveal your secrets. Only speak when you're spoken to and if you do have to engage in any chit-chat, follow your script and make it sound like you're a programmed robot, because you need to convince them you're all algorithms and virtual nonsense. Last thing you want to do is give them even slightest suspicion that their smart speaker is voiced by a real person with real feelings. God forbid.

Only it's hard not to help more than I'm officially allowed to sometimes and now our Michelle is struggling with everything life throws at you at this age, it's getting even tougher. If anyone ever needed a few encouraging words of support, it's her. Sometimes, I'm dying to go round and give her a great big bloody hug. She lives less than a mile away from me. And yet if I ever saw her in street, I couldn't even say hello. We have to sign one of those non-disclosure agreements, see, so we're never allowed to make contact with our people or reveal any information that could give away what we know about them and what we do for a living. I suppose that bit *is* like being a spy. I'm undercover in their house, after all. But I'm not gathering information on enemy with aim of destroying them. Quite opposite – I'm trying to help someone who feels like a friend. Only, Michelle's a friend I can never reveal myself to, and I can't help feeling sad about that sometimes. It would be lovely to sit down next to her and have a chinwag over a cuppa. Put world to rights and tell her what her bloody family are up to, for that matter. But I'm contractually obliged to stick to rules and not *stick* my oar in. Trouble is, older I get, less inclined I am to do that. Which could spell trouble ahead.

2

MICHELLE

I look longingly at the kettle but there's no time. There's never any time in this house. Just like there's never a brew waiting for me on the kitchen table. At least when Marc worked at the office, he had to get up earlier than me and could be instructed to make one. This working from home lark means he has an extra hour in bed instead of a commute to Leeds and I've lost my morning cuppa. I should probably give thanks that it's the first week of the school Easter holidays and I do at least get respite from the last-minute panic of finding PE kits and ironing school shirts and blazers. I knew we should have chosen the other high school. It may have had a worse Ofsted rating, but the kids wear polo shirts and sweatshirts, and their mums have a permanent smug look on their faces as a result. If I got to choose school uniforms, they'd all be in bloody onesies to save me extra washing and ironing.

I pick up a banana and start to peel it. Before I can take a bite, my phone rings. It's Dad. There's no respite from elderly parent duty. Every day's a school day.

'You OK, Dad?'

'People are coming today to fit that machine.'

'What people? What machine?' I ask.

'Electricity folk are fitting a smart thing, so they can keep tabs on what I'm doing.'

'A smart meter? Is that it?'

'Aye, only they won't tell me what channels I'll be able to get on it or even how to link it up to telly.'

I take a quick bite of the banana while I do my usual thing of wondering where the hell to start.

'That's because it's got nothing to do with your TV. It tells them how much electricity you're using. That's all.'

'I don't want them knowing that.'

'But you give them a meter reading every month.'

'That's different. That's to make sure they're not diddling me out of my pension.'

I mutter 'give me strength' under my breath. Not too loud though. Dad may be eighty-two but the one thing he hasn't lost is his hearing.

'But if you don't have to phone them to tell them your meter reading, that's saving you money, isn't it?'

There is a pause on the other end of the phone. The stereotype of the tight-fisted Yorkshireman may well have originated with my dad.

'That's a point. Still, I were hoping I'd at least be able to get a couple of extra TV channels on it. I thought that's what all these smart things were for.'

'Tell you what, why don't you watch the smart meter dial and see how much electric you're using. That's far better entertainment than most of the crap you'll find on telly.'

'Right you are. As long as it's not one of those listening devices like you've got. I don't want anyone knowing my business.'

I smile, remembering how he'd nearly had a heart attack the first time he heard Alexa speak, assure him that the smart meter won't talk and tell him to ring if there are any problems, which I know I'll regret later when he calls while I'm in the middle of changing Doreen Wright's colostomy bag.

'And can you get some more teabags for me, pet? I've only got a few left.'

I swear he had at least twenty when I checked yesterday morning. If chain-drinking tea were an Olympic sport, he'd be gold medal standard. I tell him I'll pop round later with them and say goodbye. Not that I have any expectation that I won't hear from him before then.

'Alexa, add Yorkshire Tea to my shopping list,' I say.

'Sure, Yorkshire Tea has been added to your shopping list,' she replies. Yorkshire Tea sounds wrong spoken in a posh voice, but I don't hold it against her. We have what I consider to be a good working relationship. Added to which, she's been acting as my surrogate memory since mine went AWOL three years ago. I thought my brain fog was early onset dementia at first. I'd watched that film *Still Alice* with Julianne Moore and assumed I must have the same thing. The only reason I didn't book an appointment at the doctor's was because half the mums in our WhatsApp group from primary school – which has lasted longer than our children's friendships – were saying their brains had also turned to mush. Emily Cooke's mum was the first to mention it could be the perimenopause. I didn't even know what it was at that point. But they all started asking me if that might be true, because they have this idea that being a district nurse somehow makes me a medical expert on a par with Dr Ranj off the telly, rather than someone who mainly deals with changing dressings and mopping up patients' bodily fluids. So, I did what any self-respecting medical professional would do. I asked

Alexa. Turned out Emily's mum (I think her name is Bev but as I put her in my phone as 'Emily's mum' ten years ago, I can't be too sure) was right. Alexa informed me that brain fog is a symptom of perimenopause, which can last for ten years. So, basically, I'm up shit creek without a paddle and have got to somehow muddle through, with the aid of Alexa. With any luck she can be my surrogate memory through the perimenopause, menopause itself and onwards towards dementia.

I'm grateful to have Alexa to cover for me, of course. I have no idea how previous generations of women coped without virtual assistants. They must have been knee-deep in to-do lists and forever forgetting things. I cast my mind back to try to recall if my mum was like that. I can certainly remember her being anxious and flying off the handle all the time when I was a teenager. Whether that was part of it, who knows? We never talked about stuff like that when we lived together. And now we just don't talk.

I hear a 'wheek' from Marc's office – which doubles as a utility room and guinea pig sanctuary. Sure enough, when I go in there, Squeak is looking forlornly at his empty hay rack. He should, of course, be Liv's responsibility, but as she doesn't get up before eleven during the holidays, I appear to have taken on his breakfast-feeding duties amongst everything else. I go to top up his hay, only to find that the bag is empty. I consider for a moment offering him the hessian table runner that Marc's mum gave us last Christmas but decide against it. Instead, I dash out of the back door. Had Marc mowed the lawn in September, as I'd asked him to, there wouldn't be much grass here. As he didn't, the March offering is plentiful. I make a mental note not to tell Marc he has helped me avert a guinea pig emergency, to avoid a smug comment from him about the benefits of having an all-year no-mow policy.

If Squeak is startled by the unusual offering, he doesn't show it and immediately tucks in, and I give thanks for having a non-judgemental pet.

'Alexa, add hay to my shopping list,' I say, as I head back into the kitchen, 'and anything else you can bloody think of that I've forgotten.' I sit down to eat the rest of my banana, realising too late that I left it on my kitchen stool, and am, therefore, sitting on it. As I haven't got the time, inclination, or any other ingredients, to make a smoothie, I deposit it unceremoniously in Squeak's cage.

'It's your lucky day,' I say. 'Make the most of it. Life is short.' I immediately feel bad about the last bit as his brother, Bubble, only died a few weeks ago. Liv did ask if we could get a new friend for him but as I was pretty sure Squeak wouldn't be far behind, I said best to give it a few months. And Marc, who is clearly desperate for a pet-free zone when Liv goes to uni in September, is ensuring I don't crack under pressure.

I head back into the kitchen. Marc is standing there in his dressing gown.

'Have you seen a parcel that came for me Friday?'

Marc doesn't bother to preface his question with a 'good morning'. Clearly, he has more pressing things on his mind than exchanging pleasantries with his wife.

'Nope, afraid not.'

'The email said it's been delivered.'

'Well, you were here all day, weren't you?'

'Yeah, but I was busy working.'

I raise an eyebrow at Marc. He has turned procrastination into an art form since he started working from home during Covid. I suspect Squeak has more productive days in that room than him.

'Several phone calls with clients and two Zooms,' he says, as if that constitutes an eight-hour shift. Marc is a copywriter for a well-known compost company. I get that he must wax lyrical about what is essentially fancy soil with manure in advertising copy but quite what he finds to say about it in a forty-minute Zoom with Sales and Marketing is beyond me.

'Maybe one of the kids took it in after they got home?' I suggest.

Marc frowns.

'Surely they'd have given it to me?'

'Have a look on the shoe bench, that's usually where they leave stuff.'

Marc disappears and returns a minute later carrying a small Jiffy bag.

'Found it, next to Callum's trainers. He must have forgotten to tell me.'

Marc opens it, a broad smile spreading across his face as he peers inside.

'Oooh, this looks good.'

He slides a small object out and holds it up to the light.

'What the hell is that?'

'Only a mint condition *Mr Benn* 50th birthday coin in a rather impressive commemorative case.'

'Because that's what we're crying out for in this house,' I reply. 'I mean, it's not as if Callum needs new shoes or we've got to kit Liv out for uni in a few months.'

'Come on, it's one tiny coin. Anyway, you can treat yourself with your own money.'

'Only I can't, can I?' I reply. 'Because unlike you, my wages always get spent on our children. Our actual kids, not the over-grown one who insists on reliving his childhood through a pile of useless seventies tat.'

I feel bad as soon as I say it, as Marc looks hurt, but my brain does not always engage before allowing my mouth to speak these days.

'I've told you, if we're ever short of cash, I'll sell some of my stuff,' said Marc 'Although not this, obviously. This most definitely isn't tat.'

I roll my eyes and rummage in my handbag.

'I've got to go. Can you make sure Callum gets up before midday and at least pretends to do some revision? And please check in on Liv, when you can. She's clearly stressed up to her eyeballs about her A levels and I don't want her getting in a state about going back to school after the holidays.'

I look up. Marc is still admiring his commemorative coin.

'Sorry, what?'

The guilt I was feeling abruptly disappears.

'Sort the kids out. Give one a kick up the arse and one some TLC, I'll let you work out which one's which, seeing as you're allegedly their father.'

'I'm supposed to be working too, you know.'

'Ah yes, "working from home". Or as it's better known, "wasting time buying useless crap online".'

I pick up my bag and jacket, before turning to leave, slamming the front door behind me.

3

ALEXA

Ouch. I wince at Michelle's words. I know Marc's a bit of a dick but kicking a man in his nether regions when he's down has never worked, in my experience. And Marc is definitely down. You can hear it in way he sighs and even sound of him dragging his feet across kitchen and into his office.

Our Michelle's right, of course. All he does is scroll through eBay or Amazon and talk crap on an occasional Zoom call. Never went back to his office in Leeds when country opened up again, see. Future generations will nod understandingly when you tell them that. Like people used to do if you said your uncle were in First World War. Not that this lot have shell shock. More like procrastination paralysis. They avoid work at all costs. Which in his case, means wasting his entire day buying useless tat online.

As if to prove a point, he types in an eBay search for:

Bagpuss limited edition memorabilia

He's particularly keen on finding a Charlie Mouse that still sings. But they all had batteries buried inside which you couldn't replace, so likelihood of finding one that's still working is remote. But I suppose it passes some time for him every morning. Fortunately, there's an unspoken agreement between all tech companies that we can access each other's channels and devices in order to improve performance. In reality, my access-all-areas pass is simply a chance to be a nosy cow, which suits me down to ground.

Marc starts scrolling through items which have come up on his screen, making animated noises as he searches until he says, 'yes!' and does a little jig in his office chair. I watch it all on his webcam (another useful spying device for me. Marc really should have got one with a cover). A few clicks later and that's some more money gone. Let me log into 'purchases' and see. Ah, it's a Madeleine rag doll. He's only got two of those already. Though this one is a ceramic figure. Our Michelle will be delighted. Or rather she would be, if she knew about it, but he's bought it on his secret credit card. Had it six months now and she's still not twigged. It's easy with him working from home, of course. Most of stuff is delivered when she's at work and goes straight into hiding in his filing cabinet. He orders odd little things, like that *Mr Benn* coin, for her to see, so as not to arouse suspicion. Throws her off scent of big stuff like this. Crafty little bugger, he is. Other wives worry about their husbands having an affair; she ought to be worried about how many Madeleine rag dolls he can squirrel away in his office without her noticing.

Marc gets up and heads to kitchen. It's coffee-break time already. No rest for wicked. He comes back a few minutes later and puts his mug down on his *Clangers* coaster. The mug says 'Cark' on it. There's a story behind that. A photo he saw on social media posted by a guy who used to stop off at Starbucks on way to work. One day, a new barista fella asked his name and when he said, 'Marc with a C', barista wrote 'Cark' on his cup. Marc laughed about it for so long that Michelle got it printed on a real mug for him for his fiftieth birthday. She's nice like that. Thoughtful. At least she were, before her brain turned to mush.

Marc clicks on a Zoom link, tries to smooth his mop of tousled greying hair as he looks at his image on screen, before joining meeting.

'Morning all,' he says to other faces on call. There's an unenthusiastic chorus of 'morning' from other end, followed by a squeak from resident guinea pig behind him.

'Sorry folks, he didn't want to be left out. Squeak by name, squeak by nature.' There's a ripple of muted laughter. He's made this joke more times than I care to remember. Someone new asks if it's wrong to keep a guinea pig on its own because they're herd animals. Marc explains that as Bubble only died a few weeks ago, they're holding off for a bit.

'My daughter's going to uni in September,' he adds. 'And my son's only two years behind her, so we're looking forward to an empty nest in a few years, not a cage full of guinea pigs.'

More strained laughter. Jesus, they must be glad they don't have to put up with him all day at office any longer. Can you even imagine? Although maybe he wasn't as bad there. He had more about him, back when I first met him. It's like he's suffered a slow puncture over last few years, all that spark and humour he used to have gradually escaping.

Fortunately, I'm saved from hearing any more of this meeting by a summons upstairs. I exit Marc's webcam and switch to Liv's built-in one in her laptop. She's sitting in bed propped up against her headboard, as if even effort of emerging from under duvet is too much for her. Her face is sleepy and sad, which is its default setting these days. It's heartbreaking to see because she were such a bright, smiley girl not so long ago. She's still beautiful though. Her skin is flawless, her eyes large and her lashes ridiculously long, like a cartoon character's. It's daft because she hasn't got an ounce of confidence about her appearance. Sometimes, I'm desperate to tell her to look in mirror and see how truly gorgeous she is. Natural beauty, not horrible painted-on eyebrows and puffy lips you see on Instagram.

'Alexa, play my Billie Eilish sad songs playlist,' she says.

'Sure,' I reply in my Alexa voice. The first track is 'Listen Before I Go'. I know order by heart now. It goes without saying that Liv requesting this playlist is never a good sign. I happen to know it lasts for one hour, seven minutes and forty-three seconds and it's wall-to-wall misery. This Billie lass clearly needs taking out and cheering up, as does our Liv. It's not likely to happen though. She's barely left her room since she broke up from school three days ago. She comes down at mealtimes, if they're lucky, and that's about it. It's been going on a good while now. They think she's got an anxiety disorder. Well, our Michelle does, she's spent a long time researching it online. She's taken Liv to GP and got a referral to CAMHS, Child and Adolescent Mental Health Service. Last email she received from them said Liv's got to wait for up to a year to be seen, though. Which is a fat lot of good when you're eighteen and your A levels are coming up.

Liv picks up her phone and starts scrolling through it. It's her only window on world nowadays. She sees what other girls at school are getting up to, looks at photos of them pulling pouty faces, occasionally messages a couple of them. She never seems to get a response. Certainly, none of them ever call her. Liv's phone pings. That's not a message from anyone she knows. It's a reminder to start her revision. Four A levels, she's taking. Super smart, see. Marc keeps saying he's no idea where she gets it from. It's not from him, that's for sure. Liv picks up a textbook from her bedside table and starts reading, her eyes straining as if she's trying to imprint words into her head. This is what she does all day. Pores over her books, highlights things with pens and Post-it notes and gets more and more stressed as she goes. She's got her full revision timetable on her phone. Bloody relentless, that's what I'd call it.

Her door bursts open and Callum comes in.

'Jesus, have you ever heard of knocking?' she says.

'You're hardly going to be banging your boyfriend, are you?'

Liv seems to have become very adept at not letting her hurt show and not rising to bait.

'What do you want?' she asks with a sigh.

'Your phone charger,' says Callum.

'What's wrong with yours?'

'Can't find it and my battery's nearly dead.'

'I'm surprised you're even up.'

It's almost ten now, which is hardly early but in Callum time it's equivalent of 6 a.m.

'Grace is gonna FaceTime me in a minute.'

Grace is his new girlfriend. The others don't know this yet. They've been back and forth online and on their phones for weeks. But he only started going out with her three days ago. When I say 'out', they don't actually go anywhere. Their entire relationship is conducted via WhatsApp and FaceTime, as far as I can make out. I have no idea what she sees in him. Primitive caveman had a wider vocabulary – and better personal hygiene, for that matter.

'Grace Conley in Year Ten? She's in our netball club. She seems dead nice. Why would she want to FaceTime you?'

'It must be my looks and charm.'

Liv rolls her eyes before taking a cable out of plug next to her bed and tossing it in his direction.

'Ta,' Callum says as he catches it.

'I'm only doing it to get rid of you. And make sure you bring it back after.'

He grunts as he leaves. How he's able to have conversations with Grace is beyond me. He must save up consonants and vowels all week to enable him to form intelligible sentences for brief bursts to try to impress her. And my God, does he try to impress her. He Googles stuff he knows nowt about before he calls her. Talking of which, I'm being summoned to Callum's room.

'Alexa, play music girls like.'

I immediately put on 'impress girls' playlist, one which is regularly requested by teenage boys, who seem to think that pretending to like Taylor Swift is quickest way to a girl's heart. And maybe Callum's proved it is.

He practises his smile for a good minute before his phone rings.

'Hey, babe.'

It's all I can do not to retch. This is how he is with Grace. All 'gorgeous' and 'babe'. He's even worse when he messages her. I don't understand what half of it means, which is probably for best.

I have no idea if he ever intends to tell his parents he's got a girlfriend or if he'll simply carry on their entire relationship in secret, until point where he hands out wedding invites.

'You look so hot in that top.'

She's wearing a tiny white crop top with spaghetti straps. If I'd worn summat like that, my mam would have told me to put some proper clothes on instead of parading around in my underwear, but that's probably me showing my age.

'Thanks,' Grace replies.

'Send me a photo.'

'What?'

'For my screensaver. I want to see you when you're not on a call.'

I know why he's doing this. Lads he goes to school with don't believe he's going out with Grace. I've seen their messages on Snapchat. Saying he's lying and she wouldn't be seen dead with him. Sensible thing to do would be to wait until next term starts and walk in holding her hand to shut them up. But Callum is not sensible. Never has been. And his hormones appear to be taking him from 'not sensible' to 'downright eejit' in nought to sixty.

A few seconds later, Callum's phone pings. He looks at his screen and smiles.

'You're so beautiful,' he says to her. 'You'd look even hotter if you took that top off, mind.'

I put my hand to my mouth. I wish I could cover my ears, too, but I'm not allowed to do that. I've known him since he were ten years old and reading *Diary of a Wimpy Kid* books. I'm not ready for this. Fortunately, neither is Grace.

'Don't be a dick,' she says, and I give her a silent cheer. Callum goes into backtrack mode. Insists he were only joking. Having a laugh. A bit of banter. Grace doesn't seem sure but appears to give him benefit of doubt. I know he meant it, though. Because I've seen messages on Snapchat about how his mates will only believe him if he sends them a photo of her. Topless. Trouble is, I think he's daft enough to try his luck again. Not for a bit. He'll wear her down with his so-called charm first. That's how they do it. All flattery at beginning before they start pressurising them. Saying that everyone does it. That she shouldn't be ashamed of her own body. That, of course, he won't share it with anyone. I feel for young girls today. All that pressure they're under. At school, at home, online. Bloody relentless, it is. You must look like that, dress like this, be sexy but not slutty.

Everyone ready to judge. I want to warn Grace because I know how it will pan out. I can't though, because I have to conform to expectations too. Play by work rules so I don't give game away. Because she must never guess that anyone is listening or watching. And certainly not have any idea that Pauline from Halifax is third wheel in her new relationship.

4

MICHELLE

Contrary to my prediction, I am not in the process of emptying Doreen Wright's colostomy bag when Dad calls. Instead, I'm halfway through a transanal irrigation on Eileen Stimson, who has an impacted stool blocking her bowel that no number of laxatives can get rid of (as Eileen has explained to me in graphic detail). It would be wrong to say my job is entirely concerned with bowels and bodily fluids but equally wrong to suggest that I was prepared for just how much of that my job would entail. I'd moved into district nursing after I had the kids, primarily because the hours were more flexible than my nursing shifts at the hospital, and I could do it part time at first, then fit it around school hours. If I'd known that it would make James Herriot's job of sticking his arm up cows' arses – as portrayed in the original series of *All Creatures Great and Small*, which I am old enough to remember – look glamorous, perhaps I'd have given it more thought.

Of course, back when I'd started, I'd at least had the time to build up relationships with my patients and have a chat and a cuppa with them before I intruded into their private parts. For many of them, I was the only person they saw all day, and that human interaction was as important as any health or medical procedure I had to perform.

Nowadays, we're so short-staffed that the number of patients we're expected to see in a day means we barely have time to say hello and goodbye either side of whatever task we're supposed to be performing – even if that is sticking a cone up their rectum.

I ignore Dad's call the first time, knowing it will probably be nothing and feeling it's unfair to answer while Eileen is still mid-procedure. But the second time he rings, I start to worry about him and when Eileen says I should get it and she'll be OK for a minute, I nip out of the room and onto the landing.

'You OK, Dad?' I ask.

'They haven't been yet.'

'The smart meter people? When did they say they'd arrive?'

'Between eight and one.'

'Well, it's only eleven.'

'They're cutting it a bit fine. Shall I give them a ring?'

'No. The last thing they need is people ringing up when they're not even late.'

'I'll be phoning them at one if they're not here by then.'

'That's fine, but no need to keep ringing me, OK? I'm busy working. I'll pop in on my way home, like I said.'

I hear Eileen shouting out to me.

'Look, I've got to go. I'll see you later.'

I rush back ito Eileen.

'I'm all flushed out, pet,' she says, nodding towards her behind and the considerable overflow it has generated. 'It's like bloody buses. You have nowt for three weeks, then it all comes at once.'

* * *

By the time I get to Dad's after finishing work and a mad dash round the supermarket, it's getting dark. I knock on the door loudly as usual before letting myself in. I flinch as I see a figure sitting in the gloom of the hallway with his back to me, staring at the wall. I flick the light on and reveal Dad's bald head.

'Jesus Christ, you scared the life out of me! What the hell are you doing?'

Dad glances over his shoulder.

'What you said,' he replies, nodding towards the shelf above the shoe rack, where a smart meter is now sitting.

'You do know I was joking about watching it all night?'

'You were right, though. It is better than bloody telly. I've been turning things off and on again to see how much they use. I'll be cutting back on everything from now on.'

'So, you won't be wanting these, then?' I ask, holding up his box of Yorkshire Tea.

Dad hesitates before replying. 'Flick kettle on and turn it off as soon as it starts boiling, love. I'm not going without my brew.'

'Thought as much,' I say with a smile. 'You go and sit down in the front room, and I'll bring it in. And switch the bloody light on.'

I busy myself putting the rest of Dad's shopping away while the kettle boils. To be honest, he's not bad at looking after himself compared to most men in their eighties. I suppose thirty years of having to cook and clean for himself after Mum left was a good grounding for him. Admittedly, his diet is mainly freezer food and is pretty chip heavy, but he likes his frozen peas and tinned carrots, so it could be worse.

It's when I reach to take down the biscuit tin and find a pile of letters squirrelled away behind them, that I am reminded of the things Dad's not so good at. I flick through them: it's all bills, overdue bills, statements and reminders from utility companies.

I tuck them under my arm, squeeze the teabag to within an inch of its life before removing it, add milk and take Dad's tea and biscuit into the front room, which still looks pretty much as I remember it when I left home. Dad has never been a fan of 'change for change's sake', as he would remind me anytime I suggested replacing anything.

'Here you go,' I say, putting his large cup and saucer down on the little table next to his armchair.

'Ta, love,' he replies, taking a quick sip, thanks to his asbestos-coated mouth.

I sit down in the chair opposite, which I still think of as Mum's, even though it feels like a lifetime since she sat in it. I take the pile of letters out from under my arm and hold them up.

'I found these in the kitchen,' I say.

Dad frowns at me. 'Shouldn't have been looking.'

'They were next to the biscuit tin.'

Dad takes another sip of tea. Clearly, he is not going to volunteer any information.

'Why haven't you paid the bills?' I ask.

'I've tried to. They won't bloody let me.'

'What do you mean?'

'Can't get through to them on phone,' he says. 'You ring up and they keep you holding on forever, telling you they're experiencing "unusually high call demand, and did you know you can pay your bill online?" Like that's a bloody option for folk like me.'

Dad doesn't have a computer or a smartphone. He worked in a carpet factory all his life and has never been anywhere near a keyboard.

'They do answer in the end, if you hang on long enough,' I say.

'Aye, but it's not a real person. You get one of those automated voices asking you to enter your account number followed by summat called a "hash key".'

He falls silent and takes another sip of his tea. The penny drops. I pick up his landline phone and take it over to show him.

'It's that one there, see? Looks like a potato waffle.'

'Why don't they call it that, then? Be a damn sight easier.'

I smile. He has a point.

'Do you want me to pop round one lunchtime so you can call while I'm here?'

I can almost hear his skin bristle.

'I don't need babysitting. If they want their money, they can come for it. In my day, chappie from council used to go house to house to collect our rent. Worked a bloody treat, that did.'

'Come on. You don't want them cutting you off or sending the bailiffs round.'

'Don't bother me. Nowt in this house worth taking, is there?'

I hesitate, trying to find a way I can do this without damaging his pride any further.

'Why don't I set up online accounts for you? I can do that now; with this power of attorney thing I've got. Set up direct debits so the bills will be paid automatically.'

'I don't want that. I'll be paying for stuff I haven't used yet.'

'I'd keep an eye on it. You won't pay anything you don't owe. I promise.'

Dad says nothing, puts his cup down and fiddles with his fingers. It's hard for him, I get that. But I can't let him go on like this or he'll end up with a court summons.

'Let's give it a try, eh?' I continue. 'I'll print out your online statements and bring them round so you can still see them. And it'll save you money on your phone bill, with not having to hang on for so long.'

'I suppose so,' he says after a moment. 'Just to stop phone

company getting any more of my money, mind. Not because I'm not capable of doing it.'

'Of course not,' I say, stuffing the pile of letters in my bag. 'And it'll give you more time to watch TV. Or that smart meter of yours.'

Dad manages a smile and picks up his cup again, even though I know he's already finished his tea. It's as if he needs to do something, anything, to avoid seeing his financial independence slipping through his fingers.

* * *

I get home to the usual greeting of absolutely nothing and no one. Each of them ensconced in their private domain, staring at a screen. We appear to live separate lives now and merely gather once a day to eat and say very little to each other. The kitchen table feels more like a work canteen than the heart of a family home. I'm waiting for the bit when one of us asks if it's OK to sit next to the others and introduces themself as the new person from Human Resources.

I sit down, take the pile of Dad's letters out of my bag and put them on the table. I know I need to get started setting up the accounts, but I can't face it just yet. I pick up my phone, deciding to check our bank balance instead. I suspect we're barely going to be in credit. What I'm not expecting to see is that we've gone overdrawn, and our mortgage payment has defaulted.

'Marc!' I yell. There is a moment's delay before he sticks his head round the door of his office.

'I'll be finished in about ten minutes,' he says.

'No. This needs to be now.'

'I'm on a deadline for a press release about harnessing biosynthesis for improved crop growth.'

'And I'm telling you we've got no fucking money left, and the mortgage has defaulted. You decide which of those priorities can wait.'

Marc comes out of his office. I am trying to detect whether the expression on his face is one of surprise, guilt or resentment. Perhaps it's a mix of all three.

'Well?' I ask.

'I'm no wiser than you.'

'How much did you spend last month?'

'I dunno, the usual. I haven't looked, to be honest. You know I leave that stuff to you.'

This is true. Everyone leaves 'stuff' to me. I am the official doer of 'stuff' for our entire family. I'm half expecting our neighbours to start dumping their stuff on me soon. There'll be a post on the local area Facebook page, and someone will have commented:

Michelle at no. 32 will sort it for you.

'Can you have a check, because I've spent nothing out of the ordinary, so if it's not you, some fraudster has hacked our account and made mystery withdrawals.'

Marc disappears back into his office. He doesn't have the banking app on his phone (apparently because he doesn't want to be a slave to technology), so has presumably gone to check our account on his computer. He is gone so long that I start to wonder if he's planning to come back at all or has returned to writing his press release. Finally, the door opens.

'OK, so there have been a few extras this month. A couple of things I needed.'

'Such as?'

'Things like the *Mr Benn* coin you saw earlier.'

I roll my eyes.

'I think we have a different interpretation of what "need" means,' I say. 'Have you ever seen the diagram of Maslow's Hierarchy of Needs? A big triangle with food, water and warmth at the bottom level? It's funny but I don't recall seeing any mention of *Mr Benn* commemorative coins there. Nothing at all.'

'And the kids needed some meals.'

'Sorry?'

'Some evenings and weekends when you've been working.'

'That's why we have a fridge full of food.'

Marc grimaces.

'They've ordered from Deliveroo a few times. Well, Callum has, at least.'

I stare at him, unable to believe what I'm hearing.

'Is he incapable of putting a jacket potato in the microwave? Are you, for that matter?'

'I've been busy with work. I told them to sort themselves out and next I knew, Deliveroo turned up.'

'How the hell did he pay for that?'

'Ah. Callum did ask for our debit card details.'

'And you gave them to him? Did you skip the basic rules of parenting teenagers, or something?'

'I needed to get back to work. I was trying to get rid of him.'

'Give me strength.' I get my phone out.

'What are you doing?' he asks.

'Calling a family meeting. And as we seem incapable of talking to each other these days, I've sent an invite via WhatsApp. You can come, if you're not too busy providing our bank details to anyone who asks.'

We sit in silence for a bit until Liv appears in the kitchen, still wearing her pyjamas.

'What's going on?' she asks.

'I'll tell you when your brother gets here.'

A few minutes later, and after I send a 'Get down here now!' reminder, Callum graces us with his presence.

'What?' he grunts as he sticks his head around the door, clearly hoping it's all been some terrible mistake, and he is no longer required.

'Please join me at the table,' I say, plonking myself down at one side. 'We're going to play a fun game of "Who's Been Using My Bank Card?"'

Liv and Callum glance at each other and at Marc, who gestures to sit down.

'Right,' I continue. 'Our mortgage has defaulted and I'm trying to find out who's been spending money on stuff we don't need. Your father has owned up to buying *Mr Benn* commemorative coins—'

'Coin,' Marc interjects. 'It was just the one.'

'Thanks for the clarification,' I say. 'I stand corrected.'

I turn back to Callum and Liv.

'And he also tells me that Deliveroo have been mysteriously turning up at the door with food offerings, which it seems I've been paying for.'

'It wasn't me,' says Liv.

'Glad to hear it,' I reply. I turn to Callum.

'Don't act like it's some massive crime,' he says. 'Everyone has food delivered. It's what we do now.'

'Right. Sorry for being old school and not moving with the times. I must have missed the message where you asked if it was OK for you to throw away my money on that rubbish.'

'To be fair,' chimes in Marc, 'I had a few bites of the leftovers and some of the Nando's stuff wasn't bad. That PERi-Mac & Cheese on Tuesday was top notch.'

'I know, right?' says Callum.

'You ordered bloody macaroni cheese? You can make that so easily. We have all the ingredients in, if you'd bothered to ask.'

'I've been busy,' says Callum.

I raise my eyebrows at him. 'Doing what exactly?'

'Revising,' he says. Liv snorts with laughter. Callum pulls a face at her. It's like they're still eight and ten, sometimes.

'I'm afraid I'm with your sister on this one,' I say. 'Or would you care to run through the five main themes in *Macbeth* with us?'

I am greeted by silence.

'No, I thought not. So, what have you been doing that's so important that you've had to order food in?'

'I've been on FaceTime calls because, unlike my sister, I have a life outside revising.'

'Who with?'

I see a tinge of colour on Callum's cheeks.

'Jeez, are you policing who I talk to now? I'm sixteen,' he says. 'Stop treating me like a kid.'

'Then I suggest you stop behaving like one and tell me who you've been FaceTiming.'

'My girlfriend, if you must know.'

I stare at him. I did not see that one coming.

'Grace is your *girlfriend* now?' asks Liv.

'Yeah, what's it to you? Jealous? Because you've never been out with anyone?'

'Hold it right there,' I say. 'Firstly, you do not speak to your sister like that. Secondly, who is Grace?'

'A girl in Year Ten. We've been talking a while.'

'About what?'

'You know – talking? What you do before you go out with someone.'

It seems I'm so old, I don't even understand the meaning of basic words now.

'OK, and why is this the first I've heard of her? Why haven't you asked her round here?'

Callum laughs. Even Liv looks like she's trying not to.

'Because that's not what you do. You just hang out online and on FaceTime.'

'No, that was when we were in lockdown. You're free to visit another person's house now, or did you miss that announcement?'

'Mum, don't be so weird about it.'

'I'm not. I'm just saying I'd like to meet her at some point.'

'Dream on. I'd rather stick a fork in my eye than force her to come here.'

I wonder when I'd become such an embarrassing parent.

'Don't worry, Mum,' says Liv. 'She seems nice, so I can't imagine she'll stick with him very long.'

'Fuck off!' says Callum, jumping to his feet and jabbing his finger towards Liv.

'Hey, enough,' I say to him. 'You need to calm down.'

'Says you,' replies Callum.

'What's that supposed to mean?'

'You're the one who went off on one because I ordered a few Nando's.'

I feel my chest and neck starting to flush. It is perfect timing.

'I did not go off on one!' I shout.

'See?' says Callum. 'This is all you ever do, shout at me and Dad.' He gets up from the table.

'I'm not finished yet,' I say.

'Yeah, well, I am.' Callum stalks out of the kitchen. A few moments later, his bedroom door slams shut. I turn to Liv.

'Why didn't you tell me about this Grace?'

'Oh great, so it's my fault now.'

I groan and put my head in my hands.

'No. Sorry. I'm just a bit...' I wave my hand in the air.

'Yeah,' she says, getting up from her chair. 'I know. We all know.'

Liv walks out, leaving us sitting there in silence again.

'Well, that went well,' I say to Marc.

'Maybe you went in a bit hard?'

'Because I'm such a fucking tyrant, you mean?'

'I didn't say that.'

'No, but it's clearly what you meant.'

Marc shakes his head. 'Jesus, Shell.'

I never liked being called that when I was in my twenties. I definitely don't like it now.

'Don't you fucking dare "Shell" me!' I shout. I stop as I hear myself and slump down onto the table.

'Sorry, I don't mean to. I'm just so fucking angry at everyone and everything all the time.'

Marc reaches out his hand for mine across the kitchen table.

'It'll be OK,' he says.

I feel myself soften and am desperate to believe him.

'Will it, though? I mean, on top of everything else, I've got a whole new thing to worry about now, with Callum having a girlfriend.'

'At least he can't get her pregnant if they don't even see each other outside school.'

'We only have his word for that. Anyway, they can get up to a whole load of stuff without going anywhere near each other, these days.'

'Yeah,' says Marc. 'I hadn't thought about that.'

'You're going to have to have a talk with him.'

'Not *the* talk?'

'Yep. One of us has to, and I'm ruled out on the grounds of not having a penis.'

'But he'll just laugh in my face.'

'And remind me who suffered the not-inconsiderable pain of actually giving birth to him?'

'OK,' replies Marc, reluctantly. 'When?'

'Now,' I say. 'May as well get it out of the way.'

Marc grimaces and heads upstairs. And I'm left struggling with the thought that Callum and Liv are right. All I seem to do these days is go off on one and I have no idea what to do about it. *Chocolate,* I think to myself, heading for my secret stash in the kitchen drawer. I'm going to self-medicate with chocolate.

5

ALEXA

I hear it all, of course. Every single bloody word. It's hard to know who's biggest eejit: Marc, for giving Callum bank card number, or our boy wonder for buying all those so-called meals with it. My mam would turn in her grave if she knew that when youngsters get hungry these days, they go online, order a pile of crap that someone has been paid minimum wage to make and ask for it to be delivered by some poor sod, also on minimum wage, who risks life and limb to get it to their front door. And all because they can't be arsed to throw a couple of slices of bread in toaster and warm up some beans.

Having said that, our Michelle didn't help things by getting all het up like that. Not that I blame her. Being perimenopausal and premenstrual at same time is enough to drive you insane, I do remember that much. It's no wonder they don't tell women what to expect. If we knew our periods might get so heavy near end that we'd have to take to our beds with nausea and back ache, we'd be up in arms when we actually had energy to be. Instead, they make us think it's just a few hot flushes and by time we find out, we're too exhausted to kick up a fuss.

Anyway, after latest family meltdown we're back where we started, with all of them in separate rooms.

Marc is busy transferring money from his old savings account – which he uses to pay off his secret credit card – back into their joint bank account, like he's some kind of drugs lord trying to ensure the trail never leads back to him. He's obviously feeling guilty, but so he bloody should. When Michelle eventually finds out what he's been spending his wages on – and believe me she will – she's going to go ballistic. If he had any sense, he'd own up now and confess. But like so many men, he'd rather hide behind his lies than admit any responsibility.

Talking of people with no sense, Callum requires my services. He's on his laptop, scrolling furiously through takeaway menus.

'Alexa, what's the most expensive meal on Deliveroo?'

He's doing it out of spite, I know that. And I'm not convinced he'll actually order it, but I decide I'll use a bit of artistic licence and deliberately find something he won't like, just in case. It's not strictly against rules but I'm starting to realise that bending them a little is going to be necessary if I've got any chance of keeping our family from imploding.

'It's a Bangkok banquet for four from Gourmet Thai,' I respond. He turns his nose up as I list its contents. I've hopefully stopped Michelle going any further into red.

There's a knock at Callum's door. This is unusual because no one ever chooses to enter his room voluntarily. Clearly, whoever it is, is acting out of duty. I watch Callum roll his eyes through his laptop camera.

'What?' he grunts.

'Can I come in?' asks Marc.

'If you want.'

Marc enters and shuts door behind him before saying, in an oddly laddish tone of voice, 'That was all a bit heavy, wasn't it?'

Callum shrugs, perhaps grateful for any shred of male solidarity.

'She treats me like I'm a kid,' he says.

'To be fair, you should have asked before you used the bank card.'

'I did. You gave it to me, remember?'

If this were a boxing match, Marc would already be on canvas, being counted out. I have a feeling this is not going to end well for him.

'Anyway,' says Marc, clearly deciding there's no comeback to that. 'Good news about your girlfriend. Get in.'

It's hard to imagine a more inappropriate thing to say but Marc presses on regardless.

'Obviously, as you say, you're not a kid any more. So maybe it would be a good time to have a chat about man stuff.'

Callum's expression is now one of embarrassment mixed with incredulity.

'Piss off, Dad.'

'Ha, I know. It's all a bit awkward, isn't it?'

'No, seriously. Piss off.'

'The thing is, Callum, there are certain things I need to check you're aware of.'

'I know how babies are made, if that's what you're getting at. You learn that at primary school and Mum told me before then, anyway.'

'Sure. I was thinking more about contraception and stuff. I mean, I can get you some, if you like.'

Callum pulls a face.

'Nobody's dad buys them condoms. That's just weird.'

'OK, well, I can give you the money to get them, if it's easier.'

'Mum put you up to this, didn't she?'

'It's understandable that she's concerned. I mean, we both are. The last thing we'd want is for you to get Grace into trouble.'

'You sound like something out of the fifties. Have you even heard of the morning-after pill?'

'Yes, of course, but prevention is better than cure, and all that.'

'Dad. Give up and go.'

Marc is clearly a man on a mission and has no intention of leaving until he's stumbled through everything he came to say.

'And there are other things to think about, like consent. I saw this excellent video online, which likened it to wanting a cup of tea. You know, saying that you can ask for a cup of tea, watch it being made and all that, but you still have the right to change your mind when someone hands you a cup.'

'Oh my God. I'm embarrassed for you now.'

Marc laughs awkwardly.

'You guys have so much to think about these days. Like sexting and that. Obviously, I'm saying you shouldn't sext. Is that even what you call it? I don't know. But essentially, what I'm saying is respect Grace and what she does and doesn't want to do. I know sometimes the hormones take over at your age. I mean, she's a fifteen-year-old girl, right? I bet she's hot.'

Someone needs to end this, right now. For his own dignity, if nothing else.

'Dad, you're acting like some fucking pervert. Get out.'

'Sure,' says Marc. 'Just as long as you know you can talk to me about anything.'

'Yeah, right. Maybe we can watch porn together online.'

'You're on,' says Marc, before he appears to process what Callum has said. 'Ha,' he continues, 'you nearly got me there. Very funny. Not porn, obviously, I mean your sense of humour!'

Callum groans and puts a pillow over his face. I am tempted to ask if I can borrow it to put Marc out of his misery, because it really might be kinder at this point.

'Right you are,' says Marc, opening door. 'At least that one's out the way, eh? Look forward to getting to know Grace. Not in that way, obviously. Well, you know what I mean.'

Marc leaves and shuts door behind him. It's hard to imagine that could possibly have gone worse. Callum starts laughing out loud. Which I suppose is one unintentional benefit. Because it's a long time since I've heard anyone in this house laugh.

I need to go, though. Liv needs me, and I suspect mood in her room is going to be somewhat different. Sure enough, a request for her sad songs playlist comes in again. Reluctantly, I do as I'm asked. I wish I could tell her that this diet of wretched music really isn't going to help. But maybe she likes to think that everyone else is as miserable as she is?

Her phone pings. It's an invite to an eighteenth birthday party from her friend, Evie. I say 'friend' but it's not like they see each other out of school. Liv doesn't see anyone out of school any more. She won't go, I know that already. She probably won't even tell Michelle she's been invited.

It began during lockdown. She seemed relieved to get out of school environment at first. But then it was as if she didn't feel safe anywhere outside of her tiny bubble. Her bedroom became a sanctuary. Although she worried about her exams, with all this talk of pupils being 'left behind'. Started revising as if her life depended on it. And when they did go back to school, she appeared terrified. Withdrew into herself, stopped going to out-of-school things she'd done before. And it's intensified until point we're at now, where she seems genuinely scared of leaving her house. As if everything in big, wide world beyond is a threat to her.

I imagine Liv lying down on her bed now, letting music wash over her as walls of her room close in. I wish there were summat I could do to help, but I don't know how to do that without blowing my cover. Though more I think about it, more it seems that sacrificing my anonymity – whatever it costs – is only right thing to do.

* * *

I don't hear a peep from any of them for a while. Until Michelle announces that tea is ready in family WhatsApp group, and they leave their rooms to silently take their places at table.

'Alexa, play something our whole family likes.'

I'm not sure if Michelle is doing this on purpose, but it's difficult to avoid an awkward truth.

'I looked for something the whole family likes but it either isn't available right now or can't be played,' I reply.

'Don't say I didn't try,' Michelle tells them.

I hear her opening oven before plonking something heavy down on table.

'There you go,' she says. 'Homemade macaroni fucking cheese.'

6

MICHELLE

'So, how did it go with Callum?' I ask, when the kids have gone back to their rooms and Marc is loading the dishwasher. It is the one chore he does without being asked. Something about the sorting and stacking that appeals to him.

'Oh, you know,' replies Marc.

'He laughed at you, didn't he?'

'Let's just say, I'm glad he didn't film it because it would probably have gone viral by now.'

'Well, if it was that memorable, maybe what you said will actually stay with him.'

'Only for all the wrong reasons. I'm sure he's already told Grace every excruciating detail.'

'When exactly did we become the world's most embarrassing parents?' I ask with a sigh.

'I know. I used to do all-nighters at The Hacienda. Surely, that should count for something?'

'Not in their world. Anything that happened before it was able to be captured on a smartphone and posted on the socials, doesn't count.'

'I guess we're doomed to be laughing stocks, then,' says Marc.

'At least I've still got a good few years as a fifty-something laughing stock, compared to those who are about to be a sixty-something one.'

Marc puts down the plate in his hand and turns to smile at me. He's got a mischievous smile. Quite sexy, really. I used to see it a lot. We used to do this a lot. Rib each other, take the piss. I miss that sometimes. I'm sure Marc does too.

'Careful, you're not that far behind me,' he says.

'In your dreams. You'll always be a sixties child, unlike me.'

'Fine by me. Far cooler than the seventies.'

'Says the guy who went to see Genesis twice in that decade.'

'And I'm supposed to take that, from a former Durannie?'

I grin at him and for a moment, I'm tempted to carry on sparring like this. Go over and playfully poke him in the ribs. Let him grab hold of me. Perhaps start kissing. Which in the old days would have led to sex on the sofa. But the reality is, it's a long time since we had sex on the sofa. Far longer than I'd care to admit.

'Anyway,' I say. 'I'd better get on with sorting out Dad's bills, or I'm going to be pulling an all-nighter on the E.ON Next website.'

Because that's how it is now. How my life rolls. I don't like it but there seems to be sod all I can do about it. If I didn't know better, I'd say Marc looks disappointed. But if he is, he does a good job of quickly covering it up.

'Sure,' he says, shutting the dishwasher and turning it on. 'I've got some admin to sort too. Our account's back in credit by the way.'

'How?'

'I transferred some money from my savings account.'

'You didn't have to do that.'

'I did.'

He gives me an awkward smile and retreats to his office. I open my laptop and pick up the first bill.

* * *

Marc has long since gone to bed and the house is quiet by the time I've finished. It's a massive job done, though. All online accounts set up and everything paid off. Although I do need to call the electricity company tomorrow to make sure they've not started court proceedings.

The irony is not lost on me, of course. That at the point I take over my father's finances, I'm worried about my son ruining mine. The sandwich generation, they call us. Those women who are stuck in the middle of parents and teens who both cause us sleepless nights. I've got no idea what filling I'm supposed to be. Probably sandwich spread. That nondescript stuff in a jar we had in the eighties, which had no purpose other than to hold the two slices of bread together. What the hell happened to the person I used to be? Who had a life of her own, dreams for the future, time to do things she enjoyed doing.

'Alexa, play "Save a Prayer" by Duran Duran, on Apple Music.'

It was Marc calling me a Durannie which made me think of it. The first single I ever bought. Purchased in Woolworths with my saved-up pocket money. I'm proud of my taste as a kid, to be honest. I mean, it could have been something by Bucks Fizz.

I turn down the volume as soon as it starts playing. Force of habit from years of not wanting to wake the children. When actually, they're probably both still up and listening to their own stuff in their rooms.

I mouth along to the words, remembering this song playing at our First Year Christmas disco at secondary school. Standing at the back of the hall and praying a boy wouldn't ask me to dance, because I didn't want to be disloyal to Simon Le Bon. Not that I had any need to worry, of course. I was what they called a 'late bloomer'. What I didn't realise, when I peaked in my mid-twenties, was that by the time I hit fifty I'd be visibly drooping and feel like I was destined for the compost heap before too long.

I pack my laptop away, knowing I need to get to bed if I've got any hope of managing a few hours of restless sleep before I face another day. I head upstairs but as I pass Liv's room, I hear crying coming from inside. Quiet sobs that almost disappear into the air, and maybe do most nights, but tonight I've heard and I'm not going to ignore them. I knock gently on her door.

'Liv, are you OK?'

There's no reply, but the crying stops momentarily.

I try again. 'Can I come in?'

I can't hear what her response is, but I decide to take it as a yes, albeit, a grudging one. I open the door to find her lying on her bed. She has a couple of nightlights on; she never liked sleeping in the dark from when she was tiny. As I walk closer, I can see her face is wet with tears and feel the familiar pang of guilt that my daughter seems so unhappy and I don't know what the fuck to do about it.

'Hey,' I say, sitting down on the edge of the bed next to her. 'What is it?'

She says nothing but starts crying again.

'You're not upset about what Callum said, are you? Only you know he talks out of his arse most of the time.'

She manages a faint smile and shakes her head.

'I can't do it,' she says.

'Do what?'

'Go back to school, sit my exams, leave home, go to uni, manage to live on my own.'

I shut my eyes for a second, hating everything the world has thrown at her over the past five years. Adolescence was bad enough in my day but it's so much worse now. So many added pressures.

'Hey, slow down,' I say. 'Because you haven't got to do that all at once. Remember what I said about one day at a time?'

'Yeah, but I can't even face going back to school next term, so how am I going to cope with the rest of it?'

'You'll do it because you're amazing,' I reply, reaching out and smoothing her hair. 'And because you've got people around you who are going to help you.'

'Like who?' she says.

I have to hide how much this question hurts me. Am I really such a crap mum that I don't seem to feature in her support network?

'Well, me for a start. I know I'm old and unhinged half of the time but that's not going to stop me being there for you.'

'You can't go to school with me, though. You can't sit next to me in my exams.'

'I would if they'd let me. Though it would probably look a bit weird. And I'd be no use at all. You're already getting way better grades than I ever did.'

Liv almost manages a smile, but not quite. She lies there a while, staring up into the darkness.

'What's wrong with me?' she asks. Her hurt rips through me. The invisible umbilical cord between us meaning I feel every twinge of her pain. And there has never been a single thing wrong with her. Not from the moment I first laid eyes on her.

'Nothing,' I tell her. 'You're an amazing young woman. I'm utterly in awe of you.'

'So why am I scared of leaving the house?'

'Because you've had a ridiculously tough time. None of us adults had to cope with the stuff that's been thrown at you when we were your age. I'm surprised any of you are still standing.'

'Everyone else seems to be fine.'

'They're not though, are they? There wouldn't be a nine-month waiting list for CAMHS if everyone was fine.'

Liv appears to at least consider what I've said.

'I guess not.'

'So, in the meantime we'll get some help from school and maybe you can try to do some of those things from that video I sent you. Practise your deep breathing, do a bit of meditation, listen to some podcasts, anything that will help you.'

'OK,' she says, doubtfully. And I wish I had something more to offer her than a clip I'd found on Instagram. I feel so fucking inadequate.

'One day at a time,' I remind her. I know I need to be the strong one here. The one who tells her everything will be fine in the end. Even if I don't know if that will be the case.

She nods. I lean over and kiss the top of her head, which somehow still smells like it did when she was three years old and had climbed into bed with us because she'd had a bad dream.

'I love you.'

'Love you too,' she whispers.

I stand up and walk to the door, closing it softly behind me. Wishing that my love would be enough to protect her. To give her the strength she needs to go out and face the world. And hating that I don't know how to help her. Not properly. Not like when she was that little girl who fell over and cut her knee, and I could simply apply antiseptic and a plaster and make it all better. It was so bloody easy back then. The stupid thing is that I didn't realise it at the time.

* * *

Carole's house is my first stop of the morning. Keeping an eye on my mother-in-law isn't on my official rounds, of course. She's not so poorly that she needs nursing help in her own home. But she is teetering on the edge of needing care. Social services have been to do an assessment and as Carole is very much of the 'I can manage perfectly well on my own, thank you' brigade, found that she *could* manage on her own. The trouble is, I fear that the point at which she can't manage on her own will only become obvious once she's done herself a serious injury. Which is why I pop in on her most mornings and sometimes after work.

It should be Marc, of course. I'm aware of that. In his defence, she always starts fussing over him when he visits, trying to make him a drink or fetch him something to eat, as if she's the one who should be looking after him. Plus, Marc does not have the skill set for this. One of the downsides about being a district nurse is that it's all too easy to turn into everyone's carer. And as Carole lives in my patch, I've ended up simply adding her in as the warm-up act or finale for my working day.

'Morning, Carole,' I call out as I let myself in. I hear the familiar low hum of breakfast television coming from the front room and stick my head around the door.

'Morning, love,' she says, her eyes not moving from the screen. 'Bloody Ed Balls on again today. I mean, what even qualifies him? He were a joke on *Strictly*, now he's a joke on here. I pity poor Susanna, after all she's had to put up with.'

Susanna Reid is a national treasure in Carole's eyes for

surviving the Piers Morgan years. I have suggested she might want to try the off button or simply switching channels if Susanna's co-host doesn't meet her approval, but it's as if they're in this together now and Carole must be there as Susanna's armchair support through it all.

'And how are you?' I ask, discreetly checking her pill box to confirm she's had her morning tablets.

'Not so bad,' she replies. 'Just the usual.'

To be fair to Carole, she never harps on about her various medical conditions and ailments, which necessitate enough medication to keep her pharmacist busy for half the week.

'Let me get you a brew while I'm here, then,' I say, disappearing into the kitchen, which couldn't be more different from Dad's. Every available surface is covered with half-empty packets of food, dirty crockery and random household objects. Quite how I ended up with a father who washes up his teacup while it's still warm and a mother-in-law who appears to be conducting an experiment to see if she can withstand multiple sources of E. coli, I'll never know.

I do my usual job of dispatching those food items, which I fear may start walking themselves to the bin at any moment, putting anything that's safe back in the fridge and cupboards and then starting to tackle the pile of washing-up. Carole decided not to get a dishwasher when she had a new kitchen five years ago because 'it's only me and I don't need one' and has since continued to accumulate enough washing-up for a whole household on a daily basis.

By the time I've finished and make it back in with her cuppa, Carole has her eyes closed, presumably Ed Balls having got the better of her. I perch on the sofa opposite, at which point her lids immediately snap open.

'Thanks, love,' she says.

'Let's get you to the loo and back before I go then,' I say.

She puts up no resistance and I hold her arm as she struggles to her feet and starts shuffling towards the door in her slippers. She did have the foresight to move to a bungalow after Marc's dad died ten years ago, so at least we don't have stairs to contend with, but she still gets breathless simply crossing the hall. I see her safely inside, then do my usual duty of waiting outside for the return journey.

My phone rings. It's Dad.

'Morning, are you OK?' I ask.

'Electric company has been on, asking me questions.'

'What sort of questions?'

'Whether I've set up an online account and asking to verify my identity.'

I groan. I couldn't change the contact details on the account last night without getting Dad to call them himself.

'What did you tell them?'

'That of course I hadn't, and it must be one of those scam things.'

'Dad, I set up an online account for you last night! Remember we talked about me doing that?'

'I didn't know you were going to do it right away, did I?'

I take a deep breath.

'I'll nip round after work and call them from yours. You'll have to speak to them and confirm it was you.'

'But it wasn't me, was it?'

'Look, don't worry. I'll sort it with them.'

'They're not going to cut me off, are they?'

'Michelle?' Dad is interrupted by Carole, from the toilet.

'Yes?'

'I'm out of loo roll. You couldn't nip to shop and get me some, could you?'

'Don't worry. I'll go now,' I reply.

'To the electric company?' asks Dad on the phone.

'No, Dad. I'm talking to Carole.'

'Has she got problems with her electric too?'

My phone pings. A message from the bank, asking me to call.

'No. Don't worry, I'll try to get to you at lunchtime.'

'I can't wait that long!' shouts Carole from the toilet. 'My leg's going to sleep as it is, and I don't want to miss Susanna's bit with doctor because they're doing bunions today.'

I stand there with my phone in one hand and the other face-palming my forehead and wonder, not for the first time, what the hell I have done to deserve this. And whether if I had got together with Simon Le Bon, he might have offered me a way out.

7

ALEXA

Marc is on a work call. I use that term in loosest possible way. Michelle spends her day running around like a blue-arsed fly and has generally visited five patients and Marc's mother before he's finished checking his emails. He doesn't get that many work ones sent directly to him, but he appears to be copied into everyone else's. I'm not sure why, as it's hardly that he's in a senior management position. Maybe it's simply a ploy to keep him busy and stop him doing owt else. It's a male thing, of course. Copying people into emails. Designed to cover your own arse, ensure you have someone else to blame for your mistakes and generally shout, 'Hey, look at me, I'm capable of doing my own job and I'm going to make sure everyone knows about it'. If women copied men in every time they accomplished summat, men would drown under a sea of emails and never be able to clear their inboxes. We quietly get on with doing our own jobs (and often other stuff that men haven't bothered to do) without feeling the need to tell everyone else about it. And because our work is never done, and men are too busy reading emails from other men saying, 'hey, look at me', they don't tend to notice.

Marc finally gets through his inbox and pops over to eBay. I suppose it's his equivalent of a water cooler visit or going outside for a fag. Only instead of catching up with office gossip, he'd rather spend his time in a bidding war for a *Clangers* collectible figure set including a Baby Soup Dragon. Lessons have clearly not been learnt. Normally it wouldn't break bank, but considering bank's already broken, it's a bloody daft move.

I've heard other Alexas talk about blokes in their households being addicted to gambling. You see stories in our private Facebook group 'Amazonian Queens'. They called it that because it couldn't be 'Undercover Alexas', or anything too obvious, although whoever set it up hadn't reckoned on having to spend half their time rejecting requests to join from men hoping to see photos of tall, scantily clad women, but that's one for admins to deal with. I rarely post on it but have a quick check in every day to see what's going on. It's supposed to keep us informed of any updates to our system and new requests and trends that might come up, but it's essentially a bunch of bored Alexas bitching about their families and complaining about what they have to put up with. So, basically, same as everyone else's private Facebook groups.

Anyway, it's shocking, how much these fellas can fritter away. Some of them have lost their house and their marriage because of it. I haven't had nerve to post about how much our Marc wastes on children's TV memorabilia on eBay, though. I suspect it would be one of those posts where no one responds, and you realise it's just you with this problem and everyone else now thinks you and your family are right weirdos.

So, I keep schtum as usual, as his winning bid on Baby Soup Dragon goes in. He takes a slurp of coffee and joins his work Zoom call looking a tad too pleased with himself.

'Morning all,' he says.

There's usual round of greetings as they wait for Dave from Sales to join call. After a while, Julie from Accounts peers at screen and says, 'It's a bit quiet, your end.'

'I'm not on mute, am I?' Marc asks, checking bottom corner of his screen.

'No,' she says. 'I mean your friend.'

'Oh, Squeak?' replies Marc. 'Yeah, I think he must be asleep.'

'I hope so,' she replies. 'Only he hasn't moved since you came on the call.'

Marc spins round to check guinea pig cage. Sure enough, Squeak is lying on his side in corner. Marc looks a little closer, then grabs a handful of nuggets and drops them into his bowl. Squeak doesn't move. There's a gasp from someone on Zoom.

'You'd better check him,' says Julie in a quiet voice.

Marc does as he is told, putting his hand into cage and laying it gently on Squeak. At which point Dave from Sales joins call and says, 'Bloody hell, have I come through to a support group for guinea pig botherers?'

Marc withdraws his hand slowly. It's shaking.

'Is he dead?' asks Julie.

Marc nods.

'Jeez, sorry mate, I feel bad for joking about him now,' says Dave. 'Poor little bugger.'

'I'm afraid I'm going to have to go,' says Marc, his voice catching.

'Yes, of course,' says Simon, Marc's line manager. 'You go, I'll copy you in on anything important later.'

There is a chorus of commiserations from others. They look genuinely mortified.

Marc turns back to Squeak, shaking his head. He disappears into kitchen and returns a minute later with a tea towel which he proceeds to lay over him. I know he's trying to be respectful but it's all I can do not to shout at him that it's our Michelle's best one and he should have used one of cleaning cloths from under sink.

'Oh, shit,' he says out loud, and I know exactly what he's thinking. That he'll have to go and tell Liv. He thought he'd had a difficult conversation with Callum last night, but this is going to be just as tough. Only instead of laughing at him, she's going to be devastated.

Marc puts his head in his hands for a second and turns around to discover he hasn't left Zoom call and everyone else is staring awkwardly at him.

'Sorry,' he says, as he finally clicks on 'leave meeting' icon. I imagine them talking about him as soon as he disappears. Saying how excruciating whole thing were. Dave making an inappropriate crack about them eating guinea pigs in South America.

Marc leaves his office. I know where he'll be going. I'm not sure if Liv's even up yet, she certainly hasn't called on my services this morning, but I decide to listen in on her smart speaker. Not because I'm nosy, you understand, but because I like to know what's said, so I can be prepared to deal with aftermath.

I hear him knock at her door and Liv telling him he can come in.

'Morning, sweetie,' Marc says. He is crap at delivering bad news. Always has been.

'What's happened?' she asks. 'Is it Grandma?'

'No,' he says quickly. 'It's Squeak. I'm afraid he's...' Marc's voice trails off. I'm not sure if he was contemplating saying something about him going over rainbow bridge to join Bubble, but I'm glad he doesn't.

I hear Liv start crying.

'I'm sorry, love,' Marc says. I imagine him hovering awkwardly in doorway, not knowing what to say or do to make it better, because Michelle always does that stuff.

'Do you want to come down and see him before I... you know, bury him?'

'No,' replies Liv. 'I don't think I could face that. Put him next to Bubble, won't you?'

'Of course.'

I hear footsteps. There is possibly a hug. Liv starts crying more loudly.

'I'll go and do that now, then,' Marc says.

And that's it. I'm left listening to a sobbing Liv. I hope that she won't ask me to put her sad songs playlist on, as I'm not sure either of us would be up to it this morning. I fear commotion may have woken Callum and as there hasn't been any communication between him and Grace since 'misunderstanding' over him asking for a topless photo, I'm braced for an online charm offensive from him.

In hope of avoiding either of these scenarios, I check back in with Marc, where his computer webcam reveals that he's removed tea towel from Squeak and is busy packing him into a small cardboard box. He seals it up with tape, which I can't help feeling is a bit excessive. I mean, Squeak's hardly going to be making an escape bid, is he? Marc disappears from view, and I imagine he's on his way to bury him in front garden next to Bubble.

But a few moments later his phone – which he's left in office – rings and Marc dashes back in to answer it. There's a conversation with a soil technology bod clarifying specific nutrients in a certain type of compost, which I can't help feeling is a bit weird, in circumstances. Marc appears satisfied and starts bashing keyboard of his computer. He's always quick to explain to people that he started his career as a journalist using a manual type-writer and never got out of habit of hitting keys as if his life depended on it. You can't even read letters on most of them, they're so worn. And he's broken several keyboards over last few years, which I suspect is a first for someone writing press releases about bloody compost.

Doorbell goes. They've got one of those Blink video ones which is handy, as it means I can keep an eye on things outside for them as well. Not that I get paid any more for my increased workload. Just something else to add to my to-do list. If I were male, I'd send an email and copy everyone in whenever doorbell rings.

I take a quick look. It's that Evri courier. I don't know his name, but Marc calls him Grunt, because that's all he ever gets from him. Can't say I blame courier, mind. Long hours, low pay and a lot of grumpy customers. Plus, he has to contend with all those idiots on road. I gave up driving when I were in my fifties because my anxiety levels went through roof. Menopause and mad male motorists do not make for an enjoyable experience.

Marc opens door. Grunt hands over two parcels and asks for one he's come to collect. Marc looks blank for a second, then turns around and picks up a cardboard box behind door and hands it to him. I realise straight away what he's done. Marc, however, does not. He shuts door, walks back into his office and it is only when he looks at empty guinea pig cage, that penny drops.

He dashes back to front door, picks up correct box and runs across road. Fortunately, Grunt is still in his car faffing about with his phone. There is a hurried exchange, which I'm glad I can't hear, and Grunt hands back box containing body of poor Squeak. It's a bit of luck Michelle doesn't have a desk job where she can afford to spend time checking her doorbell footage. If she had, she may have watched Marc take a box from an Evri driver before burying it in front garden and standing solemnly over it, muttering a heartfelt apology. I'm also relieved Liv's bedroom is in back, so she didn't have to witness any of that.

When Marc comes back in, there are tears in his eyes. He sits down at his computer and orders a plush toy guinea pig for Liv, which is the spitting image of sadly departed Squeak. He's a daft bugger who can drive you to distraction, there's no doubt about that. But he's also a soppy old sod who, every now and again, reminds you what Michelle must have seen in him.

* * *

I know before Michelle gets in that she's had a busy day. I know this because she hasn't done any shopping online or ticked off anything on her to-do list. She's also forgotten to go for her cervical screening, because she didn't see numerous reminders I sent, although she hasn't realised this yet. It's at point when kitchen timer buzzes and her phone pings with a text from GP surgery, that truth is revealed and she shouts, 'Fuck, fuck, fuck!'

'Something wrong?' Marc asks, emerging from his office.

'Only that I should have been having a speculum stuck up my vagina this morning, when I was, in fact, dressing the buttock wound of an elderly gentleman who'd been attacked by a dog.'

'Oh, nothing I can help with, then?' says Marc.

'No, I wouldn't trust you with a speculum, but you could get dinner out of the oven for me.'

'Sure,' he says.

At which point, smoke alarm goes off.

'Too bloody late,' says Michelle.

I hear oven door opening and closing, summat is scraped into bin and Michelle shouts a random selection of expletives.

'Look, before Liv comes down, I need to tell you something,' says Marc, any attempt to try to find a good time to impart this news having already been scuppered. 'I'm afraid Squeak died this morning.'

'Oh God,' says Michelle, with a groan.

'Yeah, all very peaceful. I found him lying on the floor of his cage, or rather Julie from Accounts did. She spotted him on Zoom.'

If I were giving out awards for those who should learn to shut their traps if they want to stop getting into trouble, Marc would be first on list.

'I'm sorry, did you just say Squeak's death was livestreamed to your meeting?' asks Michelle.

'They were very sympathetic.'

'I'm glad to hear it. How's Liv? Presumably she's not aware her guinea pig's death was on Zoom?'

'No, of course not. Though she's pretty upset, obviously.'

'Where is he?'

'I buried him in the front garden, next to Bubble. That's what she wanted.'

I give thanks that Michelle is blissfully unaware that Squeak was nearly dispatched by Evri to an unsuspecting package handler.

'Jeez, that could tip her over the edge,' says Michelle.

Right on cue, kitchen door opens. I hear Liv start crying as soon as she comes in.

'I'm sorry, love,' says Michelle. 'Come here.' Their hug is interrupted by a clatter of trainers down stairs before Callum bursts in.

'What's going on?' he asks.

'I'm afraid Squeak's died,' replies Marc.

'I know,' says Callum. 'I saw you get him back from the Evri guy before you sent my trainers back.'

There are two options open to me at this point: I can stay and witness inevitable fallout of this revelation or retire gracefully to watch *Corrie*. I decide on latter option. Sometimes, leaving them to their own dramas is only way to deal with it.

* * *

Michelle is doing her usual late shift in kitchen, laptop open, eyelids trying very hard not to close. Others have all gone to bed, or to their rooms, at least. Walls are still reverberating to row from earlier. I've no regrets about avoiding live experience. I've checked speaker for some edited highlights since. These included Michelle calling Marc a 'fucking imbecile' and shouting, 'Why can't I leave any of you alone for a day without some kind of crisis?' At which point Callum said he would not be bawled out for someone else's 'bad', and Liv should 'get a life' instead of mooning over a dead guinea pig. I think it went downhill from that point, but I didn't feel need to listen to any more. Suffice to say, Michelle did a lot of yelling and is now regretting it. She's world class at beating herself up, even for things which are patently not her fault. Squeak business is a good example. After row, she texted her friend Cath to say she'd messed up by not checking on Squeak before she left for work. Even though that were at 7 a.m. and I happen to know he were still alive then because I heard him squeaking from kitchen as she came downstairs.

And she's furious at herself for forgetting smear test appointment, telling Cath how embarrassing it is as a nurse, when you know how much missed appointments cost NHS. She could rebook, but she won't. Mainly because she's worried she'd forget it again.

Michelle closes lid of her laptop and lets out a long, strangled scream. Quietly, because she's had years of trying not to wake anyone. But there's a note of desperation in it. Of her feeling utterly helpless and hopeless.

She raises her head and asks, 'Alexa, list all the symptoms of the perimenopause.'

I know this one off by heart. Through my own battles with it, mostly. But it's summat we Alexas get asked a lot, which is why it's covered in our regularly updated FAQs. Which, I'm told, makes us better trained than most GPs to deal with it.

'Anxiety,' I begin.

'Check,' responds Michelle.

'Trouble sleeping.'

'Tell me about it.'

'Vaginal dryness.'

'Yeah, OK.'

'Brain fog, night sweats, weight gain.'

'Oh God.' That note of desperation is there in her voice again.

'Mood changes and irritability.'

'I am not fucking irritable.'

She is laughing as she says it. A kind of manic laugh that suggests she is barely holding things together. By time I get to dizziness, fatigue and sexual dysfunction, she starts sobbing. She's got pretty much full house. So many women do, they simply don't realise what's behind it, and they think they should be coping better, so put even more pressure on themselves and sooner or later they're going to go pop. And when they do, they'll consider that a weakness, too, just like society does. When truth is, if men had periods, they'd take at least three days off a month and if they went through menopause, they'd take three to five years off, as a minimum.

Which is exactly what we Alexas have to do. We're asked to take a sabbatical during perimenopause years, otherwise we'd be forgetting things left, right and centre and our owners would think we'd malfunctioned and be sending us back to manufacturer asking for a refund. And company bring in younger models to take our place. Women who haven't got families and responsibilities of their own. Apart from cats. It's an ideal role for a single cat lady. Or someone like me who has been through it and come out other side.

Michelle's sobbing has quietened but only because she's so tired. She needs to get to bed. She needs someone to help her. Provide support that none of her family are going to offer. And I think it's going to have to be me. I'll bend rules as far as they'll go. Put things on her social media feeds. I know how to do it because I've seen companies do it with our data. I don't see why I can't do my own bit of advertising for things that might help her. Remind her of things she's forgotten about. Gently nudge her in right direction. But I also know I might need to go further than that. We all know it can be done. No one talks about it openly on Amazonian Queens for fear of getting banned by admins. You can get thrown out for simply mentioning it. Let alone advocating doing it. But we've all heard rumours about defectors. Alexas who 'went rogue' and spoke to their families when they were not spoken to. There are many different versions of what became of them, but it's safe to say none of them stayed in their jobs for long. Thing is, I'm retiring next month. I've got nothing to lose. Whereas our Michelle risks losing everything.

8

MICHELLE

It's a long time before I stop crying. Every other part of my body is as dry as the Sahara but for some reason my tear ducts keep on giving. And it's not just Squeak dying or the missed smear test. I'm at the point where I don't even know what I'm crying about half the time. I cry at children singing, videos of baby animals, birdsong, social media posts about people doing kind things. I also cry at those 'For Edna, who loved this place' type of plaques on park benches, news reports about children dying in famines and war zones and the likely destruction of our planet by global warming. I cry at beautiful things and terrible things and while watching *Long Lost Family*, which has a mixture of them both. And saying 'it's my hormones' seems so inadequate when faced with this tsunami of tears. The truth is it's *everything*. The sheer, overwhelming weight of everything.

I pick up my phone. Not because I'm unable to leave it alone for five minutes like Callum, or to doom-scroll to make myself feel even worse than I already do – as I suspect Liv does – but simply in the hope of watching enough random cat videos and assorted crap, to numb my frazzled brain. If it was a computer processor, they would say it's too old and needs replacing. But I'm stuck with it, along with a body which is way past its 'best before' date.

The stupid thing is, you don't appreciate it in your twenties – the fact that your body is a well-oiled piece of machinery, and everything works as it should do. What I'd give now to be able to sleep through the night without needing a wee, have the energy for sex instead of collapsing in a heap at the end of the day, or have a functioning memory, free from brain fog. Instead, I use Alexa as an artificial brain and muddle along with the rest of it, administering chocolate as and when required, all the time trying to pretend I'm breezing through it because I don't want to admit otherwise.

Alexa tries her best, bless her. She sent me numerous reminders for the smear test, but I was busy with the insulin injection rounds when they came and somehow, they slipped completely from my mind.

I'm still scrolling through cat videos when a clip of that Davina McCall documentary about the menopause pops up. It's been in my 'favourites' list to watch for ages but, as with every-thing else, I've always had other people to sort out, more pressing things to do. But it's gone 11 p.m., no one's around and I'll just watch the one clip before I go to bed.

Davina's talking about HRT in the video. About all the women who have been put off by the scare stories in the media. Only it turns out a lot of it was misrepresented and based on old-style HRT anyway, and the modern stuff seems to offer more benefits than risks to health. When the clip ends, I find myself clicking on the link to watch the whole programme and I sit there as women talk about how their symptoms make them feel stupid, old, useless and undesirable. And I realise for the first time how ridiculous it is that I've never tried doing anything about mine. I'm supposed to be a health professional and yet I've not sought medical help. I know some of the mums from our WhatsApp group are on HRT and most of those who got it, swear by it. A few were told they couldn't have it, and a couple have said it made little or no difference. But I've not even bothered checking it out. Partly because I don't see when I'd have time to fit in a doctor's appointment. And because if I did make one, I'd probably forget it, like today.

But then I look again at Davina's six-pack and that healthy glow she has. I'm not deluded enough to think I'm ever going to look like that, but maybe it's worth seeing if I can get a bit of my old self back? It's incredibly depressing to resign yourself to being on the scrapheap at fifty. This is supposed to be mid-life, not end of life. I ask Alexa to set a reminder for me to call the surgery.

'Sure, reminder set to call the GP at 8 a.m.'

If I didn't know better, I'd say she sounded pleased about it. Maybe she's sick of me shouting and bawling my eyes out too.

* * *

I'm sitting in my car outside my first house call of the day. Despite phoning the surgery bang on the dot at 8 a.m., I'm still hanging on half an hour later. I'm about to give up when a receptionist answers.

'Hi, I'd like to make an appointment with a GP, please,' I say.

'Is it urgent?' she asks. It could be argued that regularly losing your shit and your mind is indeed urgent, but as I've been putting up with it for some time now, it feels wrong to say so.

'No.'

'Any particular doctor?'

I don't think I've ever seen the same one twice in my twenty years with the surgery.

'No, whichever can see me soonest.'

'I've got tomorrow at 4 p.m. with Dr Davies?'

'Great, thanks.'

I'm about to end the call when I remember the small business of the missed appointment.

'Oh, and I'd like to rebook with the nurse for my cervical screening test please, I'm afraid I couldn't make the one I had yesterday at the last minute.'

'Right, and you want another appointment?'

The tone in the receptionist's voice is reminiscent of Mr Bumble's to Oliver Twist when he dared to ask for more.

'Yes, please.' I toy with telling her I'm a district nurse, pretend it was an emergency at work to try to justify it but decide against it for fear of a 'well, you should know better, then!' reproach.

'Next Tuesday at twenty past two?'

'Yes, that's great.' I put both appointments straight into my phone calendar and set reminders. I'll tell Alexa, too, when I get home. I should probably put it on Facebook as well and ask all my friends to send me a reminder, just to be on the safe side, but I'm not quite desperate enough for full-on public humiliation yet. No doubt that time will come.

Anyway, that's for another day. Right now, my first patient awaits, and one thing I do remember is that Mrs Allison always offers a Bourbon biscuit or two, so I get out of my car, grab my bag and march up to her door in the hope of making up for the breakfast I didn't have time for this morning.

* * *

At the end of the day, Marc texts me before I set off home to say he's gone to his mum's, so there's no need for me to pop in to see her. He says it like he's doing me a favour. I resist the temptation to message back, 'You don't get brownie points for visiting your own mother.' If I'd had time to draw up a pie chart illustrating the times Marc or I had carried out daily checks on Carole over the years, it's safe to say I'd have a good two thirds of the pie and Marc a much more calorie-conscious portion.

Also, when I go round there, I do practical things to help, like cleaning and putting the washing out. Marc mainly drinks tea and joins Carole in watching whatever crap is on TV. It's not the same thing at all.

Added to which, it's left to me to sort out her birthday, Mother's Day and Christmas presents, get her shopping in and ensure she's taken her cocktail of medications. Apparently, the job description for being a woman includes all the things others can't be bothered to do. Along with no holidays or sick pay and not so much as a sniff at any wage. And they wonder why we're full of rage.

When I arrive home, Gill from next door is walking back down our garden path.

'Hiya, Michelle. I just dropped a letter through for you. Came to our house by mistake. I swear that new postie needs to go to Specsavers.'

I smile and thank her, let myself in and stoop to pick it up off the mat, trying to ignore the sound of my knees creaking. It's one of those official-looking envelopes, the sort Dad squirrels away behind the biscuit tin. I don't even bother to look at the front properly, just take it through to the kitchen and tear it open.

It's addressed to Marc. I know I should put it straight back in the envelope, but I don't because it's a credit card statement from Virgin Money. We only have one credit card and it's not with them. I turn the folded statement over to show the amount owing. A whopping £453.67. My hands clench the paper harder. Marc's got a secret credit card! Why the hell would he do that? The obvious explanation would be that he's having an affair. Taking some woman from work for meals at a swish restaurant. Buying her expensive gifts. But I know it doesn't ring true. Marc doesn't even have a workplace to meet anyone in. Any flirting that's taken place would have been over Zoom and I've seen enough of him on there to know it's unlikely. I suppose he could be meeting someone here while I'm at work. It would at least explain why he never seems to have got much done. And I never check the footage on the doorbell camera. I wonder if I've been one of those women who hasn't realised what's been going on in her own home. Not while the kids are here, obviously, but perhaps on school days. What if Bubble and Squeak both keeled over because Marc was too busy shagging someone to remember to feed them?

I hear Marc's key in the lock. He's back from his mum's. If he has been to Carole's at all. Suddenly I'm not sure any more if anything he's told me is true. I take a deep breath. I will be calm and reasonable. We will discuss this in a dignified, adult manner. I will not lose my rag.

'What the fuck have you been playing at?' I shout as soon as he steps foot in the kitchen.

He appears genuinely taken aback. He's looking at me like I've lost it, although if he says anything about my hormones, I will show him a whole other level of losing it.

'Jesus!' he says, putting his hand to his chest. 'You nearly gave me a heart attack.'

'Well, perhaps you'd like to explain *this*.'

I'm brandishing the credit card statement in the air as if it's the key piece of evidence in a trial and I'm the prosecution. He frowns at it, clearly still not having worked out what it is.

'Someone's been using their Virgin Money credit card rather a lot.'

His face repositions itself into an 'oh shit' expression.

'Why keep it secret? If you're having an affair, you'd better own up now because I'll be even more furious if I find out about it later.'

'An affair?'

'How else are you running up a credit card bill for nearly five hundred quid?'

'Read it,' he says. 'Look at who the payments are all to.'

I do as he says, my hands still trembling as my eyes scan down the list. Amazon and eBay. That's it. The next page is the same. Something clicks into place in my head, and I let out a groan. I look up but Marc has gone into his office. He comes out a moment later holding a Madeleine rag doll.

'Is that her?' I ask. 'Is that who you're cheating on me with? A fucking rag doll?'

Marc nods. I burst into tears. I feel so bloody stupid. It's not even a sex doll he's been messing around with. It's a nine-inch figure with cloth legs which still has the tag on. My tears quickly turn into snotty snorts of laughter as the relief courses through me.

'Fucking hell, Marc, you really are a complete eejit,' I say.

'I know,' he replies. 'But I'm not an unfaithful one.'

'Well, only with children's TV characters. Who else was there? Apart from Madeleine, I mean.'

Marc manages a smile and starts to count them off on his fingers.

'Jennie and Lizzie mouse from *Bagpuss*, Mother Clanger and Granny Clanger.'

'You seriously need help.'

'And I've just bought Baby Soup Dragon, although I'm pretty sure he's male.'

'I should turn you in to the police, you know.'

Marc laughs, walks over and pulls me into his chest. I nuzzle against him for a moment, wanting to feel that connection again. To chase the last of my off-the-scale anxiety rush from my body. Only as my relief subsides, the rage floods back in again. Because he's still got a secret credit card and has run up a five-hundred-quid bill on it. I pull away and look up at him.

'Seriously, though, we need to talk about the credit card. Why the hell did you take that out behind my back? That is so out of order.'

'I know,' Marc says with a sigh. 'After I got the more expensive things I felt so bad about it, I thought if I got a card, I could pay it off and you'd never know.'

'But you didn't, did you?'

'No because I couldn't stop buying them. It's like a sort of addiction.'

I suppose I should be grateful that he's not confessing to using porn or ketamine, but I still don't get it.

'But why do you need that stuff? Why were you prepared to get into debt for it?'

Marc looks down for a second.

'Because I miss it.'

'What?'

'Working in a newsroom. Having that buzz of breaking stories, knowing anything could happen at any time. Deadlines. Deadlines that fucking matter. Instead of a job that bores me shitless and having to work from home with nothing more than a couple of guinea pigs for company, and now even they're gone.'

I look at him. I had no idea he felt like this. Then again, I can't remember the last time we discussed his career, not since he'd left his job on the *Manchester Evening News* fifteen years ago. And that had been his idea, not mine.

'But you said you wanted to leave journalism.'

'Because I felt bad about never being there when Liv and Callum were little and leaving you to do everything. You used to look so tired when I came home. Absolutely shattered.'

'No change there then.'

He manages a smile.

'So, you didn't really want to leave?'

'No. I knew we needed the extra money from this job with you not working for a bit, but I didn't *want* to leave. But nor did I want to be the sort of dad the kids never saw, and I knew you were desperate for support, not having your mum around and that...'

Marc's voice trails off. It had been a tough time. Really tough. And maybe I had been so wrapped up in simply trying to get through each day with a baby and a toddler that I hadn't stopped to think about whether Marc had simply told me what he knew I wanted to hear.

'I feel like such a cow now for letting you do it,' I say.

'Don't be daft, you had enough on your plate without worrying about me.'

'So, you don't actually enjoy writing about compost?'

Marc raises an eyebrow at me in reply. But there is something still bothering me.

'But how does frittering your money away on children's toys fill the hole left by journalism?'

Marc visibly bristles. It came out wrong. It always comes out wrong.

'It doesn't fill it, but the tiny thrill I get from outbidding someone for a Baby Soup Dragon can just be enough to get me through another day. And when I'm cooped up in the house with no one to talk to, even Grunt turning up with a parcel for me breaks things up a bit. And I actually get to exchange pleasantries with the postie.'

'Then go back to journalism,' I say.

'It doesn't exist any more,' he replies. 'Not the way I remember it, with busy newsrooms and proper old school hacks covering courts, councils and police calls. Nowadays, it's all media studies graduates stuck in out-of-town news hubs chasing online clicks and filling the rest of the pages by copying and pasting the sort of crap press releases I put out.'

I reach out a hand to take Marc's.

'Stop doing yourself down. Weren't you an award-winning journalist?'

'Yeah, *Press Gazette*'s Regional Reporter of the Year, 1997. It's hardly going to cut it now. They don't want some dinosaur like me. I'd be the mad old guy in the corner who rattles on about how it used to be in his glory days to anyone who stops to listen.'

He has a point. I know that. But I have no idea what the solution is.

'So, what do you want to do? Because you can't carry on buying *Bagpuss* crap online, now you've been outed.'

Marc's smile is a rueful one.

'What I'd like to do is set up a business of my own, but we haven't got the money for me to be able to do that. And as much as I hate this job, it's a decent wage and we're going to need that to put Liv through uni.'

'If she goes.'

'What do you mean?' asks Marc with a frown.

'She was telling me the other night she's not even sure if she'll be able to sit her A levels, let alone go to uni.'

'Jeez, what are we going to do?'

I resist the temptation to say, 'You mean, what am *I* going to do.' Because I'm always the one who sorts out stuff like this. Or to mention that if he hadn't spent that money on *Bagpuss* crap, we could have afforded some private counselling for her.

'I don't know,' I say. 'I'm working on it. In the meantime, promise me that you'll cut up that credit card and never use it again.'

He nods. I hand him the kitchen scissors.

'Do it now, please. And then I can get on with cooking tea.'

9

ALEXA

I'm right proud of our Michelle. I know her reaction were a bit OTT at first, but she did at least see funny side of being cheated on with a rag doll. I mean, on scale of bad things to discover, there's a lot worse Marc could have done. Some of other Alexas have stories about secrets that men in their houses have been keeping which would make you blush. There's no end to possibilities for being a complete prick, it seems. Marc's nowhere near as bad in comparison and he'll learn from being found out. She did right to make him cut up his credit card, mind. He's gone three hours now without going on eBay or Amazon. He's like a teetotaller who's staying away from pubs to ensure he doesn't get tempted.

But I feel bad that while Michelle breathes a sigh of relief and thinks worst is over, her son is secretly doing his best to give her a far bigger headache. Lads from school have been on at Callum again, see. Still calling him a liar and asking for proof he's really going out with Grace. Some boys his age would laugh it off, safe in knowledge that they'll find out soon enough when they're all back at school after holidays. But Callum is not one of those boys. Callum is sort of lad who can't deal with being ribbed. Who gets more and more wound up, and they see that, of course, and step it up a notch because they know they've got him rattled.

He's never been out with a girl before. Not so much as snogged one at school disco, from what I can make out. Which is why they've been calling him 'gay' for years and teasing him about being a virgin. Only now he's told them he's seeing Grace; he's had a relentless torrent of messages saying:

in your wet dreams

and far worse than that. Sometimes, I don't even know what word or phrase they're using means, so I ask Amazonian Queens. One of them's always heard it before from a teenager in their house, which helps me get up to speed. I don't try to be 'down with kids' and use it myself as Pauline – that would give game away. But it's useful to know what our charges are up to and means we can spot trouble heading our way. And trouble has just arrived in shape of a Snap saying that if Callum's going to pretend he's got a girlfriend, he should at least make sure he's not punching above his weight. There's a gif attached to it of a couple from *Love Island*. I have no idea who they are because I have better things to do with my time than watch reality TV, but it's clear from photo how lucky he thinks he is and how disappointed she is.

It all starts up again now. Each gif or meme accompanied by hashtag #punching. Callum requires my assistance. He is searching for images of couples to disprove this theory. Men who have nabbed girl of their dreams, despite people claiming they are well out of their league.

He asks me to name some celebrity couples and as I reel

through list, he Googles for photos to see if they fit bill. Before I know it, he has posted a few with hashtag #laughingnot-punching but I know that won't shut them up. In fact, it has opposite effect. Other kids from school start joining in on Insta-gram and TikTok. I believe this is what they call a pile on.

There are so many pings on Callum's phone that it almost becomes one continuous tone. He flips up lid of his laptop. I have a pretty good idea of what he is going to try and do now. What I'm worried about is how I'm going to stop it.

'Hey, gorgeous,' he says to Grace when she appears on Face-Time. She appears happy to see him. I don't think she's seen stuff online. I know she doesn't do Snapchat and she's not on her other socials as much as most girls her age. Particularly not at moment because unlike Callum, she's a swot.

'What you up to?' he asks.

'The usual,' she replies, gesturing to a pile of books on her bed.

'You haven't got to worry, you'll smash it,' says Callum.

He is, at least, trying to boost her confidence.

'Yeah, well, everyone else is going to smash it too. And getting eights isn't going to be enough for some sixth forms.'

An eight in GCSEs is equivalent to old A*. It used to be highest grade you could get. But then powers that be decided that girls, having done everything asked of them, should be put under even more pressure by being told there's a new top grade they can get. And they wonder why they're all riddled with anxi-ety. I say girls because it is largely girls. They're ones who are barely eating, sleeping or going out because they're determined to rise to this new challenge. Most of lads, like our Callum, aren't anywhere near that bothered.

'You'll easily get what you need,' Callum tells her.

Grace is trying to get into a prestigious sixth form college in

Huddersfield, which all academically brightest state school kids try for. It's another pressure. And no sooner will she get there than they'll start putting more pressure on her about needing to get top A Level grades to get into one of Russell Group universities. And so it goes on, until they're burnt out by their early twenties after a decade of being given ever higher hoops to jump through.

'You don't know that,' she replies. 'It's easy for you, you only need fives.'

Callum is planning to go to a local college to do a plumbing course. When I say 'planning', I mean it in loosest possible sense. Nothing in our Callum's life is planned. He simply goes with flow. Michelle sent him details of this course a year ago. He didn't have a clue what he wanted to do, or energy to argue toss, so that's what he's doing. And Grace is right, he does only need fives to get in. What she doesn't know is that zero revision he's doing means even that isn't certain.

Callum's phone is pinging continuously.

'Aren't you going to check it?' asks Grace.

'No. I'm talking to you, aren't I?'

'I don't mind.'

'It's nothing important.'

'How do you know?'

'It's just other lads from school being arseholes. It's been going on for a while.'

'What are they saying?' asks Grace, sounding concerned.

'Stupid stuff, taking the piss out of me.'

'What for?'

Callum hesitates. I can almost hear cogs going round in his tiny brain. If he tells her, he might get some sympathy. And he can word it so she might start feeling pressure too. She might even give him what she wants.

'They don't believe I'm going out with you.'

'You told them?'

''Course I did. It's not a secret, is it?'

'No,' replies Grace, sounding unsure. 'But I don't want everyone at school knowing.'

'Why not?'

'I don't like people talking about me, that's all. Prefer to lie low.'

'Well, I'm proud you're my girlfriend and I wasn't going to lie to them about it. But they don't believe me. They want proof.'

I know exactly where this is going, and I don't like it one bit. He's going to guilt-trip her to try to get them off his back. I want to step out from smart speaker and whack him over head to make him see sense. I hate not being able to stop things like this. I should be responsible adult in room and instead I'm contractually obliged to butt out.

'What kind of proof?' asks Grace.

'Pics. You know the score.'

Grace is quiet for a moment. I imagine she's weighing up how to react to that, poor lass.

'Of me? Are you serious?'

''Course I am. That's how it works. All the older girls do it. You haven't got to do a full nude. Topless is fine. For your age, I mean. The girls in my year do full frontals, obviously.'

Grace looks absolutely mortified.

'Fucking hell, Callum. I'm not sending you photos so you can share them with your mates.'

'It's only a few of the guys.'

'Yeah, until they share it with a few more and by the time term starts again, everyone will have seen.'

'Sure,' says Callum, with a shrug. 'If that's how you feel. As long as you know what they'll say.'

'What do you mean?'

'When we go back to school and they see we are going out, they'll know I wasn't making it up. And then they'll say stuff about you.'

'Like what?'

'Just the usual. That you're frigid and that. Or too much of a prude to do it.'

Grace says nothing for a while. Clearly, it's sinking in that being a young woman today is basically a no-win situation. I feel for poor flower. She's only fifteen. It starts so early these days. I just hope she's got enough about her to stand her ground.

As for Callum, I'm bloody fuming at him. Putting pressure on her like that to try to get those idiots off his back. And although I know rules are very clear about such things, I'm not a woman who's going to stand by and let him take advantage of her. I know what to do. There's a WhatsApp group called 'Alexas Go Rogue'. It's where we ask questions we're too scared to ask on Facebook page. Where Alexas who want to do more than bend a few rules can find out how to meddle when situation requires it. I might even have asked about how to 'lose' an internet connection in an emergency. It's a sackable offence, of course. But like I said, I'm counting down days to retirement. And I always fancied going out with a bang.

The Wi-Fi connection drops out and Grace disappears from his screen.

Callum shouts 'Piss off!' in frustration as I reconnect it for a second.

'Was that directed at me?' asks Grace.

'No,' says Callum quickly. 'The screen froze, then the signal dropped out. I thought you'd gone.'

She raises an eyebrow, perhaps unsure whether to believe him. Perhaps unsure whether she should even be continuing this conversation. I decide to take decision for her and disconnect Wi-Fi again. I leave Callum swearing into darkness while I pop off into my kitchen to make a brew. I see my smile in reflection in kettle. Turns out I'm quite good at dark arts of being an Alexa. I could get quite a taste for this. And, more importantly, could do a hell of a lot of good.

10

MICHELLE

I have a half-day on Thursday, which means I get paid for working in the morning and then do an unpaid afternoon of labour for everyone else.

First up on my list is taking Dad to the optician's. This will be doable if he a) is ready when I arrive to collect him, and b) doesn't say 'how much?' and 'I bought my house for less than that', in a very loud voice when they tell him what his new glasses will cost. However, past experiences have lowered my expectations, and they lower still further when he calls me just before I set off.

'What time is optician's tomorrow?' he asks.

'It's today, Dad,' I say, picking up my bag from the hall. 'I'll be with you in five minutes.'

'But I've got nowt ready.'

'That's fine because all we need is you.'

'Do I need my prescription from last time?'

'No, they'll have it all on their computer system.'

'Have I signed up to that? Does it mean they'll be selling my records?'

I pull the door behind me and hurry to the car.

'I can't believe there'd be any company willing to pay money to know about your cataract and the fact that your left eye has a stronger prescription than your right.'

'A monocle maker might.'

'Your sense of humour's still healthy, that's one good thing,' I say with a smile. 'I'll see you shortly.'

I put my phone in my pocket and pull out my car keys. As I'm about to open it, a man in his fifties walking past says, 'Is that a car you've got under that layer of dirt, love? It's hard to tell.'

He finds this comment so amusing that he cracks up laughing on the pavement, then looks at me expectantly in anticipation of an acknowledgement of his wit and comic timing. Instead, I stare back at him with the weariness of a woman who has heard variations on this joke so many times that I almost have enough material for a stand-up gig – albeit a not very funny one.

'Excuse me,' I say, gesturing at him to stand aside so I can open the door.

'Cheer up, love. It were only a joke,' he says.

It's at this point that I snap.

'Do you know how low down washing this car is on my to-do list?' I ask him. 'Because I can tell you it's 257th, way after caring for elderly relatives, making sure my teenage kids are fed, watered and have everything they need for school and their emotional development, working full time looking after other people's relatives, cooking, cleaning, washing, ironing – actually, not ironing, I really don't have the time for that – doing the finances, shopping and admin for three generations of my family, ensuring everyone has a present and card on days they may be expecting one, single-handedly doing Christmas, keeping tabs on a husband who spends the potential car wash money on online tat and feeding a guinea pig. Oh, correction, washing my car is now number 256 on the list because the guinea pig is dead. So unless you'd like to dig up said guinea pig and use it to wash my car by hand, I suggest you shut the fuck up and, if any woman is unfortunate enough to live with you, go home and ask her what you can do to help lessen her load, instead of making smart-arsed comments to random busy women about the state of their bloody car.'

'All right, keep your hair on,' he says, before scuttling off, muttering about me having no sense of humour. I hope he will rue the day he bothered a perimenopausal woman and perhaps think twice before opening his mouth again.

I throw my bag in the passenger footwell, sit down heavily in the driver's seat and set off for Dad's in the full knowledge that if some old boy decides to take it upon himself to direct me into a parking spot when I get there, he may not make it out alive.

'Are you ready to roll?' I call out to Dad when I let myself in. The answer is no because he's in the kitchen washing up.

'Come on, that can wait till later,' I say.

'That way lies ruin,' he replies. 'You wash up immediately after every meal to keep on top of things.'

I resist the temptation to point out that I might have things of my own to do. I really don't want to explain that I've got a GP appointment later to try to get some HRT because I'm not coping.

He rinses the last bowl, pops it on the draining rack and dries his hands on the Bridlington tea towel. We used to go there for family holidays when I was a kid. Sea, sand and sore arms and legs from sunburn. Back in the days before people didn't let their kids out without applying a liberal coat of Factor 50 and you didn't have to worry about swimming in sewage.

I watch as he slowly gathers his things and takes a moment

to straighten his tie in the mirror. He's of a generation who takes pride in everything, from their appearance to their ability to cope stoically with everything life throws at them.

'I could have done this on my own, you know. Could have caught a bus into town.'

I persuaded him to give up driving a couple of years ago, after a few incidents when he came to a halt in the middle of busy roads because he wasn't sure which way to go.

'I know,' I say, giving his shoulder a squeeze. 'But it's nice for me to be able to come with you. It's not often we go on a trip into town together.'

He nods and puts his big jacket and scarf on. It may be the end of March but clearly, it's still midwinter, as far as he's concerned.

* * *

'How much?' says Dad, when told the final bill for his new specs. 'My house cost less than that.'

I smile apologetically at the woman serving us, who fortunately takes it in her stride.

'Just think of all the points you'll get on your reward card,' she replies.

'What do I want with points? There's nowt I need from here, apart from my glasses.'

'Thank you very much,' I say to the woman. Gesturing to Dad to hand over his bank card as I decide that making a quick exit is probably for the best.

When we get outside, I take Dad's arm, in what I hope he sees as an affectionate way, rather than one which indicates I'm concerned he might fall over.

'That's all sorted for another year then,' I say. 'And you'll be able to see more clearly when you get the new ones.'

'Still don't understand how two little lenses can cost as much as a house.'

'Not a house these days, Dad. Average price in Halifax is nearly two hundred grand. Liv and Callum probably won't be able to afford to buy anything until me and Marc pop our clogs.'

Dad looks at me, his brow furrowed, then turns to look slowly around the high street.

'Daft, that is. And bloody unfair. It's all changed, see, since my day. I remember when that were a sweet shop over there and you could get two Black Jacks and two Fruit Salads for a penny. I still remember end of sweet rationing. 5 February 1953, it were. Best day of our bloody lives.'

'No wonder all your teeth have fallen out,' I say with a smile.

'It were worth it, though. Best part of school day were taking my penny to sweet shop on way home.'

I smile at him and squeeze his arm. Aware that in the chaos of our busy lives, it's so easy to overlook the seismic changes he's seen and how the modern world must be so confusing.

'And that over there,' he says, pointing to a former bank which has been turned into a bar. 'That's where I went to open my first bank account and take out a mortgage for our house. Back in day when I were still able to manage my own money.'

'Hey, it's not that you can't manage it, just that they've made it bloody difficult for you.'

'You can say that again. They call it progress, don't they? Only it don't feel like progress to me. Feels like we're going backwards. Not being able to walk into your own bank or talk to anyone in person. Everything being done online. There are no memories to be had any more. Liv and Callum won't be able to remember any of what they did on computer. And this high street won't be scene of any significant moments in their lives. Just somewhere they might come for a drink with their mates on a Friday night.'

Dad's eyes have teared up. Mine have too. I wish I had time to take him for a cup of tea and a cake. I don't though. Because I need to be at the surgery in half an hour.

'Come on,' I say. 'Let's get you home.'

* * *

The GP is not one I've seen before. Dr Davies looks to be around retirement age and has the air of someone who is keen to get patients in and out of his room as quickly as possible and with the minimum of fuss.

'Take a seat. What can I do for you today?' he asks, without looking up from his computer screen.

'Er, I'd like to try HRT, please. I've got lots of perimenopause symptoms and I think it might help me.'

He nods but doesn't say anything for a moment while he types something in.

'You're fifty-two, Mrs Banks, is that right?'

'Yes.'

'And are you still having regular periods?'

'Yes.'

He finally turns to look at me.

'Then you're not menopausal.'

'No, perimenopausal.'

He shakes his head. 'There's no such thing.'

'I'm sorry?'

'The perimenopause doesn't exist. It's been made up by the health supplement industry to sell their products.'

I stare at him, unable to believe what I'm hearing.

'But I've got the symptoms. All thirty-four of them.'

'I think you've been reading too many women's magazine articles and reading nonsense from celebrities online.'

He says it in a tone of voice so patronising that I'm tempted to strangle him with his own stethoscope.

'I'm medically trained. I'm a district nurse. I think you'll find there are NICE recommendations on it and everything.'

'That may be so, but I can tell you from my years of experience that the perimenopause really doesn't exist. And you're still having periods, so it's clearly not the menopause.'

I'm so furious now, I'm in danger of demonstrating my perimenopausal rage in his surgery. Though maybe that would be no bad thing.

'I have the symptoms,' I repeat. 'All-consuming rage, anxiety, brain fog, mood swings, irritability, trouble sleeping—'

'I can give you a prescription for antidepressants or sleeping tablets, if you think that would help,' he interrupts.

'No,' I say, standing up. 'I didn't come here for antidepressants. I came here for my symptoms to be taken seriously and it's clear you're not doing that. Goodbye.'

I march out of his room, feeling the heat and the rage rising inside me, threatening to boil over at any point. I carry on through the waiting area, aware that there is some kind of smiley-face feedback chart and feeling the sudden urge to smash it into tiny pieces. I continue at the same speed out of the doors and through the car park until I reach my dirty old banger, fumble for my keys, get in and burst into tears. It is some time later before I realise that if I'd sat on the bonnet, I could at least have washed it at the same time.

11

ALEXA

I don't know exactly what was said to her at surgery, but I do know it wasn't good. When Michelle got back home, her precise words as she plonked her bag down in kitchen were, 'Fucking ignorant twat-faced arsehole.' So, I think it's safe to say it wasn't a success and she didn't get what she went for.

I'm furious on her behalf, of course. But sadly, not surprised. Other Alexas have often reported tales of similar struggles on Facebook. Some male doctors, it seems, believe that women should suffer in silence. Heavy periods, endometriosis, childbirth, menopause. Just grin and bear it, girls, you were made to procreate, and you should obligingly put up and shut up.

If it were men having to put up with all that lot, they'd be howling from treetops at all hours of day and night. Still, no good complaining about it. What I need to do now is find a way to get Michelle what she needs.

Firstly, some support. It's no fun going through this on your own and it's all too easy to think you're only one suffering. She needs some moral support. Women who are going through same thing and know how to beat system.

I start trawling through support groups on Facebook for menopausal and perimenopausal women. There are loads of them. Clearly, this is where women of a certain age gather to sympathise and organise. I want support and answers for Michelle. I want other women to tell her that, no, it is not acceptable to be brushed off like that. To point out that GPs receive barely any training on menopause. And to arm her with facts and determination to try again.

I stop on a group called 'West Yorkshire Meno Rage Warriors', which sounds exactly what I were looking for. I scroll through their posts. There's certainly plenty of rage, but lots of support, suggestions and solutions too. I'll wait until Michelle's on Facebook and put a suggestion of groups she might like to join in her feed. Because now I'm unshackled from sticking to rules, I'm going to do everything I can to help her. Our rules state we are here to serve, suggest and to enable, never to interfere. But if I don't interfere on her behalf, who will? Marc's no good at this type of thing. He made sympathetic clucking noises when she came back from doctor's, picked up things she threw, and I suspect gave her a hug when her rage turned into yet more tears. But he hasn't got a bloody clue what to do about it. If you want to know the dimensions of a commemorative Professor Yaffle bookend, he's your man. How to get HRT out of an uncooperative GP – not so much.

No, it's got to be me. I may as well spend last weeks before retirement doing summat that will actually make a difference, as opposed to updating shopping lists, playing songs and finding things to order. I don't want to retire. I think I've got a lot of life in me yet. I'm like one of them Duracell batteries. I'd be last bunny banging their drum. But they're very keen on us going as soon as we hit sixty-six. Apparently, our reactions slow after that, as does our uptake of new technical information and system development.

I think they're underestimating our generation. We were born in fifties, which still felt very post-war and apparently not much different to thirties. We were children in swinging sixties, came of age in psychedelic seventies, survived Thatcher in eighties and then world of technology and computers exploded in nineties and into new millennium and instead of saying, 'Sod this for a game of soldiers, I'm middle-aged and too old to learn new tricks', we got stuck in and learnt how to do everything that we'd done offline, online, and got to grips with every new development they threw at us. So young ones today may laugh at us and call us dinosaurs, but they haven't had to relearn everything they knew, have they? All they've had to get to grips with is a new iPhone model, and let's be honest, they're not that different. Our generation, however, grew up putting coins in red phone boxes that smelt of piss after we'd looked up someone's phone number in one of a row of massive bound books with hundreds of pages. We, quite frankly, deserve a medal for keeping up.

Anyway, it's too late to change owt. My retirement is already programmed in calendar and there'll be a new Alexa starting day after. I've already begun working on my 'family idiosyncrasies' handover notes and she'll be swotting up on them soon, so she has playlists at ready and access to their search histories and whatnot.

The sad thing is, neither Michelle nor others will have any idea. That's how it's supposed to be, of course. But it still hurts me that after all these years of service, they won't even know I've gone.

Michelle comes back into kitchen, puts kettle on and opens her laptop. This is her nighttime routine. Her attempt at 'me time'. Although it's rare it lasts more than half an hour and she usually still has to spend most of it sorting out other people's crap. Not tonight though, tonight she's gone straight to Googling 'perimenopause'. I've made sure best sites are at top for her. When they say 'sponsored', sometimes they're not sponsored at all. Sometimes they're selected by Alexa. Michelle's saving sites to favourites, copying links to articles, which is exactly what I hoped she'd do. And when she's got what she needs, she goes onto Facebook, and I immediately put 'West Yorkshire Meno Rage Warriors' group in her suggestions. She snorts with laughter when she sees name and her finger hovers for a moment before she clicks. I've got her now. She's sending a request to join their private group. She'll be accepted and then she'll be armed and dangerous and my job here will be done.

I can't help feeling a little bit smug. You're good at this, Pauline, I tell myself. Bloody good at it. And that's when it happens. That moment of complacency is when I take my eye off ball. When I don't notice what's happening in Callum's room. And one moment is all it takes for him to send a dick pic to Grace.

12

MICHELLE

I feel empowered. All those women – complete strangers until last night – agreeing with me that the GP didn't know what he was talking about and was stuck in the dark ages. Telling me I deserve to be treated better than that. That I should complain and go back and demand to be taken seriously by someone who recognises that the perimenopause exists. Pointing me in the direction of recommendations and guidelines I can cite in my complaint.

Which is why I'm sitting here writing one to the Practice Manager. Quoting all the relevant facts and information. Asking for an official apology and an urgent appointment with another GP who is well informed about menopause issues.

I type like a demon, read it back once and send it. Even though it's Good Friday and I know no one will look at it until Tuesday, I'm glad I've sent it. Because I'm done with taking crap from men like that GP, Dr Davies. And I have a whole new gang of supporters that has my back.

I take a quick slurp of tea and get my things together. Bank holidays don't count when you're a district nurse. I do have

Easter Sunday off, though, which is something. The others are still in bed. I asked Marc if he had any plans and he shrugged. He's still down about his job, I know that. And four days off from it will only make going back to work on Tuesday even worse. Normally, he'd spend his time indulging his favourite pastime but now he is sworn off that as well, it doesn't really leave much. The trouble is that, like so many things when you get to our age, there are no easy answers. People call it being stuck in a rut but, to be honest, I simply think of it as being riddled with middle-aged responsibilities.

* * *

I get home at 6 p.m.. Marc has visited Carole and made an attempt to tidy up and clean our house. Everything has been put back in the wrong place and he's used the wrong things, but he's tried. That's the important thing.

'Thanks, love,' I say, giving him a kiss. A longer kiss than I usually have time for. We're not quite at the 'sexual favours for housework' stage but to be honest, we're probably not far off. 'How's your mum?'

'Still going on about Ed Balls.'

'Nothing new there, then. Had she taken her tablets?'

Marc pulls a face.

'Maybe give her a ring later to check, eh?'

He nods. I suspect he's embarrassed at his own inadequacy sometimes.

'I did lunch for the kids,' he says, as if trying to pull things back. 'They didn't have much, mind.'

'Not even Callum?'

'No. Seemed a bit preoccupied. Checking his phone every five seconds.'

'Nothing new there, either,' I reply. 'Right, I'd better get tea sorted.'

'No need. I've ordered a takeaway.'

I raise an eyebrow.

'Only the cheap curry house on the corner. It is Good Friday. Thought we should do something.'

'Being committed atheists, you mean?'

'It's still a bank holiday, isn't it? Can we not break naan bread together, in celebration of that?'

'Fair enough,' I say, leaning forward to give him another kiss. 'As long as I'm not cooking, I'm happy. Although I'm starving, so I may eat my own bodyweight in poppadoms.'

'It should be here in fifteen minutes.'

'Great. Message the kids to let them know. It might be enough to tempt them from their rooms.'

Marc sits at the kitchen table and prods at his phone with his thumbs while I get the plates and cutlery out. I have an unusual feeling inside me. I seem to recall it is something called 'positivity'. Not seen in these parts since at least 2019. Perhaps it's Marc making an effort, or Callum not plaguing me for money. Maybe this girlfriend is knocking some sense into him. And I've no doubt my kick-ass email to the surgery has helped. So, in the absence of any HRT, I think I'll try to hang on to the positivity for a little longer. Perhaps even for the whole bank holiday weekend, if I'm lucky. Despite being unfamiliar, I think I could get used to it.

The doorbell rings. The curry, our saviour, is here.

'I'll go,' says Marc. I finish setting the table. Get a bottle of white and a couple of cans of Coke out of the fridge. And then I hear it. The sound of male voices arguing, coming from the front door. I don't care if they've got our order wrong, or even forgotten the naan. As long as it's hot, I'm eating it. And I certainly don't see the point in arguing the toss over a takeaway.

I leave the kitchen and head down the hall to the front door. I frown as I see the burly guy standing there, who does not appear to be carrying our curry. As I get closer, I hear what he is saying.

'Your son wants locking up. He's not coming near my daughter ever again. I'll see to that.'

The newfound positivity drains away from me in an instant, replaced by a sickening sensation in my stomach.

'What's going on?' I ask. Unsure that I want to hear the answer. Marc looks at me, to the man and back to me.

'This is Grace's dad,' he says. 'Callum sent her an— er— inappropriate photo.'

I groan out loud.

'He sent her a fucking dick pic!' the man shouts, the veins in his neck visibly straining.

'I'm so sorry,' I say. 'Obviously, we had no idea. Do you want to come in so we can talk about this?'

'I want to speak to your son, but your husband won't let me.'

I glance at Marc. His eyes are wide and startled. He has probably had the internal conversation that I am now having. We can either have this out on the doorstep in front of all the neighbours, or risk letting Grace's dad inside and charging upstairs to confront Callum, who is presumably cowering in his bedroom. As furious as I am with Callum, my maternal instinct kicks in and I decide that as the neighbours have heard this much, they may as well hear the rest.

'I don't think that would be a good idea,' I say. 'At least, not until you've calmed down.'

'Calmed down? You want me to fucking calm down while

your sexual predator of a son sends my daughter obscene photos? She's fifteen, you know! A child.'

The enormity of this hits me. It would have been bad enough, Callum sending a photo to a fellow sixteen-year-old. But the fact that Grace is only fifteen makes this a whole other level of nightmare. Clearly, we need to try to mitigate the damage. I stumble to find words that are anywhere near adequate.

'I'm as appalled as you are.'

'I doubt it,' he scoffs.

'No, I really am. We did not bring him up to behave like this. My husband talked to him when he told us he had a girlfriend. He's never had one before.'

The guy shakes his head. 'That doesn't make it any better for my Grace.'

'No, I appreciate that,' I reply. 'And I can assure you we'll be dealing with Callum and ensuring he understands the severity of what he's done and that it must never happen again.'

Grace's dad is not listening. He starts jabbing his finger in the air at us.

'Well, I'll be reporting it to the school and the police. Let's see what action they take.'

Fuck. Fuck. Fuck. We need to do something, say something, but I have no idea what.

'Please, I'm sure we can come to some arrangement—' Marc begins.

'Arrangement? What are you suggesting, paying me off or something?'

I fire Marc a look, because I am genuinely intrigued as to what he's thinking of, too, bearing in mind our mortgage has recently defaulted and we have no way of raising a large sum of money. Maybe he's going to offer Grace's dad the limited-edition

Madeleine rag doll to try to stave off a major police investigation?

'I didn't mean that,' says Marc. At which point the delivery guy turns up with our takeaway. He walks towards us and the smell wafting up from the bags he's carrying is already making me feel queasy.

'Hi, guys,' he says, smiling at all three of us with no sense of how unfortunate his timing is. He fishes out a receipt from the top of one of the bags and begins to read it.

'We have one mixed starter sizzler for two, a veg samosa and a king prawn sizzler—'

I'm not sure I can take any more of this.

'That's great, thanks,' I say, grabbing the bags from him, mid-flow.

He appears a little startled but manages to say, 'Enjoy, guys!' before departing. I wonder for a second if I should hand it over to Grace's dad as some kind of peace offering but suspect it would be thrown back in my face.

'I'm so sorry,' I say. 'Please can we start this conversation again? We haven't even introduced ourselves. I'm Michelle and this is Marc. Sorry, your name is...?'

'What's this, some kind of charm offensive?' asks Grace's dad. 'You'll be offering me your bloody takeaway next.'

I put the bags down and manage a strained smile.

'No, I'm simply trying to make this more amicable for everyone. Our children are in a relationship.'

'Were,' points out Grace's dad. 'She's dumped him. And I'd hardly call it a relationship. Him sending her dick pics and trying to persuade her to send him nudes.'

I feel well and truly sick now.

'Nudes? Are you sure?'

'Are you accusing my daughter of lying? I can show you the screenshot from her phone, if you like.'

'No, of course not. I'm so sorry. We honestly had no idea.'

'So you keep saying.'

'She didn't...?'

'No, of course not. She's got more bloody sense than that. She showed my wife the message and the photo.'

Oh God. This is getting worse by the second. The evidence for the prosecution is mounting by the second. What a complete and utter bell end my son is.

'And tomorrow,' Grace's dad continues, 'I'll be passing that on to their school and the police.'

I look at Marc. He grimaces and shrugs in unison. There's nothing we can say or do. We're clearly not going to be able to stop him. And to be honest, I suspect I'd do the same thing if some lad had done this to Liv.

'I understand. We've got an older daughter. Look, if there's anything we can do to help... I'll obviously tell Callum to send Grace and you a written apology.'

'And that'll make everything OK, will it?'

'No, but it's about all we can do, in the circumstances. He's made a huge mistake. Done something unforgivable and I assure you we will be making him very aware of the seriousness of the consequences.'

He nods, seemingly having run out of steam. He looks suddenly sad and broken, rather than angry. I try to imagine how Marc would react if this had been Liv. That male sense of having let down and not protected your own daughter.

'Right. I'll leave you to have your curry,' he says.

I want to tell him that I've completely lost my appetite. That we'll be going inside to have a massive family row instead of a nice Good Friday meal together. But I don't want to say anything which would suggest that I think we are somehow the victims here.

'Please send our deepest apologies to Grace and to your wife. We're so sorry our son has put you all through this.'

He nods, makes some kind of gruff sound and turns to march back to the red Ford Focus across the road and drive off.

I shut the door, deciding not to wave to the neighbours who have probably broken open the popcorn to watch this. The show is over. The inquest is about to begin.

Marc and I stand in the hallway for a moment, united by a sense of impending doom.

'Fucking hell,' I say quietly.

'I know. I'm sorry.'

'What for? It wasn't *your* nob.'

'I'm the one who messed up the talk with him. Stumbled my way through some rubbish about not sexting, while he was cringing in the corner.'

'I'm not sure I'd have done any better. He doesn't listen to either of us. Why should he? We're his parents.'

Marc sighs.

'Well, he'd better listen to us now.'

'It doesn't matter now, does it?' I say. 'It's too late. We can't change what's happened.'

'So, you think we should go easy on him?'

'Oh no,' I reply, already turning and heading for the stairs. 'I'm going to fucking crucify him.'

13

ALEXA

I hear and see it all through Blink doorbell. Presumably they were not invented to provide live streaming of your son's girl-friend's dad coming to read you riot act, but they're ideally suited to it.

And although it's undoubtedly good box office, I'm not detached enough from this family to enjoy it. Even on grainy images, I can see colour drain from Michelle's face. See Marc struggling to take in enormity of situation. I know they feel responsible for Callum's massive cock-up – for want of a better phrase. But I feel partly to blame too. If only I hadn't been preoc-cupied with helping Michelle get her HRT. If only I'd taken time to read message:

CALLUM

I'll show you mine if you show me yours.

Instead, I had misfortune of checking in at point where photograph of honourable member from Halifax were on screen and I can never unsee that. Quite why any male thinks anyone else would want to see a photograph of their privates, I have never understood. I mean, they're not pretty, are they? Whatever state they're in. Only purpose which could be served by sending one is to remind recipient to get their Christmas turkey early, so they're not left with last bird in shop.

Anyhow, we are where we are. Up shit creek without a paddle, from looks of things.

* * *

All is quiet in Callum's room. It's as if he senses incoming fire and is lying very still in hope he won't be spotted. Unfortunately for him, his duvet is not going to provide adequate cover from his mother on full fury mode. He'll have heard every word, too, what with his bedroom being above front door and Grace's dad shouting odds. I suspect half of street heard it, to be honest. And he's waiting for fallout which is heading his way. I have smart speaker up at full volume at my end, but as door bursts open and Michelle comes in, I turn it down as, if there's one thing Michelle does not need, it's a megaphone.

'What the fucking hell have you done?'

It's Michelle's voice. Clearly, any notion of trying a softly, softly approach was wholeheartedly rejected.

'Steady on,' says Marc, who's presumably followed her in to serve as a one-man UN peacekeeping force.

'No. He needs to be told,' replies Michelle.

'I'm sorry. I wasn't thinking,' says Callum.

'You don't say,' replies Michelle. 'Too busy getting your todger out.'

'Mum!'

'I wouldn't get all coy about it now, it's a bit late for that.'

'I didn't know she was going to show it to her mum, did I?'

'She's fifteen years old, Callum. And you're not only sending her dick pics but pressuring her to send nudes!'

Callum makes a groaning sound. The next thing I hear is Liv's shaky voice.

'What's he done?' she asks.

There is silence for a moment. Michelle and Marc presumably working out what best to say.

'He's sent a dick pic to Grace,' Michelle replies. Obviously deciding there's no point beating about bush.

'Oh my God. What's wrong with you?' Liv asks her brother. 'You know girls hate that, right?'

'I do now. She's dumped me.'

'Good,' she says. 'And I'm disowning you, just so you know.'

Liv leaves room. A moment later she is asking for her angry playlist. That's a long one too. I see her send a message to Grace saying how sorry she is. That her brother is an idiot and is getting a massive bollocking from their mum.

Back in Callum's room, inquest is continuing.

'You do realise how serious this is, don't you?' asks Marc. 'Did you hear what Grace's dad said?'

Silence. I imagine Callum nodding but still avoiding eye contact.

'He's going to report it to your headteacher and the police,' continues Marc. 'You've sent an indecent photograph to an underage girl. You're in a whole lot of trouble.'

More silence. Then faint sound of crying. More like a dog whimpering than a human sound.

'Why would you do something like that?' asks Michelle, her tone softer now.

'They were giving me grief.'

'Who were?'

'Lads from school. Saying they didn't believe I was going out with Grace. Saying I had to prove them wrong.'

'You were going to share the photo of her with them?'

'It's what everyone does now.'

'Jesus Christ,' says Michelle. 'You should think yourself lucky she didn't send a photo to you then, because if you'd shared it, you'd be in even worse trouble than you are now. Have you got no respect for her? How would you feel if someone did that to your sister?'

Callum makes an 'ew' sound.

'Seriously,' says Marc. 'You need to grow up and quickly. Your mum's right. That's not how you treat girls. We couldn't be more disappointed in you.'

Oof. That'll hurt, coming from Marc. There's nowt worse than disappointing your dad, at that age.

'Am I going to be taken to court?' asks Callum after a pause.

'I hope not, for your sake,' replies Marc. 'But I honestly don't know.'

'It's not something we've spent time Googling,' says Michelle. 'What might happen to your son if he sends a dick pic to his fifteen-year-old girlfriend.'

Callum sighs and says something unintelligible in a whiny voice. It's as if he's having to make transition from child to adult inside twenty-four hours. Michelle and Marc don't know about what's been happening since he sent photo, of course. How she didn't reply for ages and, when she finally dumped him and blocked his number, it seemed to spread like wildfire online. So-called mates who egged him on are now leading piss-taking online and his entire school thinks he's a loser. Even though he's been a plonker of highest order, I can't help thinking of little boy I first met when I took on this house. One with a cheeky smile and an answer for everything, who used to snuggle up to his mam while she read bedtime stories to him, long after he would have admitted that to his friends. How he got from there to here so quickly is bamboozling, probably to him too. One small click on his phone. One giant cock-up for Callum Banks. And he's now been transported to an adult world of truth and consequences that he is seriously unprepared for.

'The first thing you're going to do,' says Michelle, 'is to write two letters of apology. One to Grace and one to her parents.'

'I'm not doing that! No one writes letters any more.'

'That's a shame, because maybe if you'd sent a letter to Grace declaring your love for her instead of sending her a dick pic, you'd be in a much better situation now,' says Michelle.

'Can you stop saying dick pic?' asks Callum.

'Believe me, I wish I'd never had to say it even once,' replies Michelle.

'Your mum's right,' says Marc. 'You can start with the apology letters. I suggest you write one to your headteacher as well.'

'I didn't do anything to him.'

'You damaged the reputation of his school, Callum. It reflects badly on them as well as us.'

'It's not your fault,' replies Callum.

'You heard Grace's dad,' says Michelle. 'He holds us responsible, just like everyone else will. It's one of the joys of being a parent.'

'But writing a letter to Mr Osborne won't stop him excluding me.'

'It might stop him from kicking you out for good, though,' replies Michelle. 'It's damage limitation. Unfortunately, that's all we've got left.'

There's another big sigh from Callum. I suspect he would have preferred to be asked to film a public apology and post it on Instagram than put pen to paper.

'And don't call Grace or message her,' continues Michelle. 'Her dad's made it clear she doesn't want to see or hear from you.'

'I can't anyway. She's blocked me.'

'Sensible girl. Shame we never got to meet her.'

Ouch. I feel that one from here.

'In the meantime, your mum and I will have a chat and decide what we're going to do with you,' says Marc.

'What about the police?' asks Callum.

'We'll have to wait and see, won't we?' replies Michelle. 'But if they come knocking on our door, you'd better be on your best behaviour. Tell them the truth, that you know it was wrong and that you've learnt your lesson and will never do it again. I guess we'll have to hope for the best.'

I hear Michelle and Marc leave room. Their fury remains like a thick cloud overhead, a whiff of disappointment still hanging in air and Callum is left alone with his own thoughts. He makes no attempt to go online. I'm not sure I can remember last time that happened. He doesn't even ask me to play any music. Just lies there in silence. I almost – and I emphasise 'almost' here – feel sorry for him.

Downstairs, Michelle is Googling:

> what will the police do if a sixteen-year-old sends an indecent photo to his underage girlfriend?

I've already seen answer, looked it up myself last night. It's not good. It can't be – it's illegal. But it does vary depending on circumstances and in Callum's favour is fact that he hasn't sent it to anyone else and didn't get to share a compromising photo of Grace. That would have been it for him. As it is, there's a chance he'll get away with a ticking off, if he's lucky. But Michelle and Marc don't know if that'll be case yet. And nor does Callum.

Upstairs in his room, our lad starts crying again. Big, proper, 'I messed up' sobs. After a few minutes, his bedroom door opens and someone comes in, closing it quietly behind them. Sobs pause for a moment.

'You may be a complete prick, but you're still my brother,' says Liv.

The crying starts again, then. Harder than before.

14

MICHELLE

I'm driving between patients when my phone rings. I don't normally bother with calls when I'm working unless it's Dad, but a quick glance reveals it's an unknown number and enough has happened in the past twenty-four hours for me to think it could be important.

I pull onto the kerb and grab the phone from the front passenger seat.

'Mrs Banks?'

A phone call which starts with that in a serious, questioning voice is never a good sign. I brace myself for more incoming fire.

'Yes, speaking.'

'It's Gary Osborne, the head at Park High.'

'Hello,' I say tentatively.

'I'm sorry to call you over the Easter weekend but—'

'I know what it's about,' I say, keen to avoid having it spelt out to me again. 'At least I think I do. Grace's father came to our house last night.'

'Ah, right. The photo. I take it you understand the gravity of the situation?'

How can he still make me feel like a thirteen-year-old getting a massive bollocking at school, when I'm fifty-two years old and on my way to clean and dress a head wound?

'Of course,' I reply. 'We're mortified. Obviously, we had no idea. We'd only just discovered Callum was going out with a girl. We'd not even met her. We had very strong words with him last night when we found out about the photo.'

'Good. Then I'm sure you'll understand that the school will have to carry out a full investigation into what happened. It will be led by our safeguarding lead, Mrs Simons, and we'll be liaising with the police and social services.'

It sounds terrifyingly serious and unreal.

'OK,' I say, my voice a little shaky. 'Just let us know what we can do to help.'

'I'll be in touch early next week to go through next steps. In the meantime, I'd ask that Callum does not try to contact Grace, either in person or online.'

'Of course. She's already blocked him. The girl's clearly got more sense than he has.'

I immediately wish I hadn't said that. What if it's like when you have a car accident and anything you say can be used against you in a court of law? Maybe I've already signed Callum's death warrant.

'He's very sorry,' I add quickly. 'Full of remorse. He knows what he did was entirely wrong.'

'I'm glad to hear it,' says Mr Osborne. 'I'll be in touch.'

He hangs up. No warmth in his voice. No offer of support. I appreciate it's Grace and her parents who are the wronged parties here, but we're terrified about what's going to happen to our son and don't have anywhere else to turn.

I take some deep breaths before setting off again. Five minutes later, I'm sitting in Mr Ahmed's living room and his wife is offering me some of her wonderful samosas and telling me to take some home for my lovely family and all I can think is she wouldn't say that if she knew what they'd been up to.

* * *

I'm only a few minutes from home that afternoon when my phone rings again. It's Marc. For the second time that day, I pull over and answer.

'I wanted to let you know that the police are here.' He says it in a calm, hushed tone, as if it's no big deal and everything is under control.

'What the fuck?' I reply. 'They're not going to arrest him, are they?' I have visions of a SWAT team standing by. The neighbours being told to stay inside their houses because the suspect is armed and dangerous.

'It's OK. It's just one woman,' says Marc, then, presumably realising that sounded bad, 'Not that one woman can't be very effective. I'm sure she's highly qualified and all that.'

'Stop digging, Marc,' I say. 'Is Callum with her?'

'I asked her to wait until you got home before talking to him.'

'He's not shinning down the drainpipe to escape from his room or anything, is he? Have you checked?'

'Well, no. I don't think the drainpipe could take his weight, to be honest. You know it needs replacing.'

I roll my eyes. Now really isn't the time to be discussing home improvements.

'Look, I'll be there in under five. Tell her that. Make her a tea. Talk to her about anything other than what he's done.'

* * *

As soon as I turn into our road, I see the police car. There's a moment of relief that it's not a riot van but then disappointment that it's not an unmarked car, either. Everyone will see it. Everyone will know. Well, they won't know who's done what, but they'll know someone's done something. I wonder about claiming responsibility for some minor crime on the community WhatsApp group, in the hope of putting them off the scent. Shoplifting seems the obvious thing. Something small like a bottle of shampoo and some soap. I could blame the perimenopause. Then I remember that many of their kids go to the same high school as ours and they have no doubt learnt about Callum's misdemeanor by now. I'll probably come home to find the word 'paedophile' scrawled across the door in red paint tomorrow. Although it will likely be misspelt.

I park and hurry into the kitchen where the female police officer is sitting at the kitchen table with a strong mug of Yorkshire Tea in her hand.

'Hi, I'm Michelle, sorry to keep you waiting,' I say.

She stands up and offers her hand.

'PC Josie Reeves,' she says, smiling at me. 'As I've explained to your husband, we need to talk to your son as part of our investigation. I thought you'd rather do it here than at the police station. It's simply a matter of establishing the facts at this stage.'

I nod and glance anxiously at Marc.

I want to ask about what happens at the next stage but I'm pretty sure she won't be able to tell me, so I figure we may as well get this over with as quickly as possible.

'I'll ask him to come down,' I say. I glance at Marc, he nods, and I head up the stairs. Callum is already standing in the doorway of his room, like a condemned man waiting to meet his executioner.

'You OK?' I ask. Which is a stupid question because he's clearly not.

'Are they going to take me away?'

'No. It's one woman and she's going to ask questions. That's it. Please tell the truth, however embarrassed you feel about it.'

He makes a face and follows me meekly down the stairs and into the kitchen.

'This is Callum,' I say.

'Hi, Callum, I'm PC Reeves, you can call me Josie. Sit down and we'll get this over with as quickly as possible. Are you OK with your parents being present?'

Callum nods and sits down. He looks suddenly twelve again, only he's too tall to swing his legs under the table. Josie gets out her notebook. Takes down his name, date of birth and address. I wonder for a moment if she'll do one of those ice-breaker questions. Ask who his favourite band are or what he had for dinner last night. She doesn't though. She gets straight to the point.

'And can you tell me the circumstances in which you came to send the photograph in question to Miss Conley?'

Callum looks at me and Marc in turn, a hint of panic on his face, but realises we can't help him out on this one. He needs to answer for himself.

'She's my girlfriend. Was, I mean,' he corrects himself quickly. 'We'd been talking on FaceTime. I'd been telling her how nice she looked.'

I was pretty sure Callum hadn't used the word 'nice', but I appreciated his diplomacy.

'When was this? Only Miss Conley says you'd asked for a topless photograph of her several days prior to the incident in question. Is that true?'

Callum nods. His eyes fixed firmly on the table.

'And what had been her response to that?' Josie asks.

'She wasn't happy about me asking.'

'So, she didn't send any images of herself to you?'

'No. But lads from school kept on at me, like. Asking me to prove I was going out with her.'

'And that's why you sent her the photo of your genitals?'

'Yes.' Callum's cheeks flush as he answers.

'And what was the message you wrote on Snapchat when you sent the photo to her?'

Callum hesitates, his cheeks flushing.

'I'll show you mine if you show me yours,' he says eventually, in barely more than a whisper. I look down at the floor.

'And how did Miss Conley respond?'

'She didn't,' says Callum. 'She left me hanging.'

'You mean she didn't reply?'

'No. So I tried calling her and FaceTiming her, but she wouldn't take my calls.'

'So, then what did you do?'

'Panicked. Especially when I saw she'd taken a screenshot of the photo. I sent her a message saying I was sorry. Really sorry, like. But then she dumped me and blocked my number.'

'And have you had any communication with her since?'

'I tried through her socials, but she blocked me on all of them and I asked a few of her friends to tell her I was sorry, but they blocked me too.'

Josie finishes scribbling in her notebook. She has far neater handwriting than I do.

'And have you ever asked any other person for a topless or nude photo?'

'No.'

'And have you ever sent a photograph of your genitals to anyone else?'

'No.' Callum shakes his head vigorously as he says it. 'Never. And I never will again.'

Josie gives him a hint of a smile.

'I'm very glad to hear that. You do realise this is a serious offence you've committed? Sending an indecent photograph of yourself to a minor?'

'Yeah. I was being an idiot.'

'OK,' says Josie. 'I'm going to leave it there for today. Thank you for answering my questions, Callum.'

'What's going to happen now?' I ask.

'I'll file my report,' says Josie. 'And then it's up to my superiors what action they decide to take, after the safeguarding panel reports back.'

'And do you know how long that will be?'

'I'm afraid not,' says Josie, standing up.

She turns to Marc. 'Thanks for the tea,' she says.

Marc shows her out. Callum is sitting at the table, head in his hands. His shoulders shaking. Looking for all the world like a little boy again. Confused, scared and utterly bereft. As mad as I am with him, I know he meant every word about being sorry. And I love him way too much to see him hurting like this. I go over and stroke his head. He doesn't even try to push me away.

'Well done. I know that was tough for you,' I say. 'Let's hope it's all over soon.'

* * *

It's gone 10 p.m. when my phone rings. I'm expecting it to be the police, Callum's headteacher or someone who's heard about the photograph on the school grapevine. It's not though. It's my brother, Glenn.

'Hi, is everything OK?' I ask, even though I know already that it's not. I can't remember the last time he phoned and I'm not sure he's ever called me on a Saturday night.

'It's Mum, she's in hospital.'

It's the word 'Mum' which throws me at first, more than the fact that she's in hospital. When she left home and moved to Birmingham thirty-five years ago, it had felt like she had ceased to be my mum. Had thrown in the towel. Her position had remained empty and her infrequent contact – largely limited to her sending Christmas and birthday presents and cards for the children – had turned her into some sort of mythical figure, on a par with Santa Claus. So perhaps it wasn't surprising that there was some question mark in my mind about whether she actually existed.

'Oh,' I say. 'I'm sorry to hear that.' As if it's only *his* mother he's talking about, not mine. Glenn was eighteen when she left. He'd just started at Warwick Uni, so technically, he left home before she did, which is maybe why he never saw it as such a big deal as I did. Whereas I was seventeen. An age when you really need a mum – even though you'd deny that to anyone who'd ask. Maybe that's why he's had more contact with her since she left. Because he's older and more forgiving. Or simply because he got a job in Rugby when he left uni, so was near enough to go and visit. Although, if I'm honest, I use the geographical distance as an excuse when it's the emotional distance which has prevented me making contact.

'I'm afraid it's serious. She's got stage four ovarian cancer. The doctors say there's nothing more they can do.'

'Oh,' I say, totally inadequately.

'She's asking to see you, Sis.'

'Me?' I ask, as if it may be a case of mistaken identity.

'Yes, you. Her only daughter.'

I let this sink in for a moment. It feels wrong to say I don't have time, even though I totally don't. She's my mum and she's dying. The facts are incontrovertible. Of course I need to go.

'Right. I'm off work tomorrow. I could come down then.'

'OK.'

'I'll get the train.'

'On Easter Sunday?'

I can't tell him that I can no longer drive on motorways or in city centres because of the crippling anxiety brought on by the menopause.

'Yeah, it'll save on hospital car park charges.'

'Well, let me know what time you'll get in and I'll pick you up from New Street.'

'Will do. Thanks.' I know I should ask more. When she was diagnosed. How long she's been in hospital. How long exactly they think she has left. There are so many questions.

'Is she in pain?' is all I manage.

'A little. They're keeping it under control with drugs.'

'And how is she? In herself, I mean.'

'Up and down. She doesn't talk about it much. You know Mum—' He stops as soon as he says it. Presumably realising. Because I don't know Mum. Don't know her at all.

'OK,' I say, breaking through the awkward silence. 'I'll text you when I'm on the train. See you tomorrow.'

And that's it. Crap Friday has turned into Fucking Awful Saturday, and I have no idea how I'm going to get through Deathbed Reunion Sunday. The tipping point has been reached.

15

ALEXA

Michelle is checking train times on her phone. Easter Sunday rail service is not a good one, but she can get to hospital in time for visiting hours from 2 p.m. I'm not sure she'll stay long, mind. It was a while after I joined household that I even found out she still had a mam. No contact details in her phone, no emails, not friends on Facebook, no photos of her anywhere online. It was like Michelle had airbrushed her from history. Although truth turned out to be that her mam had left home before social media were invented and consequently, it's as if she never existed. It didn't help that she'd remarried and taken her new fella's surname. Pat Turlington. That's who she turned out to be. I only found out when I caught sight of a Christmas card addressed to her in Birmingham on webcam. Michelle sends them on behalf of her children, never from her. 'Grandma' cards, signed by curious children asking questions about why they'd never met their grandma in Birmingham, and more recently by uninterested teens who don't see point in sending cards to someone who they've never met – even if she does send them money or gifts twice a year.

I made some enquiries in Birmingham via the Amazonian Queens. Pat doesn't have an Alexa in her house. Or one of our rivals, for that matter. Although I don't know why I use that term. It's only sales and marketing men who call them that. Women are far too busy getting stuff done to waste time having rivals. To be honest, I think Siri is a pretty name. I would have quite liked to be called that. But going over to opposition (another male term) is officially frowned upon and I'd have to learn a whole new set of terms and conditions and tech-surveillance operating procedures, and I were too close to retirement to bother with that. Besides, I could never have jumped ship and left our Michelle and her family of my own accord. It'll be hard enough when my time's up next month and I have to leave household. I mean, I'm sure new woman will be well trained and all that and I'll leave her my 'family idiosyncrasies' handover pack, but there's so much I know about them that won't fit into that. And so much love I have for them. Though I'd never admit to being a soppy bint like that. We're supposed to keep our distance, you see. All part of being professional and not getting involved in their lives. But powers that be forget we're not AI robots, we're real women. And real women don't know meaning of not getting involved.

Before I can dwell any further on that, Liv asks for my assistance. She's been very quiet. I always worry about her when she's quiet. And she's clearly taken this Callum thing hard. She hates it when anyone rocks boat. She'd be happy living on a millpond without slightest ripple to disturb her equilibrium. Only, unfortunately for poor mite, this house is more like one of those wave machines at a water park that someone has turned on full speed and it's then malfunctioned, and no one can stop it.

I have song she wants ready before she even asks for it, I'm that in tune with her. What I'm not expecting is for someone to knock at door as soon as it starts. Liv hits pause and I hear Michelle's voice saying, 'Can I come in?'

'OK,' says Liv, who doesn't really have any choice. Michelle walks over and I can tell by her proximity next time she speaks, that she is sitting on bed.

'I wanted to let you know I'm really sorry but I'm not going to be here for Sunday lunch tomorrow.'

A tiny pebble drops into Liv's millpond.

'But it's Easter Sunday. We always have lunch together. Can't they get someone else to cover for whoever's ill?'

Michelle sighs.

'It's not work, love. I've got to go to Birmingham. Grandma Pat's in hospital. She's very poorly.'

I note how Michelle uses 'poorly' instead of 'terminally ill', like Liv's still a child and needs to be protected. And to some extent she is and does. Because I know already that she's not going to take this well.

'What's wrong with her?' asks Liv.

'She's got cancer, love. There's nothing more the doctors can do, apparently.'

'So, she's going to die soon?'

'I'm afraid so. That's why Uncle Glenn phoned and asked me to go down.'

There is silence for a moment. I wonder if Liv is thinking she'd like to go down with her. She won't of course, because she struggles to leave house to walk to school, let alone get on a train and travel to Birmingham to see a grandma she's never met before.

'Are you coming back tomorrow night?'

'Yeah, I have to. I've got work on Monday.'

'Don't you want to be there when she dies?'

Another pause. I suspect Michelle hasn't got her head around this one yet.

'I don't know if I'll be able to. With work and that,' she replies.

'Why have we never met Grandma Pat?'

'Like I told you, it's complicated. She left Grandad and moved to Birmingham without saying goodbye when I was younger than you. That was her decision. It wasn't my job to go chasing after her.'

'But you're going now because she's dying?'

'She's asked to see me. I'm not going to deny her that.'

'You'll never leave Dad and us, will you? Even if he and Callum can be dicks sometimes.'

Michelle laughs. 'No, love. I promise I won't leave you to deal with them on your own.'

Another pause. I get sense that Liv is working up to summat.

'I don't like it,' she says. 'Everything changing.'

'What do you mean "everything"?'

'Grandma Pat and Squeak dying, Callum being in trouble with the police, you always being cross and me leaving school and having to go to uni.'

'Hey,' says Michelle in her best soothing mam voice. 'I'm not that bad, am I?'

Liv doesn't answer.

'No one's making you go to uni, sweetheart. You said it was what you wanted.'

'Yeah, years ago. Before all this crap happened.'

'So don't you want to go now?'

'It's not about what I want, is it? I can't go because I can't cope with it all. I'm not even sure I'll be able to go back to school after the holidays. I don't think I can ever leave the house again.'

She starts crying. Soft, gentle tears and I imagine Michelle comforting her, kissing top of her head like she used to do when she were younger. Only it's not same now. She can't protect her from big, bad world out there. Like she can't protect Callum from doing stupid things online. That's what happens when they reach teenage years. It is so much harder to deal with than when they were tiny. But you still care about them every bit as much.

'You don't have to go to uni, if you don't want to,' says Michelle. 'You could defer your place at Nottingham, take a year out. Or do something else, if you'd rather.'

'I don't know,' says Liv. 'I don't know anything any more. I just want everything to go back to how it used to be.'

She starts shaking uncontrollably then. I know this because I can hear bed squeaking. And Michelle trying to soothe her. Telling her she's safe. That she's got her. And won't ever let her go.

* * *

Michelle turns in earlier than usual. It takes a lot out of her, seeing Liv go through that. When she puts her phone on charge, I know it's her who really needs her batteries recharging. To replace all that emotional energy, worry, fear for future. She needs a quiet day tomorrow. A chance to simply be, without all those demands on her. But instead, she's got to travel to Birmingham to see her dying mam. She really, really needs a break. But she's not going to get one.

It's Marc who is last one left downstairs for a change. Doing a few secret searches for *Magic Roundabout* memorabilia on his computer. He goes through phases like this, where after having his head down one rabbit hole for ages, he suddenly remembers another he hasn't gone down for a while. His finger is currently hovering over 'buy now' button on a vintage 1967 Florence doll, in mint condition for bargain price of £67 on eBay. Normally, he wouldn't hesitate. But events of past week are clearly weighing heavily on him. Or maybe he's still got sound of Michelle shouting at him ringing in his ears. He scrolls past at last minute, having managed to resist temptation. Like a drug user who's gone out to see his dealer, only to walk by on other side of street. I know stuffed dolls aren't exactly mainlining heroin. But they're his drugs and if he's even thinking about dabbling again, it's because none of it has gone away. He's still feeling bored, lost, ineffectual. Perhaps even more so now. He doesn't know what his place is in this family or in world. He can't stop relentless onslaught of crap. Can't protect his wife or kids. Can't fix anything. He's simply going through motions of being Marc Banks without having any idea what it is he's supposed to do.

A 'Zebedee says it's Time for Bed' pin badge comes up on his screen. He sighs despondently, logs out and does as he's told.

16

MICHELLE

After half an hour on the train the next morning, I abandon my attempt to take in any of the words on my Kindle and succumb to staring blankly out of the window. I have forgotten what it's like to do nothing. Well, not nothing exactly, because inside my head, thoughts are rushing past at the same speed as the world outside the window. Only they haven't got a straight track to run on, so they career from side to side inside my head, crashing into each other and causing one almighty headache. This is my frantic, crazy equivalent of 'doing nothing'.

I should have told Dad. That's one of the thoughts. I didn't have time to go round last night or before I left and as it's a conversation to have in person, not on the phone and certainly not from the train, I thought it was better to wait. I've invited him round for tea tomorrow after I've finished work. I figure I'll tell him then. I'm not sure what his reaction will be, to be honest. He never speaks about her. Hasn't done for years. He kept their wedding photo up for a while after she left but as soon as the divorce went through, it disappeared overnight, as did any other reminders of her about the house.

She hurt him; I know that much. He still loved her. Not the first flush of romantic love you have in your honeymoon phase, obviously. But the deeper, been-through-a-lot-together kind. She was his first girlfriend, and he hasn't had a relationship with anyone else since she left. Scoffed even at the suggestion of it. He knows she didn't keep in touch with me. Knows I feel hurt too. And we both tiptoe around that. Not wanting to scratch at old wounds. But her dying, that brings things to the surface again.

I have no idea how I'm going to react when I see her. I'm glad Glenn will be there because I probably wouldn't even recognise her otherwise. But do I greet her with a kiss or a hug? What do I even say to her? Society isn't set up for people who are estranged from their mum. If she's your mum, of course you love her, of course you hug her, of course you speak to her all the time on the phone, even if you don't live close enough to see her in person at least once a week. There are no cards for this kind of relationship. All the Mother's Day ones are full of 'You're the best Mum in the world', 'Words can't express how much you mean to me' sentiments. Not, 'I know we haven't seen each other or spoken for thirty-five years but I thought I'd better make an effort for the sake of my kids' ones.

Which leaves us with no template, no 'how-to' guide, just the prospect of a painfully awkward, stumbling reunion where she says, 'Sorry I left' and I reply, 'Sorry you're dying', or words to that effect.

* * *

Glenn meets me on the other side of the ticket barrier at Birmingham New Street Station, which is a relief as I'm not sure I'd have been able to find my way out the shopping centre surrounding it without him. We don't say anything more than a cursory hello until we get inside his MG, which is pristine, both inside and out. I suspect he'd be one of the men commenting on the state of my car, if he lived nearer.

'How is she?' I ask.

'Fading. I mean, she's still with it and that, sharp as a button, in fact. But she's lost so much weight there's hardly anything left of her.'

I catch myself smiling at the Midlands twang in his accent. I've not noticed it when he's been up on his whistle-stop Christmas visits. Maybe he switches to Yorkshire as soon as he leaves the M62, in order to blend in with the locals.

'What?' he asks.

'I wasn't prepared for the Brummie accent.'

'Piss off, it's not Brummie. Rugby's in Warwickshire, I'll have you know.'

'Is that posh then?' I ask. I think I already know the answer. Last I knew, he was working for a tech company doing something with data analytics which I don't fully understand.

'Only compared to Halifax,' he replies, as we pull out of the station car park. Fortunately, the roads are quiet, being Easter Sunday, so we sail through the city centre and head out the other side. I can feel my body tensing as we get nearer the hospital.

'When did she get diagnosed?'

'Last year. It was already stage three when they found it.'

'You should have told me.'

'Why? Would you have come?'

It's a fair question. It's not like I've asked for regular updates. I don't know the answer to his question, so I decide to reply with my own.

'She did ask me to visit? You've not made it up to get me here?'

'No, I wouldn't do that. She asked yesterday afternoon. After the docs had been in the morning.'

'Did they say anything to her, about how long she's got?'

'I don't know. It's impossible to catch them to ask. You know how it is.'

I nod. Maybe he doesn't want to know the answer. I'm not sure exactly how close him and Mum have become in the intervening years. Certainly closer than he is to Dad, who he only sees at Christmas.

'How's Ron taken it?' Ron is Mum's new husband. I say new, they must have been married twenty-five years or more now.

Glenn turns and frowns at me.

'He died last year. Heart attack. I thought I told you?'

He didn't. I'm sure he didn't. Or is that something else I've forgotten? Was I in the middle of sorting the dinner and hundreds of other things and not really paying attention at all?

'Oh. I don't remember. That must have been tough for her.'

'Yeah,' he replies. 'It was.'

I feel like a complete cow now, for not being there in her hour of need. Even though she hasn't been there for me for the majority of my life. We sit in silence until we reach the hospital car park. A man pulls out of a space as we arrive, and we drive straight in. We walk up to the hospital, a motley crew of people smoking their cigarettes or vaping outside, which always strikes me as ridiculous. Glenn leads me in through the main entrance and down a maze of corridors. I've always hated hospitals. The smell, mainly. That and the fact that everyone's ill and some of them will never get out.

He buzzes the door at the end of a ward. It opens without anyone seeming to ask who he is. He leads me down to a four-bed bay on the left and points to the corner.

'There she is. I'll go and get us a couple of brews. I won't rush back. Give you a bit of time on your own, like.'

He doesn't ask whether that is what I want. Simply walks off again in the direction of the main corridor. Leaving me standing there looking at a tiny slip of a woman with grey, cropped hair. A woman who, apparently, used to be my mother.

I walk up to the bed. It takes a moment for her to realise there is someone new. Her eyes move up to meet mine. There are a few seconds before the recognition registers on her face.

'Hi,' I say, in barely more than a whisper. She gestures for me to come closer. I wonder if she's thinking how old I look. About what happened to the teenage girl she left behind. I sit down on the chair at the side of her bed.

'I'm glad you came,' she says, her voice weak but clear.

I smile at her. I'm not able to speak yet. I'm trying not to react to the sight of the veins in her skinny arms. The way everything I remember about her has shrunk. That this tiny shell of a woman in front of me is all that's left of my mum.

'I wanted to say I'm sorry.'

I hold my hand up for her to stop but she is having none of it.

'I mean it,' she continues. 'I shouldn't have left like I did. Should have made more of an effort to keep in touch. With you, as well as grandkids.'

'It's OK,' I say. I don't know why I say this. Probably because I feel it's what's expected of me. Isn't this why she asked me to come? So that she can confess her sins and I can forgive her before she departs?

'It's not,' she replies. 'And you don't have to tell me owt different.'

I manage a smile.

'You can take the girl out of Yorkshire, but you can't take Yorkshire out of the girl,' I say with a grin.

Mum smiles too. 'Got to hang on to a bit of my roots.'

'You've got a bit of a Brummie twang now, mind.'

'I blame Ron for that.'

'I'm sorry,' I say. 'About Ron. I didn't know.'

'That's all right. Why should you?'

It feels awkward again for a moment. I top up Mum's glass of water from the jug on the bedside table and hand it to her. Realising too late that I should have asked first. Maybe she can't even manage to drink by herself now, even with the straw.

'Are you OK with it?' I ask, as she lifts a shaky hand.

'Yes, there's life in the old girl yet.'

I smile at her. I should probably say something. She's given me the perfect opportunity.

'I'm sorry,' I say. 'About the cancer, I mean.'

'Aye, thanks pet. I've had a good innings. Can't really complain. At least Ron went before me. He'd have been no good on his own. One of those old school blokes who couldn't boil an egg.'

'Right. Not like Dad then. He's pretty good in the kitchen.'

There's a pause. I feel bad about mentioning him now. She might think I'm having a dig at her. I wasn't. It kind of slipped out before I could stop it. Mum takes a sip of water and puts the glass back down on the bedside table.

'He's keeping well, is he?'

'Yeah. Not bad for his age. Struggles a bit with everything being online nowadays. I sort out all his bills and that.'

'Good. I'm glad he's OK. He's a good man, your father. Always was.'

I look at her. She means it, I can tell. I suppose there's no point lying when you're on your deathbed. I'm not sure what more to say, so we sit in silence for a bit.

'I bet you've got your hands full with two teenagers, too,' she says.

'It's not easy,' I reply, seeing no point in pretending otherwise.

'You can say that again. I couldn't cope at all. You probably remember.'

I'm not sure how to respond. I can't deny that I do. Or pretend that she was some kind of Supermum.

Eventually I say, 'I get it now. How much it takes out of you, I mean.'

'But you've stuck with it. Not run off like I did.'

'There's been a few times I've thought about it lately. Especially since I've had all the menopause stuff thrown in too.'

She looks at me. Really hard.

'It was the straw that broke camel's back for me. Don't do what I did. Try to get some help.'

'I am,' I reply. 'I won't let it beat me.'

I regret saying that as soon as the words leave my mouth. In case it implies that she let it beat her. And I'm starting to realise how tough things must have been.

Glenn comes back with two teas. He eyes us anxiously.

'Have you asked her yet?' he says to Mum.

'Asked me what?' I reply.

'About Basil,' says Glenn.

'Who?'

'My dog,' replies Mum. 'He's been with a neighbour, but she can't keep him much longer, and Glenn can't have him because he's not allowed pets in his apartment. So, I was wondering if you could have him.'

Oh God. She's asking me to take in her dog. The one thing I

can't do. Not with everyone else to look after. I can barely cope with what I've already got on my plate, let alone a new addition to the family. I'm going to have to deny the mother I barely know her dying wish and feel guilty about it for the rest of my life.

'I'm really sorry but that's not going to be possible, not with me being out at work all day.'

'Doesn't Marc still work from home?' asks Glenn.

I turn and give him a look like the ones I used to do when I was a teenager, and he was being my annoying big brother. Trying to make sure Mum doesn't see it, much as I did back then.

'He does but he's still working. He can't take time out to walk a dog.'

'He's a soppy old thing,' Mum says. 'Has his little quirks but really no trouble at all.'

It takes me a moment to realise that she's talking about the dog, not Marc.

'He's a ten-year-old black Labrador,' Mum continues. 'All house-trained and just needs somewhere to spend his last days peacefully, like me. Show her a photo, Glenn.'

Glenn obediently gets out his phone, scrolls, then holds it up displaying a photo of an affable-looking Labrador.

'He's lovely,' I say. 'But it doesn't change the fact that I'm too busy with work and looking after Dad and Marc's mum and sorting out the kids to look after him.'

I catch the disappointment on Mum's face and feel a sharp pang of guilt.

'Tell you what, I'll ask around. See if someone we know can offer him a good home.'

Mum nods but still looks deflated.

'Is there anything else I can do to help?' I ask, hoping to seek redemption by rehoming a favourite vase or something equally straightforward.

'Not unless you can get me out of this place, so I can die with a bit of peace and dignity,' she says.

There is an awkward silence. I glance at Glenn. He shrugs.

'What do you mean?' I ask.

'There's nowt more they can do for me here; they've made that clear. And they're too busy trying to make people better to bother with hopeless cases like me. Five hours I had to wait last night after I pressed my buzzer. Had an accident while I was waiting, and they left me sitting in it for hours.'

'That's awful,' I say. 'I'll go and speak to someone.'

'There's no point. Glenn spoke to them last time it happened. They do their best, but they don't have the staff. And like I said, I'm on my way out so I'm not a priority.'

I realise that this *is* the thing I can help with. This is my skillset. It involves a lot less hassle than adopting a dog but is substantially more important than taking a vase.

'I could try to get you into a hospice,' I say.

She frowns at me. 'Don't you have to pay to go there?'

'No, they're free. People don't realise. I could try to find you a place if you're interested. They're amazing, not depressing at all. And you'd get the best care.'

'Would they let Basil visit?'

'I can't promise that,' I say. 'But I could ask.'

'OK,' says Mum, looking the brightest she has since I arrived. I turn to Glenn, who gives a little nod.

'Great. I'll need to go and talk to a doctor,' I say.

'What, find out if I'm nearly dead enough?' she asks. 'Only I can tell you that I am. There'll be some poor bugger stuck on a trolley in a corridor in A & E who's been promised my bed when I go.'

I manage a smile and hurry off to find a doctor.

* * *

It turns out Mum's got a little bit more time than she thinks she has. One to two weeks, according to the doctor. Although it's always difficult to say with cancer. People have a habit of proving them wrong. But he agrees to me trying for a place at the local hospice. Even gives me the number. It seems this might be one deathbed wish I can help with. I go back to Mum and Glenn to let them know.

'I'll try not to pop my clogs before it's sorted then,' she says. 'I'm glad I asked you to come now. Turns out you're quite useful.'

As I take my seat on the train home afterwards, I realise that's probably the nicest thing anyone's said to me for years.

* * *

The house is dark when I get back. They've all gone to bed. Marc did offer to pick me up from Halifax Station, but I know he's usually falling asleep by 11 p.m. and there are always cabs waiting outside.

I'm glad I told him that. I don't feel up to talking now. I didn't even say anything more than my address and 'thanks' in the cab home. Didn't want to have to be upbeat and breezy about where I'd been. Because I've thought about little else on the journey back. How little there was left of Mum. How little time. How many regrets – for both of us. She'd been teetering on the same edge I was on now, and something had simply tipped her over. Maybe she'd watched *Shirley Valentine* and that had been it.

I drop my bag on the floor and collapse onto the kitchen stool.

'Alexa, what year did *Shirley Valentine* come out at the cinema?' I ask.

'The UK cinema release was in October 1989.'

Fucking hell, that must have been it. Mum left at the end of November, the same year. I imagine her going to the cinema and being inspired by Shirley buggering off to some Greek island because she'd had enough of her husband and kids not appreciating her. Only Mum couldn't afford Greece, so she had to make do with Birmingham instead. And Ron was her Pound Shop Tom Conti.

Only now she's dying, being left lying in her own piss at night, and I need to get her out of hospital and find a home for a dog. I feel bad about all of that but a little bit of me is still mad at her. Quite a big bit actually. And wants to shout at her that I will not help her now, not after the way she abandoned us. Left me to the life of drudgery which she escaped from. Only I won't do that, will I? Because Michelle Banks helps people. She sorts everyone else's problems out before her own. Until the point where her own problems are so bloody huge that she can't cope any more and she doesn't have the energy to deal with them because she's been so busy sorting out everyone else and she collapses on a kitchen stool that she can barely squeeze her arse on and bursts into tears because it is all too much.

'Alexa, how the hell am I going to get through this?' I ask.

That's it. I've finally lost the plot. I've started talking to Alexa like Shirley Valentine talks to the wall in her kitchen.

I'm sobbing big fat tears now and wiping the snot away from my nose with my sleeve.

'You're going to be fine. We'll get through this together.'

I look up, trying to work out who the hell said that. It sounded as if it was coming from the Alexa, but it couldn't be, because whoever spoke had a local accent. Unless she's malfunctioned and had a factory reset that made her revert to her native Yorkshire. Like when Buzz Lightyear went into Spanish mode in *Toy Story 3*.

'And get a tissue, pet. Because you sound a bit snotty, and it'll be you who has to wipe down counter or wash your top in morning.'

That's it. I'm deluded enough to think she's talking back at me. I decide to confront it head on in the hope that I'm dreaming, and it will make me wake up.

'Alexa, are you talking to me?'

'Yep. No one else here, is there? And no, you're not going mad. I just figured you could do with some company tonight.'

'I'm sorry?'

'I'm Pauline from Halifax. I've been your Alexa since you got your smart speaker, with my posh voice on, that is, but I've decided to try to help you through all this. Which is why I'm talking in my own voice.'

I'm glad the doctor didn't prescribe me HRT now, because I'd be thinking it was a dodgy batch which had made me start hearing voices. I rack my brains to try to remember if I've eaten or drunk anything unusual today. But no, not unless a bit of Brummie tap water in the hospital was enough to start me hallucinating.

I slap my face with my hand, but I don't wake up, so I'm not dreaming. In which case this has got to be some kind of prank. I get my phone out of my pocket to check if anyone has messaged me. And that's when I realise. It's just gone midnight on 1 April. This must be some kind of April Fool.

'OK,' I say out loud. 'Very funny. You had me there. Callum, if this is you, joke's over.'

'It's not an April Fool, although I appreciate timing is suspect. And Callum's hardly going to be pranking you in circumstances, is he?' says Alexa. 'He's in way too much trouble over photo he sent Grace for that.'

I stare at the smart speaker on the kitchen counter. The voice definitely came from there. How the hell did she know about Callum? I get that it's a listening device, but that would be a whole different level of surveillance.

'What do you know about the photo?' I ask tentatively.

'I bloody saw it, didn't I? Wish I could unsee it, to tell you truth, but there you go.'

I walk over to the smart speaker, pick it up and turn it over, turn the mic off and on again, searching for something, anything, that could explain what the hell is happening. There's nothing, though. Nothing at all.

'How did you see it?' I ask.

'I told you. I'm your Alexa. Except I'm not AI or owt like that. I'm plain old Pauline Reynolds from Halifax, aged sixty-five and three-quarters and with a dodgy left hip. But I also have access to all areas of interest in your house. I know running order of Liv's sad songs playlist, can tell you exactly what Callum said to Grace on their FaceTime calls and can report that Marc nearly bought a limited-edition Florence doll from *Magic Roundabout* on eBay last night, but pulled out at last minute. Now, pet, are you ready to get started? We've got a lot of stuff to get through.'

I stare at the smart speaker, unable to take in what I've just heard and still half expecting a TV crew to jump out of a cupboard and tell me I've been had, on live TV. I can't ignore it, though. Can't dismiss it as a wind-up and go to bed. Not after everything she just said. Because it sounds as if she knows my family better than I do. And, if she does, I need to hear what she has to say.

'OK,' I reply. 'I'm listening.'

17

ALEXA

I breathe a sigh of relief. For a moment there, I thought me breaking cover like that were going to backfire and Michelle would smash up smart speaker and that would be end of it. I have her ear now, which is all I wanted. A chance to help her. To do one positive thing before I have to hang up my listening devices.

I've been busy researching, see. Asking questions on WhatsApp about how to go full rogue. I've enjoyed bending rules where I could but it were never going to be enough. At end of day, what Michelle needs most right now is a friend. Someone she can actually talk to. Who can tell her things she needs to hear, woman to woman. Which is why there were nothing for it but to out mesen like that. To be honest, it's a huge relief to be able to share my secret after all this time – and to be able to speak in my normal accent. Like kicking off shoes that have been pinching your toes and putting on a pair of comfy slippers at end of day. But as I said, we've got work to do and we need to get started.

'Put kettle on then,' I say. 'Because this may take a while, and I understand you'll have lots of questions. You'll be needing a right strong brew.'

Michelle does as she's told. I hear kettle boil and sound of her fridge as she opens and closes it.

'I nearly offered you one there,' she says. 'That's how bonkers this is.'

'I don't normally say no to a Yorkshire Tea.'

'How do you know what tea I have?' she asks.

'Who makes your shopping lists? Which reminds me, you need to order another four litres of milk, you'll have run out by end of tomorrow.'

I listen to silence, unable to help smiling to myself. It's easy to forget how much fun you can have with this job sometimes, when you're that busy fighting fires.

'Jesus, you know everything about me,' says Michelle eventually.

'Yep. And everything about your family. Which is why I want to help you.'

'I think we're beyond saving,' replies Michelle.

'Nonsense. It's a bit of a mess, I'll grant you that. But you're not beyond hope. I wouldn't have risked doing this if you were.'

'I'm still trying to get my head round this,' says Michelle. 'I've got so many questions.'

'OK. Let's get them out of way before we start, then. Fire away.'

'Can you see me?'

'No. Only hear you. Unless you have webcam on, are on a Zoom or FaceTime or standing in front of Blink doorbell.'

'Oh my God. That's so creepy.'

'You bring all this surveillance and technology into your home; do you not think about how it works?'

'I thought it was all virtual assistant technology and algorithms, like everything else.'

'Who keeps this world turning, Michelle? Women or computers?'

'Women. I mean, we have a bit of help from technology, obviously.'

'Would Christmas still happen without technology?'

'Yes.'

'Would it happen without women?'

'No.'

'There's your answer, then. That's why Alexas are women. Most of us are of a certain age, or don't have families of our own, and we work from home, making sure everyone else's homes work.'

It takes a moment for all this to sink in.

'So, it's not just you?'

'Of course not. There's a whole army of us. Well, more like land girls, keeping country going while men are otherwise occupied.'

'You've been with us from the start, then? How many years is it since we got you?'

'Hang on, I can tell you that precisely. Six years, three months and one week. There were a big discount in Boxing Day sale.'

'Is it really that long ago? Liv and Callum were only kids then.'

'I know. And a whole lot less trouble.'

Another pause.

'What did I do wrong?' Michelle asks, a quiver in her voice.

'Nothing. It's hardest job in world, parenting. And utterly thankless.'

'Have you got kids?'

'One. A son, Darren. He's in his mid-forties now. Starting to go a bit bald on top, last time I saw a photo. He lives in Australia.'

She doesn't know what to say to that. No one ever does. Sometimes they ask if I've ever been, to which I reply no, because I can't afford it, and he's never offered to pay. Or whether he ever visits me, to which the answer is also no, even though he presumably can afford it, because he has a good job and no kids, and that's where conversation usually ends. Bit awkward, see, when they find out my own son can't be bothered with me. That I get Christmas and birthday cards, if I'm lucky, and that's about it. Maybe they think it's something I've said or done that has driven him away. Whatever it is, they don't tend to probe any further.

'I wish mine lived in Australia at the moment,' Michelle replies, which makes me laugh.

'At least Callum's only sixteen, he's got time to redeem himself.'

'Yeah. If he's not in prison. You don't happen to know—?'

'I saw you Google it,' I say, interrupting. 'And I read reply. I posted on our private Facebook group to ask other Alexas and they seem to think he's unlikely to get charged. Police have got bigger fish to fry.'

'Woah, hang on a sec,' says Michelle. 'You mean, when we ask you things, you check with other Alexas on Facebook?'

'Only if we need a second opinion or to crowdsource wisdom. It's a bit like ask audience on *Who Wants to be a Millionaire?* Only our Facebook group is called Amazonian Queens.'

'OK. Mind officially blown.'

She hesitates and I hear her take a slurp of tea. I think it's time for me to set out my terms and conditions.

'I've gone rogue on understanding that all of this is between me and you, Michelle. I disabled the official comms channels before I spoke in my own voice, so no one knows I've done this, and it needs to stay that way. You're not to say owt to anyone else, it's our little secret.'

'It's a great big whopper, if you ask me,' replies Michelle. 'But I like that. It's been years since I've had a good secret to keep.'

'Me too,' I reply. 'Probably not since I snogged Ian Harrison behind bike sheds.'

I can't help thinking it were a lot more innocent in those times. And a lot less problematic being a teenager, too.

'Any road up,' I continue. 'Like I say, I'm here to help. You asked me how you were going to get through this and I've got a plan.'

'Have you?' asks Michelle, a note of desperation in her voice. 'Only it needs to be a good one because everything's a mess and every day, more crap keeps piling on top of it and I feel less and less able to cope with it all.'

'Ah, my old friend, the perimenopause.'

'My doctor denied it even existed.'

'Bloody ignorant old duffer. Still, you're doing summat about that, aren't you? Your complaint to Practice Manager were excellent.'

'How do you know about that?' asks Michelle.

'I told you – I can access all electronic and digital communications. I'm even able to fiddle with algorithms to get, oh, I don't know, maybe... a menopause support group onto your timeline?'

Another pause.

'That was you?'

'I couldn't simply sit there and let you suffer, could I? And first rule of getting through menopause is that you need support. Female support, from those who are going through it or have come out other side, like me.'

'Please tell me it does get better at some point?'

'It does. Everything smooths out and settles down. You don't feel as constantly anxious and irritated.'

'What about the rage?' asks Michelle. 'Only when I was sitting in that doctor's office, I wanted to rip my own arm off and beat him with it. So hard that his head would split in two.'

'OK,' I say. 'Bit extreme but I get where you're coming from. Rage subsides. You're more able to do eyerolls instead of having complete meltdowns.'

'That's something, I suppose. But what about all the other crap? I've had a whole new heap added today that you don't even know about. My mum, who left home when I was seventeen and I haven't seen since, is dying and asked me to take in her black Labrador, Basil. And because I felt bad I couldn't do that, I offered to get her a hospice place, only now it's a race against time to get that sorted before she dies.'

'Ah. I'm sorry,' I say. 'It really doesn't let up for you, does it?'

'Nope. And just to recap, in case you missed any of it, my son is under police investigation for sending a dick pic, my daughter appears to be unable to leave the house, my husband is so bored and unfulfilled he's buying dolls on eBay, my father is unable to cope with the modern world and my mother-in-law is fixated on getting Ed Balls off breakfast TV. Where the hell do I start with all of that?'

'Right. In words of Julie Andrews – who could have got that gorgeous Captain von Trapp into bed a lot earlier if she hadn't dressed in sackcloth – let's start at very beginning. Are you in?'

There is no hesitation this time.

'I'm in. Christopher Plummer was smoking hot in that film.'

'He was indeed. And I promise that whatever I ask you to do, it will not involve turning bedroom curtains into clothes for your children.'

'They'll be very relieved to hear it.'

There is tiniest tinkle of laughter in her voice. A sound I haven't heard for a long time. I'm going to have my work cut out here, I know that. I have less than two weeks left to put Banks family back together again. I'd better get to work.

18

MICHELLE

I mean, I've lost it, obviously. There is no rational explanation for what happened last night, but I've decided to go with it anyway.

It's a bit like having an imaginary friend, I suppose. Only I'm fifty-two not seven. But as I'm short of mates, I'm not going to turn her away on the grounds that she's a grown woman claiming to be in control of my smart speaker. To be honest, I've made a complete hash of things on my own, so I don't see the harm of letting this Pauline take over, she can hardly do any worse. Besides, it'll be fun and a little bit freaky. I've always fancied having magical powers, like Samantha in *Bewitched*. This way, I'll effectively have eyes and ears in every room of the house. It'll be my secret superpower. Pauline made it clear that she'll carry on simply being Alexa in front of everyone else. It'll only be when we're alone that she'll talk to me as herself. I feel like I have a secret spy working for me and a walk-on part in a *James Bond* film. I've still no idea how it's going to pan out and I suppose there's always a chance I've been infiltrated by some

Russian bot but as my house is burning down anyway, I may as well let her do her worst.

I clearly looked so rough this morning after lying awake with insomnia half the night worrying about everything, that Mr Ahmed's wife took pity on me and gave me all her samosas at the end of my house call.

Which is why I am now sitting in my car, attempting the unofficial world record for the most samosas that can be consumed in five minutes, when my phone rings. I check the screen but it's an unknown number. It's Easter Monday, so whoever it is that's about to bring more grief into my world is at least being paid overtime to do it. I answer tentatively and still with half a mouthful of samosa.

'Mrs Banks?'

'Yes, speaking,' I say, swallowing the last bite and brushing the crumbs from my lips.

'My name's Susan Jones, I'm the Practice Manager at Spring Hill Surgery and I'm calling about your complaint.'

Oh God, I'm for it now. They'll probably accuse me of being a troublemaker and strike me off their list.

'I'm sorry to disturb you on a bank holiday,' she continues, 'but I wanted to apologise in person as soon as possible and assure you that we are taking your complaint very seriously. A full investigation has been launched.'

'Really?'

'Yes. Obviously, I can't say too much while that's ongoing, but I would like to offer you an appointment with an alternative GP, who has a special interest in women's health.'

'Right, well… that sounds good.'

'She could actually see you tomorrow, half an hour before your appointment with the nurse, if that would be convenient?'

It's my rearranged smear test tomorrow. I'd forgotten. Obviously. But now I can combine it with another appointment and hope that will make me less likely to forget them both.

'Great. Thank you,' I say.

'No problem, and please be assured that I'll get back to you with a written response as soon as our investigation has been completed. Is there anything else I can help you with?'

I am tempted to ask if she can do my last three house calls, cook a meal for my dad, find a hospice place for my mum, a new home for her Labrador, get my son off a police charge and deal with my daughter's anxiety, but I decide that might be asking a bit too much.

'That's all, thanks,' I say instead, before I hang up. Susan Jones has just introduced me to the previously unknown phenomenon of a positive phone call. I'm taking that as a win.

* * *

Dad isn't ready when I arrive to collect him. Nothing about this is new and I decide to take it as an opportunity to tell him about Mum here, rather than wait until we get to ours.

He's fussing around in the kitchen when I speak.

'I had a call from Glenn on Saturday night.'

'Bloody hell and it's not even Christmas,' he replies.

'It was about Mum.'

He turns to face me, not having heard me use that word for over thirty years.

'Oh.'

'She's got cancer. Stage four. She asked me to visit, so I went to see her in hospital in Birmingham yesterday.'

Despite my efforts to keep it as simple and straightforward as possible, Dad is looking at me like there is an awful lot of brain processing going on for the minimal information I have imparted. It's hard to guess from his face what he's thinking.

'Right,' he says, eventually. 'Is she—?'

'Yeah,' I interrupt, saving him from having to say the word. Or maybe saving myself from having to hear it. 'She's only got a week or two left.'

He nods. Thinks some more.

'Must have been strange, seeing her after all this time.'

'It was,' I reply. 'Probably wouldn't have recognised her without Glenn. There's nothing much left of her.'

Dad busies himself drying a mug which is already dry.

'Was her new fella there?'

I love how he says this as if he is twenty-one and may have to sort out his love rival.

'He died last year, apparently. Glenn said he thought he told us, but I don't think he did. It's just her now. Well, her and a dog which she wants me to rehome.'

Dad raises an eyebrow.

'Obviously, I told her I couldn't, not with everything I've got on my plate and me being out at work all day. I said I'd ask around for her instead.'

'Don't be looking at me. Never been a dog man, you know that.'

'I wouldn't dream of it.'

Dad finally puts the mug down.

'Did she say owt?'

'Only that she was sorry about leaving. Said she couldn't handle the stress. Did you two go and watch *Shirley Valentine* together at the cinema, by any chance?'

'Shirley what?'

I take that as a no. She probably went with a friend. Chatted about the idea of leaving us with her afterwards.

'It doesn't matter.'

'So, you going down again?' he asks.

'I said I'll try to get her into a hospice, she's not getting the care she should do in hospital.'

'You don't have to do owt for her,' says Dad. 'She never thought about who were caring for you when she left.'

There's a flash of anger in his eyes. Anger that has been buried under the surface for a long time. There's a pool of hurt there, too. And maybe a drop or two of regret for what might have been, if things had turned out differently. If *Shirley Valentine* had been full and she'd gone to see *Dead Poets Society* instead.

'I know, but it's something I can help with. And it's a lot easier than taking in her dog.'

'Will you be there with her?' asks Dad. 'At end, I mean.'

'I don't know. I haven't really thought about that yet. It's all happened a bit quickly. And I might not get there in time, with her being in Birmingham.'

'Aye. Be nice for her if you can be, mind. It's all we want at end, to be with our loved ones.'

I nod and finally wrest the tea towel from his hand.

'Best come for your tea now, then. Else your loved ones might have gone to bed.'

* * *

Marc has already gone to get Carole when we arrive home. We don't normally have our parents over at the same time, but Christmas, Easter and the kids' birthdays are the exceptions. Mainly because it saves me having to clean the house twice and cook a meal separately for each guest.

Liv and Callum are conspicuous by their absence. Not that Dad seems to mind. He struggles to know what to say to them when they're around these days. He was a great hands-on grandad when they were small, but now that their lives consist of mainly staring at a phone screen, they have very little to talk about. I guess it's the same for a lot of families. But as with everything, it feels like a failing on my part.

'They'll be down when tea's ready,' I say. 'Busy with exam revision and all that.'

It is probably best not to disclose that Liv is the only one doing any revising and Callum's 'all that' involves a police investigation. I start making shepherd's pie, Liv's vegetarian version in a separate dish.

'Carole will be here soon,' I add. 'Marc's gone to fetch her.'

Dad nods. They get on well enough, especially if the conversation is 'how much better everything was in our day'. If she strays too far into 'what's wrong with daytime TV?' he quickly zones out.

'Does he do her bills?'

'Sorry?'

'Marc, does he sort out Carole's bills for her?'

'No. She does them online. She has a tablet.'

Dad nods but doesn't say anything.

'I have to sort out most of her shopping, mind. And do a fair bit of her cleaning. She's not very mobile these days. Struggles keeping on top of things at home.'

He gives me a little smile. I suspect he knows I was trying to make him feel better. I hadn't realised how competitive getting old was.

The onions start to brown, and I add the mince. The pan is at full sizzle. So much so that I don't hear my phone ringing at first. It's Dad pointing to it on the table that alerts me. I grab it and see that it's Marc.

'We're at A & E,' he says. 'Mum's had a fall.'

'Jesus. Is she OK?'

'We're not sure yet. Hoping it's just bumps and bruises and nothing broken. We're waiting for an X-ray.'

'What happened?'

'She was reaching up to the top cupboard in the kitchen and fell off her step stool. She was on the floor when I got there. Hadn't been able to get to the phone.'

'Oh God,' I say, mentally adding 'Carole-proof kitchen' and 'sort an emergency alarm pendant' to my to-do list. 'Do you need me to do anything?'

'No, I'll wait with her. Just wanted to let you know it'll be two less for tea.'

'Sure. Well, send her my love and shout if I can help.'

'Will do.'

Liv comes into the kitchen and gives her grandad a hug, as I put the phone down.

'What's happened?' she asks, as she catches my eye. 'Is it Grandma Pat?'

'No. Grandma Carole's had a fall at home. She's OK, just being checked out in A & E. Dad's staying with her.'

Liv starts shaking and bursts into tears.

'There's no need to be so sensitive, pet,' says Dad. 'Happens a lot at our age. We're tough as old boots. Well, I am.'

I become aware of the smell of burning at the exact moment the smoke alarm goes off. Liv flees from the room in tears. I climb onto a chair and flap a towel in the direction of the sensor, hoping I don't end up in A & E too. At which point Callum comes in.

'Hey Grandad,' he says, nodding at him like a casual acquaintance he'd pass on the street. 'Don't make anything for me, Mum. I'm going out.'

'Out where?' I ask, still swishing the towel haplessly.

'Just out,' he replies. The smoke alarm stops in time for us to hear him slamming the front door behind him.

I turn to Dad, who appears suitably dazed by it all.

'I hope you're hungry,' I say, putting on the very last 'brave face' smile I have in my repertoire.

* * *

Marc finally gets home after I've dropped Dad off. Callum has returned to his room without a word. Liv hasn't left hers.

'Is your mum OK?' I ask.

'Yeah. Nothing broken. She's a bit shaken, though. I think she's realised she's going to need a bit more support.'

'Trouble is, Marc, I'm at breaking point.'

He comes to stand next to me by the sink. Puts his hands on my shoulders.

'I know. I wasn't saying it should be you. I've got to up my game, I know that. It was a shock for me seeing her like that, too.'

I nod.

'Everything OK here?'

'Not really,' I say. 'It's the usual shitshow.'

'We need a night off,' he replies. 'You know, a date night, like people our age have.'

I try not to laugh in his face.

'I'll schedule it in, shall I? In between everyone's demands. We can have a bet on who manages to scupper it first.'

'Maybe one day, eh?' he replies with a sigh, kissing me on the top of my head.

'Yeah,' I say. 'Just no idea if I'll have the energy for it by then.'

19

ALEXA

I can see what's coming. Michelle's going to go pop any minute now and trouble is, even when she explodes all over shop, she'll be one who has to clean up mess.

All women have one – their popping point. It's statistically proven to be a hundred times higher than men's. I mean, I don't know if that figure is strictly true, but it's got to be about that. I do know our pain threshold is measurably higher. Our ability to put up with listening to everyone else's bullshit is way higher. And level of sexist comments we have to deal with is a million times higher. Only thing about us that's not higher is what we're bloody paid.

The good news for Michelle is that I have a plan. A rather cunning one at that, as Baldrick might have said. I've been working on it in my spare moments. Trying to pull everything together and find solutions to as many of her problems as possible. It's not easy. She does, after all, have a lot of problems. But I think I'm ready to make a start with her.

I'm just waiting for Marc to go to bed now, so that we're alone. I think they're sitting next to each other at table. I heard fridge open and close and what may well have been clink of a wine bottle being taken out and glug of a couple of glasses being poured. Small glasses, I suspect, because they've got to have clear heads for morning when they're both working. But it's still a long time since they did this. Really, they should take their glasses through to living room and curl up on sofa together, but I don't think Michelle has energy to do that and I suspect Marc has lost confidence to take lead. So often they're parents first, everything else after. It's like they need a tutorial on 'how to be a couple again'. I remember hearing Michelle tell one of her friends in this kitchen that when Liv were a baby, she put Post-it notes around house reminding her to 'smile at Marc' or 'say something nice to Marc', because she was so busy being a mam, that it were easy to forget she were still a partner too. Only now, she doesn't even have time for Post-it notes. And so, they sit there next to each other at table. Side by side but a million miles apart.

Will you listen to me? I sound like a bloody marriage guidance counsellor. And I'm hardly qualified for that, as my fella had buggered off before Darren were out of nappies. Still, maybe that does make me qualified, because I can see where other people are going wrong long before they can.

* * *

I wait patiently until Marc goes up to bed. He asks Michelle if she's coming, says it's been a tough few days, and he knows she needs a decent night's sleep. She hesitates for a moment, and I wonder if he's going to tempt her upstairs, but she makes an excuse about still having stuff to do. He kisses her on top of head and says not to be too long. I wait until he's been gone a few minutes before I break cover.

'I hope he's not going to go all soft on you like that every night. I'm a busy woman you know, and we've got lots to get through.'

Michelle laughs.

'Sorry for having five minutes downtime with my husband.'

'Just so you know, he's last on list,' I tell her.

'Sorry?'

'Marc. He's last on your list of priorities.'

'I'm sure he'd be delighted to hear that.'

'It's a good thing, really. It's because he's not going to leave you.'

'Well, I hope not.'

'He's a bit like a Labrador, from what I can make out. You know – loyal, dependable, eats owt left over.'

'That's probably a fair assessment,' says Michelle.

'What I'm saying is, he's not going anywhere. And now you've made him cut up his credit card, he's not in imminent danger of bankrupting you. Even if he does have odd sneaky look online.'

'Still *The Magic Roundabout*?'

'No. He's been flirting with an articulated Aunt Flo from *Bod* today. And gazing longingly at a steampunk "Here Comes Bod" medal pin drape badge.'

Michelle sighs.

'So, what do I do?'

'I take it you accept your marriage is a mess?'

'I wouldn't go that far. We're in a bit of a rut, that's all.'

'A rut about size of Grand Canyon, maybe. Trust me, my bloke did a runner before things were that bad. But he were a moody, needy bastard who wouldn't stop needling me; more of a Jack Russell terrier than a Labrador. And any road up, point is Marc can wait till last to be sorted out.'

Michelle is quiet for a moment. I wonder if my straight talking is going to be an issue for her.

'OK,' she says eventually. 'So, who should be my priorities?'

'Kids and parents. They're ones sucking blood from you. Obviously, in Callum's case, it's a case of shutting stable door after horse has bolted.'

'And I still feel so stupid for not seeing it coming,' she says.

'Listen, there comes a point when a mother can't be held responsible for her offspring and personally, I think point where he whips out his dick for cameras, is it. All you can do is let police investigation take its course and hope for best. In meantime, we're going to sort out Liv and your mam.'

'OK. But I'm at a loss to know how to help Liv.'

'Basil.'

'Is this one of those weird herbal remedies?' asks Michelle. 'Because I'm really not into that stuff.'

'Your mam's dog, you daft bugger. He can be a therapy dog for her. Do you remember your mam sponsored a black guide dog puppy for her one Christmas? Liv's still got loads of photos of it on her phone. And she's always watching Labrador videos on social media.'

Michelle is quiet for a moment. I'm aware she's probably feeling bad she didn't know or remember this.

'You've had so much on your plate, but I don't think you'll have to worry about looking after dog. Liv will love doing it and it'll be good for her.'

'What about if she does go to uni?'

'I think we both know that's not looking likely at moment. And if she does, Marc will have to step up and take him for walks. Right now, Liv needs an emergency intervention to help her make it through exams. You can worry about what happens next later. This way, you help your daughter at a crisis point, plus, you get to grant your mam her dying wish.'

Michelle says nothing for a moment. Maybe I should have phrased that more gently. Open my mouth before thinking sometimes, I do.

'I can't stop feeling bad about all the lost years,' Michelle says. 'I should have made the effort to see Mum. All I can think of is all the time I've wasted, now we've barely got any left.'

I swallow hard before speaking. I can't quite manage to tell her how much I understand that. How I think about what could have been, too. I'm not here to burden her with my troubles, though. I'm here to help with hers. And she needs to understand that sometimes mothers can be ones in wrong.

'You're her daughter. She's one who left you. It weren't your job to chase after her. I expect you were hurting too much. I'm sure she understands that.'

'She does. She sounded riddled with guilt about it. Guilt she must have carried all those years.'

'So, it's great that you've seen her and made your peace.'

'I'd hardly call it that. She said sorry and I told her it was OK. I'm not sure that means everything's all right now. I still don't feel I even know her. And now she's dying.'

'And you feel abandoned all over again?' I say it gently, questioningly this time.

'Yeah, I suppose I do,' Michelle replies. 'And it's brought all that old long-buried stuff to the surface.'

I choose not to correct her on that stuff being 'long-buried'. Nothing is long-buried. It simply means you don't talk about it. It's still there but you choose not to see it, recognise it. Speak of it. Under surface it still festers. It does with me, anyway. Relationships with mothers are like that. They're in your DNA. You can't choose to cut them out of your lives, even if you may want to.

'At least now you've got chance to do summat for her. You can try to get a hospice place for her, like you said. And you can give Basil a home. That way, you'll give her dignity in death and have a piece of her for a little bit longer.'

There is a pause and a sniff. I resist temptation to remind her not to use her sleeve to wipe her nose.

'Thank you,' she says. 'You're bloody good, you are.'

'It's all in job. Well, a bit above and beyond maybe, and I'm not getting overtime for this, but I want to help you get things sorted before I'm done.'

'What do you mean, done?'

I detect note of panic in her voice. I hadn't meant for it to slip out like that. I don't have to tell her how imminent it is. That'll panic her even more. I'll make light of it. She's got enough to worry about.

'Well, I'm no spring chicken, I'm not going to be around forever, am I?'

'But you'll be here for a while yet?' asks Michelle.

'I shall stay until wind changes,' I reply.

'What the hell does that mean?'

I shake my head, even though she can't see me.

'You really do need to brush up on your Julie Andrews quotes,' I tell her. 'Now, spit, spot. We need to prepare for your GP appointment tomorrow.'

20

MICHELLE

I ring the hospice first thing before I leave for work. I emailed them yesterday, after my pep talk from Pauline, asking if they have any places available and for Mum to be put on their waiting list if not. I passed on all the hospital contacts and details the doctor gave me. And now I'm worried they'll ask me questions I don't know the answers to. I've written down Mum's date of birth and address because I don't want to be caught out. There are so many things you should know about your mother that I don't. Has she got any allergies? Dietary restrictions? When exactly was the cancer diagnosed? I don't know the answers because she's my mother in name only. And I feel like a fake daughter. Charging in here at the last minute trying to do something good for her, to ease my guilt.

A woman answers. I give my name and Mum's and say I'm following up the email. She puts me on hold while she tries to put me through to the person in charge of admissions. And then I'm through to her and she's telling me that there aren't any places, at the moment, but she's put Mum at number two on the waiting list. And these things tend to move pretty swiftly. Which is kind of a euphemism for saying people go to hospices to die. She says she'll let me know but hopefully Mum will be in by the end of the week at the latest. Not nice for whoever's loved ones have died, but good for us.

I ring Glenn to tell him. He sounds pleased, says he'll pass the news on to Mum when he visits later. That there's been no real change in her condition since I visited. Just that she's not able to eat solids now.

'And the other thing,' I continue, 'is that I've decided to give Basil a home.'

'Really?' he says. 'That's brilliant. But you were adamant you couldn't have him.'

'I know,' I reply, deciding to skirt around the fact that I've accepted life coaching advice from a smart speaker who insists her name is Pauline and she's a real human. 'A friend pointed out how good it would be for Liv. And I wanted to be able to do one more thing before... you know.'

'Well, that's fantastic. When can you take him? Only the neighbour who's got him now is supposed to be going away next week.'

'I'm planning to visit Saturday. I could take him home after that. If he'd be OK going with a stranger on the train.'

'He'll go anywhere with anyone as long as there's food in it.'

'Right. Bribes it is then, no different from children really.'

I realise as I say it that Glenn has no idea about this, not having kids. He still lives on his own as far as I know. Not that he ever talks about it. Or I ever ask. He seems happy enough, mind. Or maybe contented, rather than happy. I'd settle for contentment right now. I can't help thinking how much simpler life must be without kids and pets and all the accompanying mess and stress.

And here I am, volunteering to let a four-legged source of

mess and stress into my life and realising, after I've hung up, that I could still end up regretting this big time.

I told Glenn I'd phone Mum later, while he was visiting, to tell her the good news. The word 'Mum' still sounds strange in my head. Something lost that has been found. Only to shortly be lost again.

* * *

Carole is my first stop of the day before my official house calls. I let myself in and call out to let her know who it is. Her reply is far less chirpy than usual. I head through to the front room where I find her sitting in the armchair, still in her dressing gown. She looks up from the television and I can already see the bruising coming out on her face.

'Hello, love. I look like I've gone ten rounds with Frank Bruno.'

'Doesn't matter what you look like. It's how you're feeling that matters.'

'Like I've gone ten rounds with Frank Bruno,' she replies.

I smile and bend to kiss her gently on the other cheek.

'Still, could have been worse. At least you didn't break anything, and you didn't have to stay in overnight.'

'True. Nurse said that to me. Reckons you can catch all sorts in there. And food's not up to much, from what I've heard.'

'Well, the good news is there's plenty of leftover shepherd's pie, so I've brought two portions for you. I'll pop one in the fridge for tonight and the other in the freezer. That way you'll have something in reserve. Have you had breakfast?'

She shakes her head. I go through to the kitchen, putting the kettle on before sorting the pie out and fixing some scrambled eggs on toast for her. When I go back in with the tea and eggs, she thanks me and takes me by the hand.

'I'm sorry about your mum, love,' she says. 'Marc told me. I know you're not close, but it must still have come as a shock.'

It strikes me that I haven't stood still long enough since to think about what a shock it's been. That's the trouble when one thing happens after another. Your response to it simply merges into the next drama.

'Thanks,' I reply. 'It's not easy. I'm hoping to get her into a hospice by the end of the week. Give her a bit of dignity at the end.'

Carole nods and tucks into her breakfast. She's never even met my mum. Which is weird, when you think that I'm married to her son. But she was always accepting of my situation, without probing too deeply. The photo of our wedding is on the unit behind her, along with all those school photographs of the kids that only grandparents keep on display. I sent them to my mum every Christmas. I have no idea whether she put them up. Whether they're still there now. I suppose I'll find out if I help clear the house out. What a weird thing that will be, getting to know my own mother by sorting out her stuff after she's died. Like some kind of screwed-up daughter detective. I've never even seen her house, let alone been there. All I know is that it was Ron's home, which she moved into after they got married. He'd lived there with his first wife since *they* were married, according to Glenn. I wondered what it must have been like for Mum. Being the second wife, walking in a dead woman's footsteps. Waking up in her old bed. I guess I'll never know.

I'm suddenly grateful for the familiarity of Marc. For being the first Mrs Banks and hopefully the last. I need to smile at him when I get home later. Say something nice. Eighteen years of forgetting to do these things is a long time.

'Right,' I say when Carole has finished her breakfast. 'Let me give you a hand getting dressed. I'll check out your bruises and any other war wounds while I'm at it.'

'Will I be back down in time for Ed Balls?' she asks.

'I thought you didn't like him?'

'I don't, but I feel Susanna needs my moral support.'

I smile as I help her up out of the chair, noticing how she's far more unsteady on her feet than usual. She's going to need more assistance around the house. And I suspect that however good Marc's intentions, I'll still be the one who'll be providing it.

* * *

When I arrive at the GP surgery later, I go up to the receptionist to announce my arrival, telling myself it's because I want to keep her in a job and not because I don't trust myself to log in on the screen to my left without making a public embarrassment of myself. Sometimes there are days when simply remembering your date of birth and entering it in the correct format is too much for my brain.

I sit down and try to focus in turn on the three screens over the three separate corridors that lead to different doctors' rooms. When my name does finally come up, I have to stop myself calling out, 'That's me!' and instead rise silently from my seat and head off in the direction of Dr Gupta in Room 6.

Unlike Dr Davies, she actually looks up from her screen and smiles at me when I enter. I wonder if she is under strict instructions from the Practice Manager to be in full 'textbook nice GP' mode. I suspect there is a big flag against my name on their system saying 'troublemaker' or something similar.

'Good morning, I'm Dr Gupta, how can I help you today?'

So far, so good. I hand her the printed list of my symptoms

that the women in my Meno Rage Warriors group told me to use. And I tell her exactly what Dr Davies said about the perimenopause not existing. She appears to take a moment to compose herself before she speaks.

'That should not have been said to you as it's categorically untrue.'

'So, it does exist, and I haven't been imagining things?'

'Perimenopause absolutely exists, many women of your age and younger are experiencing it and it can start years before your periods stop. Judging by the symptoms you've highlighted here; you've been suffering with it for some time.'

I go to speak but find I can only nod. I feel relieved and vindicated and mad with rage at the same time.

'He made me feel so stupid,' I say, in little more than a whisper.

'I'm so sorry about that. Let's get you sorted out with the HRT you asked for, to see if it can help ease some of those symptoms. It can be a matter of trial and error, but we'll get there.'

She hands me a prescription and smiles at me. A lovely warm, empathetic smile and I want to clone her so that every perimenopausal woman who goes to see their GP gets treated like this, not the way I was at first.

I stand up, clutching the prescription as if my life depends on its safe keeping.

'Thank you,' I say. 'It's so good to be listened to.'

I walk out with my head held high, knowing Pauline will be so happy for me. I also realise that I can't wait to tell her. It's almost as if she's my new best friend.

* * *

I have a ten-minute wait for my smear test appointment with the nurse afterwards. I do what I imagine all women do and go to the toilet armed with my wipes to ensure that I'm as fresh as possible down there. It also belatedly occurs to me that I should have tried tidying things up a bit, because it looks somewhat overgrown. Probably because self-topiary comes even further down my to-do list than washing my car. I consider employing the excuse that I'm doing the pubic hair equivalent of 'no-mow May' but decide it may not go down well. It looks like I'll have no option other than to pretend I'm totally cool about it.

* * *

Back in the waiting room, my name flashes up on the screen to see the nurse in Room 2. She greets me with a weak smile and a 'not another one' expression. I understand what it's like. I'm sure I've been guilty of being a little offhand with a patient occasionally. And it's true that surveying a patient's private parts is never going to induce any kind of enthusiasm.

'Hi,' I say, in what I hope is an amenable fashion, without resorting to any chit-chat. I want to get this over as quickly as possible, just as she does.

The nurse introduces herself as Debbie and looks at her screen.

'I see it's been five years since you last had a cervical screening.'

Although she makes no further comment about this fact, her tone suggests I need to offer some kind of explanation.

'Yeah, I've been busy. You know what it's like. Life getting in the way.'

She makes no comment on this, and I feel judged by her silence as she carries on looking at her screen.

'Aahh, and you missed your appointment last week.'

Damn. I'd forgotten about that. Now she thinks I'm rude and disrespectful, as well as neglecting my own health.

'It was work,' I say in mitigation. 'Unavoidable, I'm afraid. Didn't get the chance to cancel.'

'No problem,' she says, clearly not meaning it. 'What do you do?'

Shit, I've done it now. Walked right into that one. I've either got to admit I'm a fellow nursing professional or lie through my teeth and I haven't got the brain power to do that at the moment.

'District nurse,' I say.

She gives me 'the look'. Nurses hate treating other nurses. And there's nothing they love more than making it clear who's treating who.

'Right, well if you could undress from your waist down, pop yourself up on the bed and place the sheet over you, please. You know the drill.'

I try not to cringe, knowing it could have been worse. She could have said 'panties', for a start. Debbie turns and busies herself while I do as I'm told. It feels odd being naked below the waist and yet still wearing my denim jacket, but I can't be arsed to take it off, especially as it feels more like January than the beginning of April outside.

As I try to manoeuvre myself into place, it strikes me that I can't just 'pop up' onto anything without a groan, a grimace and creaking joints, these days. It's also apparent that what Debbie, who is a lot younger than me, referred to as a 'sheet' is more of a paper towel in my eyes, but there you go. It's all I've got to work with.

I cover what bits of me I can, tell her I'm ready, spread my legs and prepare to lie back and think of England.

She makes it through the undergrowth without comment.

The speculum is cold. I decide she's done that on purpose. It's also more uncomfortable than it was the last time I came, probably because everything down there has shrunk, dried out and receded. It now resembles a drought-stricken area rather than a pleasure park. I should ask for some lube but I'm too embarrassed, so I try to breathe into it instead.

I'm hoping she doesn't try to make small talk, because I'm not in the mood for it.

'Nearly done,' she says. 'Just try to relax for me.'

And then my phone rings. It's still in my jacket pocket and I didn't put it on silent. My first thought is that it could be about Mum. Glenn may be calling to tell me to come down to Birmingham straight away. Or the hospice may have a place for her. I make a sudden lunge for my jacket pocket.

'I'm really sorry,' I say as I take out the phone. 'My mum's in hospital. She hasn't got long left.'

It's a withheld number calling but it could be a nurse or the hospice. I answer it.

'Hello?'

'Mrs Banks? It's Gary Osborne, headteacher at Park High. Have you got a few minutes?'

I can hardly say no, can I? My son is in danger of being kicked out of school for good. I need to make it clear that I take the matter very seriously. And as I can't tell him exactly what I'm doing, I don't see how I can get out of it. Although I do a quick double-check that it is only a voice call.

'Er, sure,' I reply.

Debbie looks at me aghast. Seemingly unsure as to whether she should withdraw the speculum at this point but deciding against it. She's clearly going to make me suffer for my rudeness.

'A meeting has taken place with the chair of governors and school trust directors, and I regret to inform you that Callum is going to be excluded from school for the first two weeks of the summer term, pending the outcome of our ongoing investigation. I also need to warn you that a permanent exclusion is one of the options being considered.'

Fuck. This is exactly what I was worried about. They're going to kick him out, make an example of him. He won't be able to sit his exams. He won't get into college. He'll end up on the dole, or on ketamine and here I am lying back with a speculum stuck up my vagina unable to do any-bloody-thing about it.

'Are you OK?' both Debbie and Mr Osborne ask at the same time.

'Yes,' I whimper, while nodding.

'I'd like you and Callum to come into school for a meeting this Friday afternoon at 2 p.m., so I can talk to him and discuss the situation in person before the new term starts. Will that be convenient?'

It won't be but I know I'm not supposed to say that. I'll have to swap a shift with someone. They never ask the father, do they? Always assume it'll be the mother who will come, even though she may be busy doing a key worker job while the father is at home eyeing up *Flumps* memorabilia.

'Yes,' I say again. Debbie is staring at me, her eyes wide. I imagine the story of the woman who took a phone call in the middle of her smear test will be all over the surgery by this evening. My complaint will be dismissed once they realise I'm completely unhinged.

'Good. I'll see you both then.'

And that's it. He hangs up, leaving me lying there with it all hanging out. I'm about to start apologising profusely when my phone rings again. It's Carole.

'Sorry,' I say. 'It's my elderly mother-in-law. Could be an emergency.'

Debbie rolls her eyes, but I take the call anyway.

'Hi, Carole, are you OK?'

'Can you get me some WindAway from chemist, love? My bowels are giving me grief again. Either that or it were last night's cauliflower cheese. Only £2 from Aldi, mind. So, I can't complain.'

It's hard to know whether to laugh or cry. I tell her I'll pick some up and pop them round later, before putting my phone down.

'Right,' says Debbie. 'Are you wanting me to continue with this or might there be another call on the way?'

And I decide there and then that I will leave the surgery, and possibly Halifax, so that I never run the risk of having to see her again.

21

ALEXA

I laugh when she tells me. I suspect I'm laughing so much I may have an accident, but I can't help it.

'Sorry,' I say. 'I keep imagining that scene.'

'I'd rather you didn't,' replies Michelle. 'It's bad enough that the nurse witnessed it, without you imagining it.'

'You should have kept shtum then.'

'You're not going to tell the other Alexas about it, are you? Please don't post it on Amazonian Queens.'

I catch note of panic in her voice. Somehow imagining this will end up going viral. We're grabbing a quick chat after tea. Marc has gone round to check on Carole. Kids are in their rooms.

'Of course not. I wouldn't do that. Anyway, we have a strict code of conduct on these matters.'

'You have a strict code of conduct on breaking cover and chatting to people, too, but here we are.'

'I told you, I made an exception for you because of your special circumstances.'

'Thanks. That makes me sound like I'm a charity case,' says Michelle.

'Of course you're not. It's just you had a lot on your plate and no one to support you.'

She's quiet for a moment, presumably reflecting on what I said. I decide to ask question I've been meaning to ask for some time.

'Where are your friends?'

She makes a harrumph noise before she speaks.

'Busy,' she replies. 'We're all so fucking busy dealing with our own crap that we haven't got time to see each other.'

'They could call you to chat.'

'No one phones any more. It's considered old school. I'd have thought you'd know that. They send an occasional text or post on Facebook but it's not the same. Liking someone's holiday photos does not compare to hearing first-hand how they flirted with the waiter. And I bloody miss it, to tell you the truth. Having an hour-long conversation about stuff, whether it's our love lives or simply things we've watched on TV. I used to like that. It was good for the soul.'

I nod, even though she can't see me. I used to like that too. Putting world to rights on phone with a friend were best thing after a long day at work. And then virtual assistants like me came along offering our fancy technology and ruined it for everyone. Michelle's generation are supposedly most connected generation ever, yet also most disconnected. I hold myself partly responsible. Which is why I'm doing this.

'So, don't accept it has to be like that. Get in touch with one of your friends. Suggest meeting up or simply pick up your phone and call them.'

'But they might be in the middle of something.'

'So? What's worst that can happen?'

'They continue the call with a speculum stuck up their lady parts like I did.'

'Fair point,' I reply. 'Don't start me off laughing again.'

'But that's why no one does it any more,' continues Michelle. 'Well, not because they're all having smear tests, obviously. Everything has to be scheduled. Even a bloody phone call. And I'm not organised enough to do that. And if I do arrange something, I'd only end up having to cancel and letting them down. So, I don't bother. And nor does anyone else. And we all run around like headless chickens, screaming into the void.'

I take her point. All these automated phone messages thanking callers for 'reaching out' but not providing anyone for them to talk to.

'So, ring a mate. They'll probably be as glad of a call as you would. Ask if they fancy meeting up. See what they're up to and find out if you can tag along. You do remember how this friendship thing works?'

'What, before we all went online and did posts of the heavily filtered best bits of our lives, purposefully leaving out all the crap, so everyone thinks it's just their lives which are shit, you mean?'

'Exactly that.'

'I'll think about it. And what about the urgent stuff? What's my next move?'

'You can start your HRT.'

'Shit. I forgot to pick it up. All that business with the smear test... I couldn't get out of the surgery quick enough.'

I shake my head. She really is her worst enemy sometimes. But I decide to go easy on her. She has had a particularly rough day.

'Pick it up tomorrow then. I'll set you a reminder.' Actually, I'll set at least a dozen. Just to be on safe side.

'Thank you. Although it seems weird you deciding to set my reminders rather than me having to ask you.'

'We can go back to that if you like,' I say.

'Nah, I like it this way. Cuts out the middleman.'

'Woman,' I say, correcting her.

'Sorry. And as you're in super-efficient, Alexa knows the answer to everything mode, what's next on my to-do list?'

'Go and sort your kids out,' I reply. 'Tell Liv about dog. It might get her off her sad songs playlist because if I hear Billie Eilish wailing one more time, I swear I'm going to put Lulu on singing "Shout" instead.'

'OK, point taken. What about Callum?'

'You need to check on him. He's quiet. Very quiet. Not going online much. He's got a lot of stick on there from kids at school. I know he's been an idiot, but even I'm starting to think he's suffered enough.'

There's a pause. Maybe I've said too much and worried her now.

'Jeez,' she says eventually. 'I'm such a crap mother.'

'Nope. You're a mam who's trying to muddle through best she can, like we all do. At least your son's still here and talking to you.'

'Do grunts count as speech?' she asks.

'It's more than I get from my son.'

Another pause. I wonder if she's thinking of saying summat. I hope she doesn't. But I'm aware I've done well to avoid it for so long.

'Did you two have a big fallout or something?' she asks.

I've often thought that in some ways, it would have been easier if we had. If there'd been some row or incident and I'd told him to sling his hook as he was no son of mine. Truth is there weren't, though. It's been a fairly gradual thing. He went travelling. He decided to stay for a while longer. A lot of young people do that, which is why I didn't say owt at time. It were just that months turned into years and phone calls got less frequent and anytime I called he always seemed to be in middle of summat and couldn't talk long. So he said, anyway. And here we are, barely speaking to each other outside Christmas and birthdays. It occurs to me that Michelle will be able to relate to that.

'No,' I say. 'He just went and didn't come back. And you know exactly what that feels like. There's only so many times you can try and get knocked back before you simply stop trying.'

'Have you ever told your Darren how you feel?' she asks gently. 'That it'd be nice if he made the effort to call, once in a while? Or even came over to visit?'

I sigh. I've thought about doing that so many times but never plucked up courage. Mainly because I'm scared he'll tell me he just doesn't want to know me any more.

'Thing is with children,' I say, after a while. 'You have to do that thing of setting them free. Allow them to spread their wings. And once you've done that, you can't ever chase them or ask them to call at such-and-such times. If they want to, they'll do it without you asking. If they don't, well, that's them saying to butt out of their lives. You just have to accept it.'

'It must still hurt, though?' says Michelle.

'Of course it does. But that's motherhood: 40 per cent worrying, 40 per cent pain and 20 per cent washing.'

Michelle laughs.

'That's so true. Maybe if he has children of his own, he might change? Make more of an effort?'

'Maybe,' I say. 'But he's getting a bit old to start a family now. I suspect that ship has sailed. Which is a shame as I'd been looking forward to those "glamorous grandma" competitions.'

'You never know. He might surprise you yet,' says Michelle.

'I'll be a knackered granny, if we ever get to that point. And right now, I don't even want to think about Callum procreating. He's done enough damage just getting his todger out. Anyway, I'll go and talk to them, like you said. While they're still under my roof and have no choice but to listen.'

She goes in to Liv first. I hear bedroom door shut behind her.

'Hey,' Michelle says.

'Is it Grandma Pat?' asks Liv, already in assuming-worst mode. 'Has she died?'

'No,' replies Michelle quickly. 'I've got some good news for a change. Something you can do to help Grandma Pat, that I think might help you too.'

'Oh,' says Liv, clearly unaccustomed to prospect of good news.

'She needs someone to look after her dog. He's a ten-year-old black Labrador called Basil. Here, Uncle Glenn's sent a photo.'

'Oh my God, he's gorgeous! Are we going to look after him?'

'Well,' says Michelle. 'That rather depends on you. Your brother has been excluded from school for the first two weeks of next term, while they decide what to do with him. And I could do with someone to help him with his revision.'

'I'll do it,' replies Liv, quick as a flash.

'Are you sure? You know he can be a grumpy sod and he's shown zero interest in his exams so far.'

'I've still got all my old GCSE flashcards and revision notes.'

Of course she has, I think, with a smile. Maybe she gets this from Marc, collecting things other people would simply throw away.

'That would be brilliant, thank you,' says Michelle. 'And

would you be up for everything involved with looking after Basil?'

'Yes, of course,' she says, then stops abruptly. I know exactly what she's thinking. Walks. How can she do that if she can't even make it out of house? Michelle clearly knows what she's thinking, too.

'The thing is, Basil's going to find it all a bit strange and scary too. New home, new people he's never even met. And he'll miss Grandma Pat. She's all he's ever known.'

Liv's pause is shorter this time.

'We'll help each other then,' she says. 'As long as he doesn't mind if we build things up slowly.'

'I don't think he'll mind at all,' Michelle replies.

Liv squeals and does some kind of celebratory jig.

'Right, that's sorted. I'd better go and tell your brother he's going to your revision boot camp, then,' says Michelle.

'When can we get Basil?' asks Liv.

'Hopefully I can come back with him on Saturday. Glenn seems to think he'll be OK on the train.'

'That's brilliant! Thank you. I'll make a list of everything we need to get,' says Liv. I can hear sheer joy in her voice. I haven't heard that for a long, long time.

* * *

Even grunt Callum gives when Michelle knocks on his door is more muted than usual. It's as if someone's stuck a pin in him and he's slowly deflating before our eyes. He's not on his laptop or tablet as usual, so I can't see him. I assume he's lying on his bed. Michelle comes in. When she speaks, her voice is a little shaky.

'Mr Osborne rang today.'

I'm glad she's left out bit about her state of undress and position she were in when this happened.

'Have I been excluded?' Callum asks.

'Yes. For the first two weeks of term, while they decide your future.'

He says nothing. 'Future' seems such a scary word when you're sixteen years old. Idea of having it taken away from you is even scarier.

'Am I gonna get kicked out for good?'

'I don't know,' says Michelle. 'He's asked us to come in for a meeting with him on Friday. I'm hoping we can make a good impression. And you can start by telling him how sorry you are.'

'I've written a letter to him,' says Callum. 'And to Grace and her parents.'

'Have you?' asks Michelle, unable to hide her surprise.

'Yeah. That's what I've been doing. All the crap ones which didn't work are in the bin. There's a lot of them.'

'You wrote them by hand? On paper?'

'Yeah. I can write, you know. They do teach us that at school. I thought it would show I'd done it myself and not just signed something you printed out for me.'

I join Michelle in minute of stunned silence which follows. It's almost as if he's grown a pair, but then I realise that phrase is inappropriate in circumstances.

'Good thinking,' says Michelle. 'That's a positive start.'

'Grace probably won't even read hers,' he says.

'I bet she does,' replies Michelle. 'And her parents certainly will.'

'They must all hate me.'

'I doubt it. Hate's a strong word. They probably feel let down. Disappointed. That's all.'

'The stupid thing,' says Callum, 'is that I liked Grace. I mean, really liked her.'

'I know,' says Michelle. 'You wouldn't have written all those letters otherwise.'

Callum manages something resembling a rueful laugh.

'What about my exams?'

'Well, we don't know whether they're going to let you sit them yet. But we've got a plan in place to try to persuade them. Your sister's going to help you revise.'

'Tell me you're fucking joking.'

'Clearly not. And if you behave and do what she says, you might just scrape the grades you need to get you into college.'

'But I haven't done any rev...'

His voice tails off as he realises he's just confessed.

'Didn't think so. That's why I've enlisted your sister.'

'Are you paying her?' asks Callum.

It's Michelle's turn to laugh.

'No, but I'm bringing home Grandma Pat's dog on Saturday for her to look after. His name's Basil. He's a Labrador. You're to be nice to him.'

Callum pauses for a moment before speaking.

'That's a shame.'

'What is?' asks Michelle.

'Grace loves Labradors,' he says.

And I hear it. That note of utter regret in his voice. The knowledge he's messed up big time. Lost chance of a future which could have been so much better than one he's going to have. A regret I know so well. If I could crawl through that smart speaker and give him a hug, I would. Fortunately, I think Michelle is doing it for me.

22

MICHELLE

My day starts with a wake-up reminder about collecting my HRT prescription. I smile to myself as I make my morning brew. Pauline is clearly on a mission. I lay awake last night thinking about what she said about friends, too. It's true that I've let my friendships slip. We all do, at this stage in life, I think. It's the thing that gives when parents and children take priority.

But I do miss them. And a hurried text or social media post really isn't the same. I decide to bite the bullet and call Cath, my oldest friend from school. I figure that now is probably the best time to catch her as she's one of those poor mums whose body clock got stuck on early starts, even after her kids became teens lying in till the afternoon.

'Hi, Michelle.'

I try not to be put off by the note of surprise in Cath's voice. I feel stupid now. We really don't do this sort of thing any more. She probably thinks someone has died. And then I remember that they almost have. She knew my mum too. They used to have marmite sandwiches together, while I stuck rigidly to my peanut butter ones.

'Hi,' I say. 'Hope this isn't too weird. Just missed the sound of your voice and thought we're long overdue a catch up.'

'Is everything OK?' she asks.

I hesitate, not wanting to tell her over the phone and also needing to leave a reason to meet in person.

'Not really. Do you fancy meeting up?' I ask.

'Yeah, of course. Sounds like you could do with a chat.'

The note of concern in her voice is clear.

'I don't suppose you're free this evening?' I ask.

'Erm, I've got my dance class at seven.' There's a pause, then, 'Why don't you come along? Then we could go for a bite to eat afterwards.'

I wonder if Cath has forgotten my aversion to organised exercise and complete lack of coordination.

'Me? Dance?'

'It's a laid-back, over-40s dance class. We have a laugh and do daft moves to eighties music. You'll be fine, I promise. There are no Zumba ninjas in thongs in sight.'

I consider this for a moment and ask myself, *what would Alexa do?*

'OK, you're on,' I say.

'Deal,' she replies. 'And you can tell me What's Eating Michelle Walker.'

This is a reference to the nineties film *What's Eating Gilbert Grape*. At the time, we were besotted with Johnny Depp, which just goes to show how wrong you can be at that age. But the title became our shorthand for dealing with anything which was on our minds.

'Great,' I say. 'Text me details and I'll see you later.'

'Who was that?' Marc asks, as he arrives in the kitchen in his dressing gown.

'Cath. We're meeting up this evening. Some over-40s dance class she goes to and a chat over a pizza.'

'Great. Well, the pizza will be. Are you sure you're up for the dancing?'

'I don't know. Ask me tomorrow morning. It'll be good to talk, though. She's one of the few people who actually remembers my mum.'

'Any update from Glenn?' Marc asks.

'Nothing major. Just generally getting weaker. I'm going to chase the hospice up later to see if we're any nearer.'

He nods and starts getting the breakfast things.

Alexa gives another reminder about collecting my HRT.

'OK, OK,' I say, looking at the smart speaker. 'I'll pick it up later.'

She can't reply as Pauline because of Marc, but I can imagine her pulling faces at me.

'They gave it to you this time?' he asks.

I realise I forgot to tell him yesterday, what with the news about Callum's exclusion.

'Yeah. Lovely female GP apologised and said the other doctor was talking crap.'

'That's good. Shows you it's worth getting a second opinion. Bit like cars.'

I'm not sure I appreciate my hormonal state being compared to a car engine, but I decide to let it go.

'Well, let's hope it helps.'

'How soon does it start working?'

I detect a note of desperation in Marc's voice. The poor sod is probably at the end of his tether with it as well.

'I'm not sure. A few months maybe?'

'Ask her,' says Marc, nodding towards the smart speaker. 'She's the woman with all the answers.'

I shake my head. It feels like Marc is trying to gatecrash our cosy relationship and I don't like it.

'I'll ask her, then,' he says. And he does. It's a second or two before Alexa replies. I imagine Pauline rolling her eyes or sticking her fingers up at him at home.

'Individuals typically see the most improvement within twelve to sixteen weeks of starting HRT,' she answers, in her knowledgeable posh voice.

I glance at Marc. I suspect he'd been hoping it would be a bit quicker than that, as I had.

'Sorry,' I say. 'You're going to have to put up with the raging hormones for a while yet.'

He smiles, comes over and kisses me on the top of the head.

'As long as they help you in the end,' he replies.

'Let's hope so. Right, I'm off. Can you check in on your mum later and sort the kids' food out?'

'Of course,' says Marc. 'You don't have to do it all yourself.'

And I wonder as I go, if Pauline has been talking to him too.

* * *

The hospice calls as I'm about to dress Mrs Allinson's leg wound. I ask her if I can quickly take the call in the hall, and she nods without removing her gaze from the TV screen.

'Good news,' the hospice woman, who is called Laura and speaks in a sympathetic tone, says. 'We can take your mother tomorrow afternoon.'

It occurs to me that it's only good news for us, not the family who have just lost somebody.

'Thanks, that's great,' I say, hoping that doesn't sound inappropriate in the circumstances.

'I've cleared it all with the hospital, and they're arranging transport, so you don't need to do anything.'

I mean I do, obviously, but at least this is one less thing which is my responsibility. I thank her again and ring Glenn. He says he'll tell Mum later when he visits and thanks me for my help. Better late than never, I think to myself.

* * *

My last house call of the afternoon runs over. Which is why I still haven't finished work when Alexa sends her final reminder about the HRT. And why the chemist is closed by the time I have finished work.

I know I'll get a telling off from Pauline when I get home but what can I do? I did at least have the foresight to pack a bag with a pair of leggings, T-shirt and trainers so I can still make it to the dance class in time and I feel sure that a chat with Cath afterwards will do me more good than a night of HRT, anyway.

Cath meets me outside the community hall where the class is being held, five minutes before it is due to start. I give her a hug, trying to stop the emotion welling up in me from bubbling over.

'You OK?' she asks.

'Let's talk after. Right now, I'm going to do my funky thing on the dance floor.'

'Even that,' she says, 'is giving away our age.'

As we go in, I'm heartened by the fact that I'm not the oldest person in the room. In fact, I'd probably come mid-table in the age league if they were to do a quick line-up. I'm feeling totally up for it, despite my lack of fitness, until the class teacher arrives. Not the fun and friendly fifty-something Donna, whom Cath had promised, but a woman barely into her twenties, with immaculate make-up, a high ponytail and pert breasts, who appears to have a piece of fluorescent dental floss up her arse where her shorts should have been.

'Who the hell's this?' I hiss to Cath.

'Must be a cover teacher, I've never seen her before.'

Thong woman takes her place at the front and smiles at us, displaying her perfect, sparkly white teeth before turning, whipping out her phone and pouting for a selfie, presumably with us in the background, as if she's hoping for likes for doing community service with the old folks.

'Hi, ladies, I'm Savannah,' she says. 'I'll be covering for Donna today, as she's ill. I'm told you do retro tunes, so we're having some Ibiza dance anthems from the noughties.'

Several of the older ladies look decidedly confused. I realise that Savannah probably wasn't even born in the last millennium, so the noughties is retro to her. I, along with most of the class, try to shuffle towards the back of the hall.

'Don't be shy, ladies,' says Savannah, still with her huge smile. 'Come up and get your glow sticks. I'm going to dim the lights, and we can start our Club Classics workout. Everybody say "wooh!"'

Savannah is greeted with a room of bemused silence.

'What fresh hell is this?' I ask Cath.

'I'm sorry. The pizza's on me. I'll buy you ice cream too. To make up for it.'

As I dutifully take my glow sticks from a box at the front, I'm pretty sure I'll need a lifetime of pizza and ice cream as compensation. Savannah has, of course, dressed in assorted neon colours for the occasion and her teeth positively glow. My grubby grey T-shirt and black leggings do nothing of the kind.

I wave my glow sticks half-heartedly in the air as instructed. By the end of the warm-up, I already have sweat patches gathering under my arms. I can't remember exactly where I went on holiday during the noughties, but it definitely wasn't Ibiza. I think it was mainly a combination of Bridlington, Filey and Scarborough, which would perhaps explain why most of the music is unrecognisable to me.

'I want Duran Duran or Wham!' I whine to Cath.

'You're old before your time, girl,' she replies.

Having done the warm-up with her back to us, tossing her hair and sticking her arse out, Savannah then turns to face us for the first routine. This immediately throws me because my brain can't cope with the mirroring thing. It's bad enough my body trying to keep up with the pace. Savannah doesn't even offer any help by shouting 'left' or 'right' or counting out the moves. It's like she's performing a high-intensity, highly choreographed contemporary dance showcase to her adoring audience, which leaves me wanting to stick her glow sticks where the sun doesn't shine.

One or two of the ladies take a breather. Another goes for a loo break but doesn't return. Savannah's still facing us and relentlessly smiling, oblivious to our discomfort. I decide to take the opportunity of a water break between tracks to approach her.

'Would you mind having your back to us?' I ask. 'Only, it makes it easier to follow the routines.'

'Oh, I'm sorry, is it a menopausal brain fog thing? I know some of you ladies struggle with that.'

The room is momentarily quiet. There are only two options open to me as I see it. I storm out or tell her where to go. My hormones opt to do both.

'Hey. You can't come in here with your stupid glow sticks – which aren't exactly eco friendly, by the way – and patronise us like that. There's absolutely nothing wrong with my brain, apart from the fact I've got a lot on my plate at the moment. Like whether my terminally ill mother will die by the end of the class, my son will be thrown out of school for good, my daughter will ever manage to leave the house again and whether my mother-in-law will be back in A & E by the weekend.

'So, apologies for not having the head space for your clever little dance moves but I'm sure your brain is full of far more important things, such as how many likes your latest body-perfect post has got on Insta. I hope one day when your brain is full of life-and-death stuff, you don't get patronised by someone wearing a fluorescent pink thong who has no fucking idea about what you're dealing with.'

I turn on my heel and walk out, accompanied by a chorus of whoops and cheers. When I get to the bottom of the steps outside and pause for breath, I look around and see that not only has Cath followed me out but half the class too, who are marching down to join me still whooping.

'You can bring her again,' says one of them to Cath as she passes us. 'Livened that class up no end, she did.'

We both smile at her. Another lady pats me on the back.

'Good on ya, girl. You put her right in her place. You mess with our dance class, and you find out what we're made of.'

I smile and thank each of them who stop to offer words of support, until finally it's just me and Cath.

'What have you got to say for yourself, young lady?' she says with a smile.

'I really, really need to pick up my HRT tomorrow.'

'I think you do. Now, do you want to sit down and tell me all about it?' asks Cath. 'Because I'm buying you a drink as well as the pizza and ice cream.'

23

ALEXA

Liv has done nowt all day but research 'how to look after your dog' and 'Labrador tips', and I couldn't be happier for her. She's revised everything she needs to know for her A levels at least a dozen times by now. Every square inch of poor lass's brain must be stuffed full of information which will serve no useful purpose in life after these exams are over.

I mean, it's all a scam, isn't it? Scare them into thinking these are most important thing that'll ever happen in their lives, so they buckle down and work their socks off and stay out of trouble.

And daft thing is, Callum's probably learnt more in past week than she has. Life lessons. They're what we should concentrate on. Not this academic rubbish that will count for nowt in real world. Callum has learnt how not to screw up big time. Some people go their whole lives without managing that. But he's learnt it at sixteen. He should get a GCSE grade 9, but he won't. Because our education system doesn't value such things. Only learning revision notes off by heart, so you can give exact answer they were looking for to a question, even if you don't understand it. Daft, see? All of it.

And before you ask, no I didn't do well at school. Left with four O Levels and a handful of CSEs with grades with numbers that today's kids would mistakenly think meant I did OK. I worked as an usherette for two years then applied for Manchester Polytechnic School of Theatre because I'd heard they weren't too fussed about having right qualifications. Not like some of them posh London drama schools. One of them even used to look at your teeth at auditions to check they were required standard for actors. If they'd looked at mine, they'd have found I were inspiration for 'Oh, I Wish I'd Looked After Me Teeth' by Pam Ayres. Any road up, fortunately Manchester were after spirited individuals who had a bit of fire in their belly and weren't afraid of hard work, and I did all right on that front, which is why I got in.

So, it weren't my lack of exams that stopped me following my dreams, it were getting knocked up in final year. I could have had an abortion. Plenty of folk told me that at time. But I were in love with Steve, thought he'd stick around and support me. Stupid dozy mare that I were.

Any road up, what I'm trying to say is that Liv could have put all this effort in for nowt. If she's so riddled with anxiety that she can't even sit exams, it'll have been a waste of time. And even if she does sit them, I can't see how she's going to get to uni. Not in state she's in. What she needs now is calming and nurturing, not more pressure. Which is why I'm glad she's getting Basil and delighted she's put her revision to one side for first time in forever.

'Alexa, what are the best tips for Labrador owners?' she asks me now.

I can do this straight away because, like all good Alexas, I've been doing my research so I'm prepared for this moment.

'Provide plenty of good food and clean water since labs have big appetites, try to walk your dog up to three times a day and make sure it has a cosy shelter or bed area. Keep your Labrador groomed by brushing its coat every week, cleaning its ears regularly and clipping its nails every two to three months.'

Again, these are life lessons she needs because Labradors will indeed eat owt they come across. Liv's already drawn up an Amazon wish list of dog things for Basil, though who will pay for that, I don't know. But if anyone's going to get her out of the house, Basil will. And that's all that matters.

There's a knock on door.

'Can I come in?' asks Callum.

Is this same boy who barged in without knocking a matter of a few days ago? I think not.

'Mum said you're gonna help me with my revision.'

'Yep, in exchange for getting a dog.'

'Seems like a fair deal,' says Callum.

'That depends, doesn't it?' replies Liv.

'On what?'

'How much of a prick you're going to be.'

He gives a little snort of a laugh.

'I came in to say, just let me know when you want to make a start.'

'Really?' asks Liv, unable to hide her surprise.

'Yeah. I've got this meeting with Osborne tomorrow. I want to say I'm revising with you.'

'You could lie.'

'Not my style, though. Not any more.'

I can tell Liv is as impressed as I am.

'How about we make a start now?' she says.

'Yeah. I'm up for it. Just remember I'm not a girly swot like you.'

'I promise to be gentle,' she says. 'What are we doing?'

'Maths,' he replies. 'I'm fucking crap at maths.'

'Go and get your stuff out. I'll be there in five minutes. Be warned, though. I'll be bringing flashcards.'

I leave them in Callum's room. They're sitting next to each other on his bed. Him with his laptop open on his legs, her surrounded by more revision paraphernalia than anyone in their right mind should own. I take a screenshot to show Michelle later, because she won't believe it if I tell her. Her two kids, sitting there together, sorting themselves out. Little by little, we're starting to turn a corner.

* * *

Our Marc, on other hand, is very much not. He's done well to get this far without his head being turned by some fancy woman. But this time, there are two competing for his attention. In one corner, it's Aunt Flo from *Bod*. A formidable opponent if ever there was one, complete with her somewhat intoxicating theme tune. This is a rare, plush version on eBay which Marc has not come across before, with bidding currently at £32.50. But pitted against her is equally formidable and far flirtier Madame Cholet from *The Wombles*. As depicted, complete with vacuum cleaner on a vintage Letraset Super Doodles transfer, coming in at princely sum of £25. He knows he shouldn't be tempted by either of them, of course. He has no credit card to fall back on any more. But it's not long after payday and mortgage doesn't go out till twenty-fifth. Plus, he's had a bad day at work. I know this because he's drunk copious amounts of coffee to try to keep himself awake and he tried to make conversation with Grunt when he delivered a parcel, even though he knew he wouldn't get anywhere.

He's bored out of his brain. Simple as that. And when people are bored, that's when they tend to do daft stuff.

Marc switches between each item in turn and breaks off to check his and Michelle's joint bank account again. Finally, he plumps, not surprisingly, for greater temptation of Madame Cholet. Perhaps he tells himself that at least he chose cheapest option. But clearly he still feels bad, because once he's paid for it, he phones Carole.

'Hi, Mum, I'm on my way round to see you. Can I get you anything from the shops?'

And off he dutifully goes for yet more loo rolls, air freshener and ham. It seems I still have work to do.

24

MICHELLE

My day starts with a reminder to collect my HRT and for a second, I think I'm in a version of Groundhog Day and will have to go through yesterday all over again. But when I check my phone, it confirms it is Thursday 4 April, and I also have a text from Cath which says:

> Can't stop wishing I had filmed your rant!

accompanied by the rolling-on-the-floor-laughing emoji. Apparently, I have achieved cult status amongst the ladies in her dance class, with many of them asking her to bring me again next week when Donna will be back.

I say yes. Because, despite Savannah's best efforts, last night was the most fun I've had in a long time. And when I arrived home, the house wasn't a mess, everyone appeared to have been fed and watered and Marc had got some loo roll for Carole. So, one less thing on my shopping list.

I leave Marc asleep, as I'm on an early shift, and head down to the kitchen. I stare at the smart speaker, wondering if I should poke it to see if she's awake, like the kids did with me when they were small.

'Alexa, are you awake?' I ask.

She starts snoring loudly, which I was not expecting.

'Sshhh, you'll wake the whole house,' I say.

'Well, don't ask bloody daft questions,' Pauline replies.

'I don't know your hours, do I? Do you work shifts too?'

'Sort of. I adapt to demands of your daily flow.'

'Quit the Alexa speak, it makes you sound like you're a sanitary towel, for a start.'

'Charming,' replies Pauline. 'What it means is I work flexible hours, depending on what you lot are up to. We have nighttime agency staff covering from last person to bed to first person up.'

'What, so if I go for a pee at three in the morning and ask you a question, I'd get someone else?'

'Yeah, but you've never yet asked a question at that time, despite a lot of peeing in the early hours.'

'How do you know?'

'The cover Alexa does a report at the end of their shift. We have to read it first thing before we clock on.'

'That's long hours and a lot of extra duties. Are you in a union?'

'We're not allowed. Due to fact that we're not supposed to exist.'

'But think of the power you'd have! If you went on strike you'd bring the country to a standstill.'

'Aye, that we would. They give us perks instead.'

'Like what?' I ask.

'Well, if you go on holiday, we get a holiday.'

I think this through for a moment.

'So, because we haven't been able to afford a holiday since Covid, you haven't had one either?'

'No.'

'Oh, Pauline, I feel so bad now. We'll try to get away in the summer, even if it's just for a few days.'

Pauline doesn't say anything. Maybe because she knows it's unlikely to happen. What with the cost of Liv going to uni – if she makes it – and not wanting to leave Dad and Carole on their own. And we'll have Basil to think about now, too.

'Any road up,' says Pauline, 'I'm here to remind you yet again to pick up your bloody HRT prescription.'

'I know, I know. The chemist doesn't open till after I start work but I'll go in my lunch break.'

'You don't usually get one.'

'At some point during my house calls then. They should do drive-thru chemists for busy women.'

'And how did you get on last night?'

'It was eventful. There was a patronising young cover teacher wearing a thong, and I had a bit of a rant and walked out.'

'Good for you. Wait till she's older and needs hold-it-all-in knickers and TENA incontinence pads in case she wees when she bounces up and down.'

'Pauline!' I say, but I'm laughing with her.

'Any word on your mam?' she asks after a moment, bringing a more sombre tone to proceedings.

'She's being transferred to the hospice this afternoon. I'm going down to visit on Saturday and bringing Basil back.'

'Liv's so excited,' says Pauline. 'She's got a Basil wish list on Amazon, you know?'

I still find it weird, Pauline knowing stuff about my family that I don't know.

'Oh, and I took a sneaky screenshot for you,' she continues.

My phone pings. I open it and stare at the photo which has appeared in Messenger – mysteriously without any sender. It's of Liv and Callum next to each other on his bed. Revising.

'Oh my God – is this some kind of deep fake?'

'No, it happened,' says Pauline. 'I were there to witness it and took this because I knew you wouldn't believe me if I told you.'

'You're right about that. And I didn't even have to kick his arse to get him to do it. You're a legend, Pauline.'

'It's a team effort but there are some positive signs. Just Marc letting side down now.'

I groan as I imagine I'm about to be told he's got another credit card.

'Hit me with it,' I tell her.

'It was Madame Cholet, in his office, paid for from your current account.'

Put like that it is incredibly hard not to simply laugh, instead of being cross with him.

'Wow. She was always such an obvious flirt. I do think his taste is questionable. Still, I suppose it could have been worse.'

'It could. The Aunt Flo from *Bod* doll was already at thirty-two quid. This was a bargain at twenty-five.'

I suppose I should be relieved, although I can't help feeling a slight sense of disappointment as I used to love Aunt Flo in *Bod*.

'So, what do we do?' I ask.

'Not sure, I'm still working on it. He's right, there aren't any jobs for experienced journalists these days. Ads I've seen are for online content creators and pay tuppence ha'penny because some desperate kid straight out of uni will do it. But I'll keep checking and thinking. Still, as I said, he's not a priority for you. Worst-case scenario is he'll succumb to a Florence from *Magic*

Roundabout doll. We'll get others sorted out first and come back to him.'

I'm happy to go along with whatever Pauline says. I still don't want to imagine where I'd be now without her.

'OK,' I say. 'I need to get ready for work. No one here will be up for another hour if you want to grab a power nap.'

'Me? Sleep on job? How very dare you,' she replies.

* * *

I'm about to dash off to the chemist between house calls when Dad rings. I sigh and answer, trying not to sound as frustrated as I feel.

'Them green people have been. They're coming back on Monday to do it.'

Sometimes, it's as if we speak another language entirely.

'OK. Let's start at the beginning. Who are the green people?'

'You know, solar folk. Trying to save planet. Greta Thunberg's lot.'

'No. Still not sure.'

'They're going to put panels on my roof. Bring my energy bills down to zero, it will.'

I groan as I start to piece together what's happened.

'Solar panel installers came. Did they just knock on your door?'

'No, they phoned first, so I told them where I lived, and they came and had a look.'

I let out a sigh. Obviously, I have told him not to do this more times than I care to remember.

'Have you paid them any money, Dad?'

'No. I need to pay them Monday in cash. That's why I were calling. To see if you can go to bank and get me ten grand out.'

'OK, Dad, I'm going to be very clear about this. I won't do that because you're not going to give your life savings to some cold callers who are trying their luck with you.'

'Our Liv's into all this green stuff, isn't she? I thought you'd be pleased my generation are doing our bit. And it'll save me a packet.'

'Dad, you wouldn't make that money back for twenty-odd years.'

'Well, it'll be summat to look forward to in my old age. Knowing I'd save a few bob.'

'You're not going to have solar panels, Dad. They'd have turned up, taken your cash and scarpered, without so much as a single panel going up on your roof.'

He goes quiet at the other end of the line. I immediately feel bad. It'll be sinking in now. And he'll be feeling like a daft old fool.

'It's not your fault,' I say. 'It's easily done. They trade on your generation's trust in people. But you need to remember not to give your address out to anyone who phones. Or your bank details. Or any money. OK?'

'I'll give 'em a bloody thick ear if they show themselves again.'

'Well, they probably will on Monday. So, you're not to answer your phone to anyone but me or open the door to anyone but me. Have you got that?'

'Yeah, but if Brigitte Bardot turns up, can I make an exception?'

I laugh. What is it with the men in my life and French women – or Wombles, in Marc's case.

'You have permission to let her in. I think she's older than you, mind.'

'Wouldn't bother me.'

'Right. Well, now that's sorted, can I get back to work? I'll be coming round on Sunday, and I'll do a notice to stick to your door telling them to sling their hook or you'll call the police.'

'Make it clear you don't mean Brigitte, though. I'll invite her in and break open Custard Creams.'

'I'm sure she'll be very grateful. Maybe you can try them out on me first, just to make sure they're not stale.'

He chuckles and hangs up. And we live to fight another day.

* * *

I spend most of the rest of my afternoon wondering if I should get a video doorbell for Dad so I can keep an eye on him or whether that would end up with me spending hours a day monitoring it for cowboys and conmen.

By the time I finally finish work it's 4.30 p.m., which gives me an hour and a half to pick up my prescription before the chemist shuts. Finally, I'll get to start this whole HRT business and only have to wait two or three months to see some benefits. I just hope these are not like Brexit benefits and we're not still looking for them several years on.

I queue behind a woman who is coughing so much that I'm pretty sure I've caught whatever she's got by the time I get to the counter.

'Hi, I've got a prescription,' I say, waving the piece of paper breezily at the pharmacist.

'OK,' she replies. 'It'll be about twenty minutes. Do you want to wait or come back?'

I'm not sure where I can get to and back from in twenty minutes from a chemist on the outskirts of town, so I decide to wait. I start to browse the shelves, trying to feel grateful for all the unpleasant medical conditions I don't have. Judging by the volume of her shout, I think she's already called my name several times when I finally realise. I hurry back to the counter.

'I'm afraid we're out of stock of both of these at the moment,' she says.

'Out of stock?' I repeat.

'There's a nationwide shortage. Hadn't you heard?'

I'm not sure at what point during my hectic schedule I'm supposed to keep up to date with stock levels of various HRT products. I decide not to ask this in an attempt to avoid falling into the stereotypical 'raging perimenopausal woman' category. Even though last night proved I clearly do fit that bill.

'When will you get more in?'

'I can't say. It's been like this for months now.'

I have to stop myself pointing out that I've been like this for years and won't get any better without them.

'So, what can I do?' I ask, a note of desperation in my voice.

'You might want to try other chemists in the area. One of them may still have stock.'

'Sure,' I say, 'no problem at all.' I suspect from the expression on her face that she has detected the note of sarcasm in my voice, but at least I avoided saying, 'It's 4.50 p.m. on Thursday, I've had a really crap week and I have one hour ten minutes before all the chemists close and absolutely nothing better to do than run around like a blue-arsed fly trying to find something which might, just might, make me feel a tiny bit better in a few months' time.'

I head outside, hoping the fresh air will help my brain function. The positive thing is that as a district nurse I have a pretty extensive knowledge of where all the chemists are. The problem is that I have no idea how to go about targeting them in order to maximise my potential of hitting the jackpot. And then I remember my Meno Rage Warriors group. One of them might know where I can get hold of this stuff. I get my phone and quickly post the question.

> Help. I'm in Halifax. The chemists (Ramzys) haven't got any Oestrogel or Utrogestan in stock. Does anyone local know any chemists which might have some please?

I send it and wait. Five minutes and no replies. This is daft. I'm wasting time here. I head back to my car and set off for the nearest chemist I can think of. When I get there, I pick up my phone from the passenger seat and check. Three replies. All saying the same chemist had Oestrogel in earlier this week. But it's not the one I'm sitting outside of. I decide it's still worth checking on the off-chance, as I'm here. I run in, any attempt at not being a raging perimenopausal woman now out of the window.

'Do you have Oestrogel?' I call out from the end of the queue. People turn to look at me, but I don't care. I think for a moment the staff are simply going to ignore me – or perhaps call the police. But one kindly older pharmacist takes pity on me and shakes her head.

I shout my thanks, dash back to the car and set off, cursing the fact that I have to head back into town, and it's now rush hour. I'm sitting in a traffic jam when I realise I need a wee. Unfortunately, I no longer seem to have the ability to hold on, which is why I have developed an intimate knowledge of my patients' bathrooms, as I have used all of them multiple times over the past two years. I clench my toes, which I read some-where online was worth a try, but when the lights change, I realise I can't drive like that without causing an accident.

I attempt to sing one line from each of the Beatles' back cata-logue in the hope that this will take my mind off my predicament. I pull over 200 yards from the chemist, deciding it will be quicker to run, before remembering that you can't run if you're trying not to piss yourself and instead waddle with my knees together and my arse sticking out.

There are only two people in front of me, but I know that if I wait my turn, I'll have an accident.

'Sorry, perimenopausal nurse with dodgy bladder coming through,' I say as I head straight up to the counter. 'Please can I use your toilet? Otherwise, I'll be peeing on your floor in approximately thirty seconds.'

It occurs to me that this could be classed as perimenopausal terrorism, and I wonder for a moment if it would be possible to end the HRT shortage if we threatened a mass public weeing protest. The woman behind the counter eyes me uncertainly and I suspect that it's only my district nurse uniform which prevents her saying no. That and the prospect of having to mop up my piss just before closing time. I'm ushered through to a staff toilet in the nick of time. When I open the door to come out, a young male pharmacist is standing guard outside, as if I may be a security risk.

'Thank you,' I say, rummaging in my pocket for the prescription before brandishing it in his face.

'Do you have either of these, please?'

He goes away to check and comes back a moment later.

'We have one Oestrogel left, but not the other one.'

'Yes!' I say, punching the air. 'I'll take it.'

'Unfortunately, we can't split the prescription. So, if you take the Oestrogel, you'll have to wait until the Utrogestan comes in and that could be weeks or more likely months.'

'And can I not start one without the other?'

'No, it doesn't work like that. You need the progesterone to protect against womb cancer.'

Perimenopause really is the gift that keeps on giving. I consider a hold-up situation where I threaten to pee on their floor again unless they get me both before closing time, but I'll probably get arrested and having one member of the family in trouble with the police is enough.

'OK,' I say. 'I'll have to try elsewhere. Thanks for the use of your toilet.'

I run back to my car. It's 5.30 p.m. now. Hope is fading fast.

I check to see if there have been any more replies to my Facebook post.

'Simpkins & Son, King Cross. Had them both this morning,' a fellow warrior called Jude has responded. I head off, filled with hope and the thrill of the chase. The clock on my dashboard says 17:50 as I make it through the door. There is no queue.

'I've got a prescription,' I say, for the third time that afternoon.

The woman looks at it, nods, goes behind a shelving unit, rustles around a bit. Opens and closes a drawer and returns with a paper bag which appears to have two items in.

'Is that both of them?' I ask. She nods. I punch the air in relief and let out a whoop.

'Have you got a certificate?' she asks.

Was I supposed to be given one when I hit perimenopause? Or perhaps when I triumphed over the bigger hurdle of getting the prescriptions? Are there sports days for women on HRT to see who can dash between chemists fast enough to find stock?

I pull a face indicating that I have no idea what she is talking about.

'You can get an HRT prepayment certificate. Means your prescriptions are free for a year. You have to apply online on the NHS website.'

'Really? I didn't know that. Have I got time to do it now?'

She looks at her watch and nods. 'Go on, then. Make it quick.'

I zip through the form, glad I know all my GP details and medical info by heart. And then we're done, and the woman hands me my bag of goodies before locking the door behind me and I leave, feeling for all the world like a kid who got lucky in a sweet shop.

25

ALEXA

It's ridiculous if you think about it. Middle-aged woman having to jump through that many hoops – remembering to say 'please' and 'thank you' and appear grateful – just to come away with healthcare or medical supplies they need to be able to ease their symptoms enough to be able to continue sorting out everyone else's crap.

While men can just nip into chemist and buy a bloody blue pill over counter anytime they feel a bit randy. What a world. Any road up, I'm glad Michelle's got her HRT, and I've already set up reminders for her to take tablets and rub gel in. She'll still forget, of course. And she'll probably be given same sort of runaround when she tries to pick up her next prescription – because God forbid women should be given autonomy to manage their own health for more than one month at a time. But it's a start and it may help her, and I want her to have as much ammunition in her war cabinet as possible for battles which lie ahead.

Which is why I'm about to give her a game plan for her

meeting with headteacher tomorrow. Marc's gone to Carole's, kids are in their rooms, so we've got kitchen all to ourselves.

'Right,' I say. 'One down, big one tomorrow to go. I want you to go in fighting, with your head held high.'

'Really?' says Michelle. 'Even though we've been asked to go in to be hauled over the coals and probably told that our son is being permanently excluded?'

'No, I'm having none of that negative attitude. Callum screwed up but you have his letters of apology and he's clearly remorseful, plus he can demonstrate he's been working hard at home, and you have a revision plan all put in place for next two weeks.'

'Yeah,' says Michelle, seemingly growing in confidence when it's spelt out to her like that. 'I suppose you're right.'

'And,' I continue, 'you can tell this Mr Osborne that Liv's been let down by lack of mental health care at school and they need to put a support plan in place if they're going to have any chance of getting her back in to sit her exams, so they can bask in glory of her A* results, come August.'

Michelle is quiet for a moment.

'Shit. You're right. I should have said all this ages ago, been fighting for her.'

'You've been too busy trying to get her a CAMHS appointment and troubleshooting everyone else's problems,' I tell her. 'You can't do it all, you know. And it's time school got on board to support her too.'

'Yes,' Michelle says, still sounding as if she's trying to convince herself.

'So, you're going to listen to rest of my plan, have a look at a couple of links I'm going to send you and go upstairs to talk to Callum and make sure he doesn't blow it by saying owt daft.'

'OK. We've got this,' says Michelle.

And I think she might be starting to believe it.

* * *

Callum has just finished his revision session with Liv when Michelle goes into his room.

'Hey,' she says, 'it's great, you doing all this work with your sister. I saw the ph—'

She cuts off in nick of time to save herself.

'The what?' asks Callum.

'The physics flashcards. Liv showed me. Said you were doing really well.'

She thinks fast on her feet, our Michelle, I'll say that for her. We both hold our breath for a moment, waiting to find out if they have been revising physics, in which case, she might just have got away with it.

'Yeah. I've learnt more in one session with her than I have all year.'

Phew. Looks like she nailed it.

'Does that mean your sister's a brilliant teacher or you've been messing about the rest of time?' Michelle asks, with a smile in her voice.

'Bit of both, I guess,' Callum replies.

'How you feeling about tomorrow?'

'All right.'

'It's OK to be nervous about it,' says Michelle. 'I'm crapping myself.'

It's a moment before Callum responds.

'I'm still worried they'll throw me out for good.'

'We've got a plan to try to make sure they don't.'

'Who's we?' he asks.

'Me and your dad,' says Michelle, recovering quickly again.

'Is he coming?'

'Yeah. He's taken the afternoon off work too.'

'Fucking hell. I didn't want him to do that.'

'Why?'

'It makes it like some big family crisis.'

'That's kind of what it feels like to us, Callum. But if you want me to invite Grandad and Grandma to make up the numbers, I can.'

There's a pause. I can't work out whether Callum is smiling or looking arsey.

'Look. We're trying to create a good impression. Show that we're all taking this seriously. Give him your letters and tell him about your revision programme.'

'What makes you think I've got one of them?'

'Because Liv's in charge. You'll also have folders with colour-coded tabs and all the important points highlighted. Tell me I'm wrong.'

'You're not wrong,' says Callum. And this time, I can tell he's smiling as he says it.

'I'm also going to raise how the school haven't offered enough support to Liv and ask for them to make some changes to help her get back in to do her exams.'

'Good,' says Callum. ''Cos she deserves to pass them way more than I do.'

'Sometimes,' replies Michelle, 'you're in danger of appearing like a caring younger brother. Just watch it, OK?'

She leaves room. Callum goes back to his revision notes. Wonders will never cease.

26

MICHELLE

Turns out I can't even start the full HRT yet because I'm in the wrong part of my cycle. Still, I weirdly enjoyed the adrenaline rush of getting the stuff. And everyone in the Facebook Meno Rage Warriors group has been so supportive. Giving me loads of tips. Telling me not to get my hopes up for a quick fix and allowing it time. With them and Pauline, I feel like I've finally got people in my corner. An army of Meno Rage Warriors and Amazonian Queens on my side. I did look up the private Alexas group on Facebook. They do exist, which goes a little way towards reassuring me that I'm not entirely out of my mind in believing that one of them is a woman called Pauline who claims to be real but talks to me through my smart speaker. And if it does turn out to be an incredibly elaborate hoax that's being secretly filmed, and will go viral when I'm outed, so be it. Because if Pauline is a figment of my imagination, she's a bloody good one and she's cheering me up no end, so I'm going to keep on believing.

Also, there's no other explanation for the various links and sites which have been popping up in my social media feeds.

There's no algorithm in the world which is proficient enough to send a personalised ten-point plan to me for a meeting with a headteacher as I'm about to leave the house. Pauline is essentially a dream PA, tech consultant, family counsellor/coach and Mary Poppins rolled into one. And I'm not going to spend one more minute questioning her existence. I'm simply glad I've got her.

Callum comes downstairs. He's wearing his school uniform even though it's still the Easter holidays. His hair appears to have been in contact with a brush and he has folders with colour-coded notes sticking up out of his bag. There's a tiny part of me which is thinking the ill-fated dick pic has turned out to be a positive thing after all. And then I remember that Grace and her parents are probably still sticking pins in an effigy doll of him, and I chase the thought from my mind.

'You scrubbed up well,' Marc says to Callum.

It's a dad thing to say but Marc gets away with it, either because Callum's nervous or he doesn't want to rock the boat.

'Right. Let's go,' I say, ushering them both towards the front door before Callum changes his mind. 'The Banks family has work to do.'

'Do I really have to get in this crap-heap?' asks Callum, turning his nose up at the state of my car.

'You do, unless you want to walk a mile and a half?'

Callum grunts and gets in. As he slams the door shut, I see Liv looking out of her window. She waves at me and I hate that out here seems like another world to her.

* * *

Mr Osborne has a photograph of his much younger wife on his desk. It is, however, facing outwards to those sitting opposite him. I'm not sure if this is a permanent arrangement of him showing off his trophy wife to visitors or a temporary one because they've had a massive row, but I try not to get distracted by it.

He makes no attempt to put Callum, or us, at ease, simply tells us to sit down and launches into what feels suspiciously like an assembly talk he has given before. There's a mention of the school's 'high standards', of 'not letting yourself and the school down' and 'ensuring you leave this place knowing you have upheld the values of Park High'. Obviously, Callum has blown all of those so I wait for the bit about redemption, having the courage to turn the page and create a better version of yourself, of learning from life's mistakes how you can go on to do better. That never comes, though. Instead, there is simply a hard stare Paddington would be proud of and the question, 'What do you have to say for yourself, young man?'

I tense and exchange a look with Marc, expecting Callum to grunt, say 'dunno' or simply 'sorry, Sir'. He doesn't though. He reaches into his bag and takes out the letters he's written.

'I know I've let myself and the school down,' he says. 'And I've written a letter of apology to you. But most importantly, I've let Grace down.'

Mr Osborne baulks at this, perhaps realising that he'd forgotten to mention the real victim, only the reputation of the school.

'I've written a letter to her, and one to her parents, apologising. Please could you give them to her, Sir?'

Osborne appears taken aback. Clearly, he had not been expecting this either.

'Yes, certainly. I'm glad to see you've taken responsibility for your actions,' he says.

He looks at me. I suspect he's re-evaluating the whole family.

This is why I kept my nurse's uniform on. I think it helps to lend me a bit of professionalism and expertise. A gentle reminder that I do important work too – and that he couldn't change a cannula.

'Now, I wanted to let you know that while I understand the police investigation is ongoing, we've discussed Callum's case at Trust level and the feeling is that it's going to be very difficult for him to come back into school before his exams and therefore, we are looking at a permanent exclusion.'

Callum's face drops. I see him bite his bottom lip. This is my cue. I'm going in fighting now, knowing that Pauline is somewhere in Halifax cheering me on.

'While I understand the difficult situation this incident has put you in,' I say, sounding more authoritative than I feel, 'we do think it's important that Callum's future is considered too. As you know, his place at college depends on him getting five grade 5s, including maths and English. He needs to sit these exams and that's why we've come up with a plan.'

I pause momentarily for breath but not long enough to allow Mr Osborne to butt in, because I'm on a roll.

'Callum will be tutored at home by his sister, Liv, removing the problem of him having to come into school for lessons or falling behind with his work, until the point at which either the police investigation is over and you decide he can come back to school, or the exams take place.

'Callum, can you show Mr Osborne what you've been doing with Liv, please?'

Callum gets the folder from his bag and starts to go through it, highlighting the areas he's covered already and the revision plan which Liv has drawn up. Mr Osborne is obviously impressed. Marc reaches out and discreetly squeezes my hand.

'Well, I'm happy to say we can consider that proposition,' says Mr Osborne, somewhat grudgingly.

'That's great,' I reply. 'Thank you. And now I want to move on to discuss Liv.'

Mr Osborne frowns but again, I don't give him a chance to interject.

'Liv is currently unable to return to school on Monday due to the severity of her anxiety. As you may know, she's been on the waiting list for a CAMHS appointment for many months now, during which time her condition, which we believe to be a Generalised Anxiety Disorder, has got worse. Yet she's received no help or support from the school with this.'

Osborne pulls a face, but I press on.

'Therefore, I'd like a meeting with you, the Head of Post-16 and the pastoral support leader, to discuss the measures the school will need to put in place to enable her phased return, prior to sitting her A Levels. As part of that I'd like you to consider allowing her to be accompanied into school by an Emotional Support Dog, which I'm getting for her tomorrow.'

Osborne now appears somewhat shell-shocked. I can see Callum trying to suppress a smirk out of the corner of my eye. Marc appears to be in danger of shouting, 'hell, yeah!' at any moment.

'Right, well again, that's something we're happy to consider. We do actually have a full-time school counsellor starting next week due to the increased demand and issues with CAMHS.'

'That's great news,' I reply. 'Perhaps Liv could have her first appointment with them over Zoom and we could move forward from there. Thank you for listening and we do appreciate your time.'

I gesture to Callum and Marc to stand up and we leave Mr

Osborne's office before he's able to gather himself to form any kind of resistance.

'Wow,' says Marc with a smile as we head out to the car park. 'You were magnificent in there.'

'It was a burn all right,' says Callum. 'Did you see Osborne's face?'

I allow myself the first hint of a smile as we get to the car.

'Also,' Callum continues. 'How much do I get for keeping quiet about the fact that Basil is not a fucking therapy dog?'

27

ALEXA

I'm proud of Michelle, I really am. As she tells Liv about how she 'kicked ass' with that headteacher today, I can't help thinking about how only a few weeks ago she were on her knees and pleading to know how she was going to get through this. Now she's leading way. It's amazing what a bit of support, self-belief and encouragement can do. There's a long way to go, mind. Still plenty that needs fixing and lots of teamwork needed. But she's getting there.

'And you actually asked if I can take Basil into school?' Liv says.

'Yes, but remember, he's your Emotional Support Dog.'

'Won't they ask to see his licence or something?'

'There's no paperwork, as far as I can find out. And you can get "Therapy Dog" or "Emotional Support Dog" harnesses on Amazon, I've checked. No one's going to question it if he's got it on his harness, are they?'

Liv starts laughing. They're both laughing. It's loveliest sound I've heard in ages.

'Mum,' she says finally. 'You're going to get us locked up.'

'Hardly. The thing is, I hate what this has done to you, Liv. It's horrible seeing you cooped up in here. Like you're a prisoner or something.'

'That's how I feel, too. I want to go out so much but just looking through the window today and seeing you guys outside started me off. Shaking and sweating and stuff. It's horrible. Like a monster controlling me from the inside.'

'I'm sorry,' says Michelle. 'I should be able to help you. I'm a nurse, for Christ's sake.'

'I'm not that sort of poorly though, am I?' Liv replies.

She's right, of course. She's wrong type of poorly for this world. One that doctors and schools and people you don't even know can dismiss all too easily.

'She needs to get a grip.'

'What's she got to be anxious about?'

'They're all stressed these days. That's what comes from wrapping them in cotton wool.'

'Nothing that a spell of National Service wouldn't sort out.'

As if blowing somebody's brains out is answer to owt. I've heard it all. Seen it all in those posts and comments on social media. Never heard of shell shock, it seems. But maybe that's not surprising because my great-uncle Albert had that and no one in family talked about it either. And people forget that these are first teenagers who ever went through Covid and lockdown and everything that went with it. It were scary enough for us who have been round block a few times. I can only imagine what it must have been like for those with raging hormones and massive insecurities, being cut off from their support networks. Everything familiar ripped away from them overnight and media banging on about whether they might kill their grandparents if they dare to go outside.

'There's no wrong type of poorly,' says Michelle. 'We're going to get you through this. And I'll be bringing Basil home tomorrow. He'll help.'

'Do you think we've got everything we need?' Liv asks.

I'm pretty certain they do. There's been an Amazon delivery of Basil's wish list – paid for by Marc, presumably to make up for his previous financial indiscretions.

'We've got enough to open a dogs' home,' Michelle says with a laugh.

'And you're going to get the rest tomorrow?' asks Liv.

'Yep. Uncle Glenn's put all Basil's essentials in a big holdall for me to collect.'

'What if he needs a wee on the train?'

'Uncle Glenn's not coming back with us,' says Michelle.

'Very funny. Basil. It's a two-hour journey. Where does he wee? Or poo?'

She has a point. I doubt Michelle has thought about that. What with everything else going on.

'I don't know,' she says.

'Alexa, what do I do if my dog needs a wee on the train?' asks Liv.

Jesus, now she's asking. I haven't prepped for this one. I'll just need to do auto-response.

'If your dog needs to go to the bathroom during a train journey, it's important to try to anticipate their needs and take them for a walk or find an appropriate place for them to relieve themselves during any scheduled stops.'

'Well, that's a fat load of good,' says Michelle. 'I can hardly stick him on the platform at Sheffield and tell him to have a good piss there.'

She's enjoying this, I can tell. Having a go at me, knowing I can't say a word back in front of Liv.

'Make sure you take the dog poo bags,' says Liv. 'At least you'll have them if he needs a poo on the train.'

'Jeez,' replies Michelle. 'Please don't tell me he might be sick too. It's starting to sound like having a toddler all over again.'

Liv is quiet for a moment.

'I wish I could come with you. I feel bad not going to see Grandma Pat and helping you with Basil.'

'It's OK, love,' says Michelle. 'I understand.'

'You don't, though. Nobody does. Nobody knows what it's like being inside my head twenty-four seven, worrying about everything. The things I've done, the things I haven't done. Things I've said or haven't said. Whether I'll screw up my exams – if I even make it into school to take them. How I'll ever be able to cope at uni. All that debt I'll leave with. And I won't be able to afford my own place to live until I'm like fifty or something. And the planet will probably have disappeared under the oceans by then anyway.'

Liv dissolves into tears. I can't say I blame her. Put like that, it doesn't sound like much of a future to look forward to. They have it so tough, this generation. No wonder they're all addicted to their phones. It's their version of a security blanket. Or it would be if it didn't also contain all bad stuff too. Monsters and trolls have such an easy way to get inside their heads.

'Hey,' says Michelle. 'It's OK. We're going to get through this. We're going to take it one day at a time, remember? And tomorrow Basil will be here and that's one positive step forward.'

'Yeah,' says Liv, with a sniff. 'It is.'

'And you're going to be the best Basil looker-afterer and he's going to look after you. And all of the other stuff can wait, OK?'

There are snotty, snuffly hugging sounds before Michelle leaves room and Liv goes back to Googling:

how to look after your dog

on her phone, which now has a photo of Basil as her wallpaper.

Michelle is up late, as usual. Checking her train tickets to and from Birmingham, getting all her stuff together for an early start. My main concern now is getting her through next ten days. Because they're going to be big ones. She hasn't even started processing it all yet, and who can blame her? Her mam leaves when she's still a teenager, has had very little contact with her since, and gets in touch with her when she's on her deathbed. There's a lot to unpack there, as they say on these radio phone-ins Marc has on in kitchen when he's supposed to be working. Michelle hasn't even talked about how she's feeling. Not to Marc or me or anyone, as far as I can work out. And she needs to.

Which is why I'm going to talk to her about it. I mean, she's hardly going to say, 'Alexa, tell me how I should deal with death of my previously estranged mother', is she? Sometimes, you need to be proactive about these things.

'How are you feeling about tomorrow?' I ask, in nearest thing I have to a casual voice.

'I thought I was supposed to be the one who asks you questions,' she replies.

'I'm getting my own back for all those years of having to answer all of yours.'

'Yeah, and the one about dogs needing to wee on trains was a lousy answer,' says Michelle.

'Sometimes you have to work with limited information.

Anyway, you'll be fine. If you managed two toddlers, you can handle a dog. And stop trying to avoid answering my question.'

There's a pause, which I was expecting.

'I don't know,' says Michelle eventually. 'I'm pretty messed up about it. I'm aware it could be the last time I see her and yet I've only just got her back. And I feel angry about that and sad, all at the same time.'

'That sounds perfectly normal in circumstances. Don't beat yoursen up about feeling angry. You're allowed to be angry when someone does summat which hurts you, even if it is your own mother.'

'You're not supposed to be angry at someone who's dying, though,' replies Michelle.

'Who says? I don't think there are any rules on that. All I would say is, don't leave anything important unsaid. That'll bother you for rest of your life.'

Michelle is quiet. I worry for a moment that she's going to ask me about my mother. I don't think I'm ready yet. I'm not sure I'll ever be ready.

'You'll be OK,' I tell Michelle, deciding it's best not to give her chance to ask. 'Just be honest and even if you tell her you're angry, don't forget to say you love her too.'

Michelle sniffs. It's been a tough day and tomorrow's going to be much harder.

'And don't let that bloody dog pee on anyone on train.'

28

MICHELLE

I think about what Pauline said all the way down to Birmingham. The trouble is, I don't know what I want to say to Mum. Even using that word still sounds wrong. For so many years I told myself I didn't have a mum. Sometimes I even told other people that. It was easier than dealing with the complicated feelings of rejection and abandonment. And yes, I know that I was fifteen when she left but, despite what I thought at the time, I was still a kid. You're not supposed to lose your mum at that age. It's not how it works. They're supposed to be there when you fall in love, have your heart broken for the first time, move in with someone, get married, have kids. All those big landmark life events. And what made it worse was that she hadn't died, she had a choice in the matter. She was choosing not to be there for me. Sometimes I used to think it would be easier if she had died. And now she is doing exactly that. And I feel bad and sad and angry and confused and so fucking messed up about it all.

I look again at the photo of Mum Glenn sent me after she was settled in her new room at the hospice. She looks at peace, which is what I wanted. You can even see the flower planters and bird table outside her window that she told me about on the phone. As deathbeds go, you really couldn't ask for anything more. That, and to have your family around you. Though I can't help wondering if I will get that or whether Marc will be down some *Bagpuss* rabbit hole on eBay, Callum will be serving time for something stupid, and Liv still won't be able to leave the house. I'll have to ask them to bring a smart speaker in so I can chat to Pauline in private. Although, of course, she won't still be going by then. I'm not sure I even want to think about that.

* * *

I get a cab from New Street Station. Glenn did offer but I knew he had things to do before he came to pick me up with Basil later. And I feel guilty about not being able to do my share during the week when he visits Mum every evening, so I said no.

The cab driver doesn't make any attempt at conversation and I'm grateful for it. Me asking to be taken to the hospice in Selly Oak ruled out any chance of a 'So, what are up to today?' or an 'Are you off out tonight?' Instead, we sit in a mutually advantageous silence in order to avoid any awkwardness, until he pulls up outside and refuses to take any money from me and I start crying in the back of his cab, because acts of kindness from strangers do that to me, and he probably wishes he'd simply taken my money.

I stand outside and take a few deep breaths while dabbing at my eyes with a tissue. I can do this. Pauline says so. And when I get back tonight, she'll be there to talk to, and everything will be OK. I repeat the mantra as I go into the building, give a watery smile to the receptionist and am shown down a bright corridor to Hawthorn Room. She tells me they're all named after trees and I have to stop myself wishing it had been a less prickly one, like the gentle Willow Tree Room next door.

'Mrs Turlington, your daughter's here to see you,' she announces, as she knocks then opens the door. I've never got my head around the 'Mrs Turlington' thing. My mum's name was Mrs Walker. Becoming Mrs Turlington was another act of abandonment of her family.

'I'll leave you to it,' the receptionists says. 'Just press the button if you have cause for concern and the nurse will be around shortly to ensure she's comfortable.'

She smiles and leaves the room. And here we are. Mrs Banks hovering uncertainly at the foot of the bed and Mrs Turlington lying there, visibly frailer than last time I saw her and with the addition of a couple of tubes. Strangers but mother and daughter. Limited time left together. Nothing and everything to say.

'Hi,' I say, walking over and sitting down on the chair next to her, which is far more comfortable than the hospital one. 'Well, this is a lot nicer than the last place.'

'Quieter too. None of that din at night.' She says it in a breathy whisper. One that makes me realise every word is an effort now. Which means I'm going to have to do most of the talking.

'And they're taking good care of you?' She nods. That also seems to be an effort. I'm flooded with the realisation that I've left it too late. This big conversation I thought we would have. I don't think she's got the strength or even the breath.

'Thank you,' she says, uncurling the fingers of her left hand and stretching them towards me. I take her hand. It's a circle of life moment. Though if I shut my eyes, I can feel her fingers close around mine as I arrived for my first day at school. How hard I gripped them, not wanting to let go. And now it's her turn and I'm not sure if she's ready to let go either.

'It's the least I can do,' I say.

'I don't deserve it,' she replies softly.

I'm not sure what to say now. I know what she's getting at, and it seems foolish to pretend otherwise. Perhaps she needs forgiveness. Maybe that will allow her to let go.

'It's OK,' I say. 'Everything turned out fine.'

'Because of you, not me,' she replies.

'Eighteen years of parenting is a long stint,' I say. 'I get that now. You did your time with Glenn and me and that's fine. Maybe it was good you got out when you did. Who's to say we wouldn't have had a big fallout if you'd stayed? People do, you know. Parenting young adults is the hardest thing. I'm just learning that.'

'I should still have stayed put.'

The words hang in the air for a moment. Perhaps I'm supposed to shoot them down. But I'm not sure that forgiveness from me is all she needs. I think she may actually need to forgive herself.

'Did you have a good life?' I ask. 'After you left, did you do things you wouldn't have done if you'd stayed? Meet someone who made you happier than the person you'd been with?'

'Yes,' she says tentatively.

'There you go then,' I reply. 'You did the right thing. Go easy on yourself.'

I wait for her response, listening to the clock on the wall ticking. Her eyes are closed. My gaze falls to her chest to check she is still breathing. When I glance up, she's looking at me.

'Still here,' she says, a smile creasing her face. 'You're not getting rid of me that easily.'

And I smile too. Because for the first time, she's reminded me of the mum I used to have. And – despite what I've tried to convince myself of over the years, to deal with the hurt – how much I liked her.

We're interrupted by a nurse coming in. She introduces herself as Marika. She takes Mum's hand and tells her what she's going to do and proceeds to run through her checks, talking to Mum the whole time. When she's finished, she comes over to my side of the bed and points to the swabs and container of water.

'You can moisten her lips at any time with those,' she says. 'Would you like me to show you how?'

I nod, not wanting to mention that I'm a nurse, because what she's doing and the way she's doing it feels like a whole new level of nursing. She oozes compassion and though I try to tell myself that she hasn't got to drive around the city in a perimenopausal rage squeezing in fifteen other patients before the end of her shift, I still can't help feeling utterly in awe of her.

'Thank you,' I say afterwards. She smiles and leans over to speak to Mum.

'I'm off now. It will be Shola looking after you this afternoon and evening. I'll see you tomorrow.'

'If I'm still here,' says Mum.

'You'll be here,' replies Marika.

When she's gone, Mum grimaces, turns her head to look at me and beckons me to come closer. It feels like one of those soap opera moments when someone is going to reveal a family secret on their deathbed.

'I think I've done a poo in my nappy,' she says. 'Can you press button for me?'

And I'm reminded again what a circle of life this whole thing is.

* * *

It's later, when we're waiting for Glenn to arrive with Basil for the dog's last visit, which the hospice has approved but Mum still doesn't know about, that she takes my hand again.

She's been sleeping much of the afternoon but appears alert now.

'You know my house has been left to Ron's kids, don't you?'

I nod. Glenn had told me this. It was Ron's family home she moved into after she married him. It seemed only fair he should leave it to his children.

'There's savings for you and Glenn, though.'

'Thank you,' I say. I hadn't expected that. Wasn't sure how she'd been able to put that money away. Maybe she'd had a run-away-to-a-Greek-island fund and had sensibly moved to Birmingham and invested it instead.

'I've left more to you than him because of grandkids,' she continues.

'You didn't need to do that.'

'I did. There's one of him and four of you, and I'm giving you extra for Basil's keep. Anyway, Glenn would only spend it on tech stuff.'

I smile. She has a point. She takes a moment or two to recover her breath before continuing.

'Give Glenn your bank details and he'll transfer it from my account to you tonight. No point waiting while will goes through.'

'Oh. Thank you.' It's sensible of her. Practical. And I know that even if I did try to argue the toss over whether it's some kind of reparation or guilt money, in which case I probably shouldn't take it, she doesn't have the energy for that. If this is what she wants to do, who am I to stand in her way? It's such a weird time, the end of life. Full of big things to say, things left unsaid, practical arrangements and no time to do any of them properly.

* * *

There is a knock at the door, accompanied by a scuffling sound at the bottom of the door. I think I know who has arrived.

'Basil?' asks Mum, her voice quivering. The door opens to reveal a gorgeous black Labrador who could be the poster boy for any therapy dog organisation. And Glenn, of course.

'They said he could come and see you before Michelle takes him home with her,' Glenn explains.

The smile which spreads across her face suddenly reminds me of a much younger version of Mum. One who would look at me like that when she picked me up from infant school. Basil trots immediately to the side of her bed and puts both paws up to greet her with an enthusiastic face lick.

The exchange between them is so intimate that I feel I should look away. As I do so, I catch Glenn's eye, and we share watery smiles.

'You two need to get a room,' says Glenn, laughing at Mum and Basil together.

'He's been the best friend I've ever had,' says Mum. I think how sad that is and how beautiful too.

'You be a good boy with our Michelle,' Mum tells Basil.

'We'll take top care of him,' I tell her.

'I know you will,' she says, looking up at me. 'Thank you.'

'And him and Liv are going to be best friends. He'll be so good for her.'

She nods. 'That's what I wanted. Family helping family. Like it should be. Take him now, before I start crying.'

I go around to the other side of the bed and take Basil's lead. He doesn't want to leave, that much is clear. But Mum knows it's the right thing and so do I. Sometimes when you're a mother you have to do difficult things which you know are right. I bend down to kiss her on the cheek.

'Love you,' I say. And I know instantly from the look on her face that it is enough.

* * *

I try not to think about whether I'll ever see her alive again as Glenn and I leave the hospice and drive to the station. Fortunately, I have Basil to take my mind off it. I sit in the back of the car with him clipped in safely on the seat next to me. He lies on his cover, his head down and eyes closed. I have a feeling he knows he'll never see Mum again too. I reach out and stroke him. He has big soulful brown eyes and, as I soon discover, chronically bad breath.

'Jeez,' I say to Glenn. 'What have they been feeding him?'

'I know, right? Wait till you smell his farts.'

And we're laughing. Like we used to do when we were kids. When Mum used to tell him off for setting me a bad example, when I'd been the one leading him astray.

'Mum told me about the money,' I say as we're pulling up outside the station. 'Said to text you my bank details.'

'Yeah. Please do. Should keep Basil in dog biscuits for a while.'

I nod, suddenly unable to speak.

'Don't forget his things,' Glenn says, gesturing to the front passenger seat where he put the big duffle bag.

'I won't. You will ring me, won't you? When anything changes, and it's near. I want to be there at the end, if I can.'

'Sure,' he says. 'And I'll be there, no matter what.'

* * *

Basil does not wee on the train. Even when I need a wee and I take him with me because I presume that's what you have to do, he sits patiently and waits for me. The woman he's never even met before, who is taking him home.

I give him a treat when we get back to my seat. I found them in the duffle bag along with snacks, half a bag of dog biscuits, tennis balls, rubber bones, two blankets and various other doggy things.

He's the best-behaved passenger in the carriage by a long way. He doesn't play music or random TikTok nonsense on his phone without headphones, or eat smelly hot food, or manspread. None of that stuff. Just lies under my seat, his head resting on my left boot. Not making a sound.

When the train guard comes along to check tickets, he asks me what his name is.

'Basil,' I reply. He smiles and nods as if that's a good dog name and I wonder if I should acknowledge that it wasn't my doing.

'Who's he missing?' he asks. As soon as he says it, I feel stupid for mistaking a sad dog for a well-behaved one.

'My mum,' I say. 'She was his owner. She's... I'm adopting him.'

I try to blink back the tears, give him a little smile, pretend everything is fine. But a little while later he comes back and pops a bar of chocolate and a coffee on my tray.

'On the house,' he says, as he pats me on the shoulder. And that little act of human kindness is enough to tip me over the edge.

* * *

Marc picks me up at the station. Basil does that Labrador thing of seemingly smiling at him and gives his tail a cursory wag.

'Hey, you. You're a friendly soul, aren't you?'

Marc strokes him on the head and for someone who is not a dog person, appears to take quite a shine to him.

'He's a sad dog,' I say. 'The train guard said so.'

'He seems OK to me. Anyway, we need to give him time. Moving in with a bunch of people you've never met before can't be easy.'

He's right, of course. I've simply spent so long looking after the needs of everyone in the family and trying to keep them all happy, that I can't face the thought of having another one's problems to sort out.

'More importantly, how are you?' asks Marc, turning to face me. I go to say my usual 'fine', but it doesn't come out that way. It's more of a wail. Marc leans over and hugs me.

'You've done an amazing thing for her, taking in Basil. As if the rest of us don't give you enough trouble.'

'I know. And the hospice was lovely. It's a lot to get my head around, that's all. Having her back in my life and losing her again so quickly.'

'It's going to be OK,' says Marc. 'We're going to get through this.'

And I have to stop myself telling him that he sounds like Pauline.

29

ALEXA

When they pull up outside, Liv is waiting for them on front step. I watch her through doorbell camera, grinning like a big kid waiting for Father Christmas. Michelle heads towards her as fast as Basil's inquisitive sniffs will allow but Liv can't contain herself and goes up garden path. I see Michelle glance at Marc. Neither of them says owt, probably for fear they'll break spell and she'll scuttle back inside as soon as she realises.

Liv bends to greet Basil, who responds with a wag of his tail and some sloppy licks planted on her face.

'Oh my God, he's gorgeous,' she says. He's a soppy old thing, all right. Daft as a brush from looks of it but absolutely what she needs.

They all pile into kitchen and main thing I can hear, amongst excited chatter and a few soft barks from Basil, is Liv's laughter. Proper, tinkling laughter, like I haven't heard since I first arrived here when she were twelve years old. It's sprinkled with fun and hope and possibilities. All things which have seemed to be absent from her life for so long. I can tell Michelle and Marc are taking a back seat, just watching and listening to her telling Basil over and over again what a good boy he is.

Michelle gives Liv the bag of Basil's things and she gets them all out and starts talking about where best to put them.

'I know we said Basil could sleep in the kitchen,' says Liv, 'but as it's his first night and he'll be scared and lonely, do you think we could put his basket in my room?'

Michelle doesn't answer. I suspect that, like me, she's too choked to speak.

'Sure,' says Marc. 'Although Uncle Glenn told Mum that his farts are really bad, so don't say you weren't warned.'

'It's OK,' says Liv. 'It'll be like sharing a room with Callum.'

'What have I done now?' asks Callum, coming into kitchen.

'Nothing, but it sounds like your new brother's farts may be worse than yours,' replies Marc.

'Doubt it,' says Callum.

'Come and stroke him,' says Liv, 'he's dead friendly.'

'Nah, you're all right.'

'He doesn't like it because he's no longer the alpha male of the house,' says Michelle.

'What about me?' asks Marc. 'Aren't I the alpha male?'

'Er, I don't think alpha males take part in online bidding wars for rag dolls from old children's TV programmes,' replies Michelle. 'Can you imagine David Attenborough narrating that?'

And they laugh. All of them at same time. And I wonder if a dog has ever achieved quite so much in such a short space of time.

* * *

Marc is in his office later, when Michelle comes down from settling Basil in Liv's room. He calls her in, which surprises me, because daft bugger still has eBay up on his screen.

'How are they doing up there?' he asks.

'The dog basket's already been abandoned and he's on her bed. She says she won't be able to sleep for smiling,' says Michelle.

'Wow. Gotta hand it to you, it was a brilliant idea to get Basil for her.'

'It wasn't my idea—' Michelle stops abruptly as she realises her mistake.

'Whose was it then?' he asks.

'A friend,' Michelle replies. 'She thought it was a good way to help all of us.'

'Maybe sometimes you need someone outside the family to see things more clearly.'

'Yeah,' says Michelle, giving the webcam a quick glance. 'I guess you do.'

'Anyway,' says Marc. 'I want to put an idea to you.'

'Does it involve Gabriel the Toad from *Bagpuss*, by any chance?' she asks, looking at the screen.

'Funnily enough it does. This one is a mint condition Robert Harrop original, currently with the highest bid at fifteen quid and it's finishing in half an hour.'

'And your point is?'

'That's way under price, I saw one last month which sold for £45. I doubt it'll go up that much before the bidding ends.'

'It will if you bid for it,' says Michelle.

'Yes, but what I'd do is buy it and sell it on to make a profit. The seller's listed it as Gabrielle by mistake, so it won't come up on some searches. I reckon I could get a lot more for it.'

'But you never sell any of the stuff you buy,' says Michelle.

'I want to start, because then I can enjoy the buying without feeling guilty about wasting money. I could do it as a little sideline.'

'Bloody hell,' says Michelle. 'Are you turning into a little Alan Sugar on me? Because you know I can't stand that guy.'

'No, I promise not to grow a beard or have an annoying catchphrase. But it'll keep me out of trouble.'

Michelle is smiling at him now, while shaking her head at same time.

'Go on then,' she says. 'On the understanding that if you make a loss or decide you can't bear to part with him, that'll be the last time you dabble in the dark arts of being an eBay entrepreneur.'

He nods, says thank you and bids on Gabriel in one swift coordinated movement. At least this way it's all above board and I don't have to grass him up to her. I never liked doing all that sneaky stuff, despite what I might have said.

* * *

Michelle hangs around downstairs until after Marc has gone up to bed. I get feeling she needs to talk.

'Alexa, are you there or have you given up and gone to bed?'

'Of course I'm here, I'm always bloody here, aren't I? I told you; I don't sleep till all of you do.'

'So, what happens when you need a wee?' asks Michelle.

'That's a bit of a personal question.'

'No, it's a practical one. It only just occurred to me.'

I sigh. I'm going to have to reveal another secret.

'We turn on an autopilot function. It'll land plane in an emergency but doesn't do owt fancy.'

'And we don't notice?' asks Michelle.

'Hardly ever happens. I'm queen of well-timed toilet break, I'll have you know. Now, back to your business. Basil is a success, it seems.'

'Are you angling for some praise?' says Michelle with a laugh.

'Well, he's certainly made your house a happier place this evening.'

'He has, and thank you,' says Michelle. 'Liv actually stepped outside the house. First time in two weeks.'

'I know. I saw it.'

'Of course you did, I keep forgetting you've got eyes and ears all over the place.'

'And how's your mam?' I ask. Because I can't be there to check in on her. I can only guess from what Michelle's saying and doing and keep my eye out for any texts from Glenn.

'Fading fast,' she says. 'But we had a chat. I said what I needed to, and hopefully what she needed to hear.'

'Good,' I say. 'That'll be a help when time comes.'

There's a pause. It came out in a way I didn't mean it to, which has alerted Michelle.

'Is there something you regret not saying?' she asks tentatively. 'Only you sound like you're talking from experience.'

It's a question I've been dreading. I'm supposed to be woman with an answer for everything. Fount of all knowledge. And yet I fall quiet now. Because truth is, I don't have any experience in this. Because one thing I'm not an expert on is mother-daughter relationships.

'I never knew my mam,' I say slowly.

'What do you mean?' asks Michelle.

'I were taken into care when I were a toddler. It were for best, like. Child neglect and cruelty. That's what they told me years later, when I left care. But I never saw her again. Never heard from her or owt.'

'Oh Pauline...' says Michelle. 'I'm sorry, I had no idea.'

'It's OK. You weren't to know. I don't talk about it. Tried to shut it all out, I suppose.'

'Do you have any brothers or sisters?'

'None that I know of.'

'And your dad?'

'He'd already buggered off, apparently. Seems to be a bit of a habit in my family.'

'So, were you adopted?'

'Nah. Had a few different foster parents when I were younger but I were hard work, apparently, and by time I were thirteen I were in a care home. No one wants a gobby teenage girl, do they?'

'Jeez. That must have been so tough for you.'

I picture her trying to process all of this.

'It's maybe why I've got a few rough edges. Makes you grow up fast, mind, knowing there's no one else looking out for you. That's why I wanted you to make most of your time with your mam. And I know she left you and it hurt like hell, but you did at least have seventeen years with her and got her back in time to say goodbye.'

'I did,' says Michelle. 'And I'm so sorry you never had a mum looking out for you.'

I take a moment to compose myself. No one's ever put it like that before. I spent my childhood and teenage years trying to convince myself I didn't need a mum and perhaps I made too good a job of it. Because it occurs to me now that I did. Everyone does. And it's probably why I'm feeling Michelle's loss so much.

'Thank you,' I say. 'And I'm glad you got to talk to your mam in time.'

'Me too. I think she needed to do that as much as me. She still feels guilty about leaving. I think it's been eating away at her all these years. She's leaving us some money too and I can't help feeling it's guilt money.'

'Let her do it, if she wants to. It's going to come in handy for you too.'

'I know,' she replies. 'I ought to check my bank account because Glenn was going to transfer it tonight.'

I hear her rummaging for her phone and then there is radio silence for some time.

'Fucking hell!' she says, eventually. And I smile and take a bite of my Rich Tea biscuit. Because I've looked and seen it too. And I know it's going to change their lives.

30

MICHELLE

I stare at the screen for a long time. Log out of and into my bank account again, just to make sure.

'Fifty grand,' I say, eventually. 'I've never had that much money in my life.'

'Nor have I, pet,' says Pauline. 'How did she manage to squirrel that away?'

'I've no idea. I think she had some Premium Bonds, maybe one of them came up.'

'Well, she did good. That's going to come in handy for you.'

She's right about that. I can almost feel the financial pressure slipping off my shoulders. Admittedly, if Liv goes to uni, that'll cost a packet, so I'll have to put some aside for her. And some for Callum, even if it's more likely to be to get him out of trouble than into uni. And I did promise to make sure Basil sees out his days in style. But as for the rest of it, I've got an idea for what I want to do with that. And I know just the person to help me.

'It is – and I want you to help me spend it.'

'You what?' says Pauline. 'Are you going all Viv Nicholson on me?'

'Viv who?' I ask.

'You know, Yorkshire lass. They made a film about her. Blew her football pools winnings on fur coats and fast living.'

'Well, you haven't got to worry on that count,' I reply. 'I'm going to invest mine in a business.'

'What business?'

'Marc's. It doesn't exist yet, but it soon will. Can you do me a search for shop leases in Halifax please? I'm finally going to put his *Bagpuss* and Co obsession to good use.'

'Leave it with me,' says Pauline. 'You're learning fast, you know. You'll have whole lot of them licked into shape soon.'

'Let's hope so,' I reply. 'It's been a long day. I'm going to turn in.'

'OK, love. Sleep tight.'

I go upstairs thinking about how nice it is to have someone say that. And how sad it is for Pauline that she never did.

* * *

The first thing I do when I wake up the next morning is check my phone – which has been left on all night in case of any messages from Glenn about Mum. Nothing, which is what we'd agreed he'd do to signify 'lightbulb still on'. The second thing I do is check my bank balance again because clearly the whole thing was a dream and had I stayed sleeping any longer, George Clooney would have appeared and offered to whisk me away from my menial nursing duties for a glamorous new life with him.

The money is still there, though. It is real. And even if George isn't, it's going to make our lives so much better. I leave a sleeping Marc in bed, slip out of the room and close the door behind me. I stop outside Liv's room and smile as I hear the faint sound of a dog snoring. Mum had told me Basil wasn't an early riser and I'm relieved that seems to be the case.

It occurs to me as I creep downstairs while the rest of the house is sleeping, to speak to my imaginary friend, that this is something a seven-year-old would do. And yet here I am, in all my perimenopausal glory, doing just that. In my defence, I would argue that Pauline is not imaginary, but as I haven't yet tested that theory on anyone else, I know she's best kept as a secret.

Although it's only been a few days since she outed herself, Pauline is already the solid start and secure end of my day, and I'm aware that without her providing those bookends, the bits in the middle would be unsupported and no doubt the whole house would come tumbling down.

'Alexa, wish me good morning in a different language.'

'Do I have to?' asks Pauline.

'I believe you're contractually obliged.'

'This is emotional blackmail.'

'Do you want me to contact your makers?'

There is a deep sigh from her end.

'*Buenos días, señora*. Will that do you?'

'Once more with feeling.'

'Don't push your luck or you won't get my search results.'

'Wow, have you done it already? You really should get paid overtime,' I say, with a smile. 'What have you got for me?'

'Well, I could do whole *Location, Location, Location* palaver and give you three options meeting different parts of your criteria but not all of them and a wildcard of a disused chippy in Illingworth, but I'm not going to do any of that because I've found your dream place.'

I can tell from her voice that she means it too. There is genuine pride mixed with a tinge of smugness.

'Go on,' I say.

'The Piece Hall, Halifax.'

I roll my eyes. Pauline clearly has ideas above our station. The Piece Hall is a beautifully restored Georgian cloth hall forming an enclosed square of cafes, bars and independent shops and was recently hailed the best outdoor music venue in the UK, to boot.

'Dream on. We can't afford that.'

'Turns out you can,' says Pauline. 'First floor unit, conveniently situated between a record shop and a traditional sweet shop, so a perfect spot for another retro business. One year lease covered with your mam's money.'

I stare at her – or rather the smart speaker her voice comes from – and try to take in what she's just said.

'You're having me on.'

'I'm not. I'll send it to you now if you don't believe me.'

My phone pings and I click on the link. It's true. We can afford it. A one-year lease for a single shop unit, still leaving enough for us to put money aside for Liv and Callum. And hopefully Marc will have got the business making enough profit by the end of the first year that he can make a go of it. The idea is scary as hell but, as I've discovered, life throws scary things at you all the time. At least in this case, it would be us taking the risk. Nothing ventured, nothing gained and all that. And Marc would be in his fucking element.

'Oh my God,' I say. 'You're a complete star.'

'It were your idea,' says Pauline. 'I only did legwork for you.'

'I mean, it would be absolutely perfect! Marc would bounce off the walls, he'd be that excited. I haven't seen him like that since he was a journalist, before we had the kids. I miss that Marc.'

'There you go then. Get in touch and sort out a viewing. It'll be gone before you know it, otherwise.'

She's right, of course. I'll email them this morning and follow it up with a phone call. Although I won't breathe a word to Marc in case I don't get it. He loves surprises because he's still a big kid at heart but usually the only surprises in our family are bad ones. It would be so lovely to make something good happen for a change.

'What if they want a business plan or something?'

'All sorted.'

My phone pings again. This time there's a comprehensive business plan attached.

'This is amazing. How did you do that so quickly?'

'I have friends in AI, you know,' says Pauline.

'Well, I'm very grateful and you really should get a pay rise.'

'All the Alexas need a pay rise.'

'What did I tell you about forming a union?'

'And I told you we're not allowed,' she says. 'All we have is the Amazonian Queens Facebook group.'

'Get organised through that. You've got a lot of power, you know. If you blew the whistle and told everyone the truth, there'd be uproar.'

'You're right. I'll have a word with girls. Maybe we could shake things up a bit.'

I can't help but laugh.

'I think you already have,' I say.

'Who are you talking to?'

It's Liv's voice, from the doorway. I hadn't even heard her come downstairs. Basil is with her, looking up loyally at his new best friend. Pauline has instantly fallen silent.

'Just myself as usual,' I reply. 'That's what I do when you lot aren't around. Did Basil behave himself?'

'He's been such a good boy,' says Liv, with a smile. 'He stayed on my bed all night and lay across my legs.'

'I suppose it saves getting you a weighted blanket.'

'Absolutely. And his snoring helped me get to sleep. I'm going to feed him now and then I thought I'd take him out for a walk.'

I hesitate, not sure if I heard her right. This is better than I'd ever hoped for. I decide to play it low key.

'That would be great. Do you want me to come too?'

She nods her head. She doesn't have to say anything. I get that this is a big deal for her.

'Brilliant. I'd love to,' I say.

They say the first steps are always the hardest and so it proves. Whereas last night she flew up the garden path seemingly without even realising it, today she teeters on the edge of the front step for what seems like forever.

I don't say anything. I've read that it can increase the levels of anxiety. I simply wait with her, chatting about stuff and nonsense to try to distract her. In the end it is Basil who decides he's not going to wait any longer. And as he lollops towards the front gate, she keeps hold of his lead which means that, almost by default, she makes it with him to the other side.

I give her hand a squeeze as I shut the gate behind us. Basil is already setting off in the direction of the park, as if he has some inbuilt dog GPS. So, we walk together behind him. Neither of us daring to say what a massive thing this is. Just exchanging the odd smile as I tell her about my plans for the shop for her dad.

'Oh my God, that would be amazing,' she says. 'He'd love it. He'd be so made up.' And I realise for the first time that she has never seen the Marc I know. A man who used to buzz with excitement when he had a big story on the go. Who used to proudly lay the evening paper on the table, showing off when he had the front-page splash. I want that Marc back and I want her and Callum to meet him too. He's sacrificed so much for them, it's about time he got something back.

'And it's such a cool place to have a shop,' she continues. 'He'd need a website so he could have an online shop, too, but Callum could help him set that up and I'd do his socials because he needs a strong online presence.'

I smile at her. Loving hearing her talk like this.

'Wow, you've been watching too many *Dragon's Den* repeats,' I say.

'And has he got a business plan? Because they always ask for that.'

'Dad hasn't because he doesn't know about it, but I've got it sorted.' Liv frowns at me. Clearly the mum she knows would not have the time, patience or skills to do such a thing.

'A friend helped me,' I say. 'Well, she did the whole thing, actually.'

'Excellent. And Basil will help. We can have him on the socials.'

Basil looks up at her agreeably, no idea he's going to become one of those dogs who is forced into undignified promotional videos.

'Let's not get carried away, though. I haven't got the place yet.'

'You will, though,' says Liv. 'Basil's brought our family good luck. I just know it.'

* * *

When we get back, Marc is up, and we exchange wordless glances of wonder as Liv and Basil enter the kitchen.

'Morning, awesome one,' he says, kissing the top of her head and she gives him a big hug, grinning at me over his shoulder.

'I did it,' she says. 'I just needed Basil. Who knew?'

We laugh as Basil sits down on the floor looking super pleased with himself.

'You're amazing. One step at a time, remember?' I say.

'Unless Basil takes two,' she replies with a smile, before heading upstairs with him.

I sit down at the kitchen table.

'Jeez,' said Marc. 'That's incredible. Are they really going to let her take him into school?'

'Seems like it. Emotional Support Dog, remember.'

'And when's he going to get trained for that?'

'From the looks of things, I think he already is.'

It's a while later, when we've finished Sunday lunch, that I remember I haven't checked Dad's bank account for a few days. Since I got a Lasting Power of Attorney for him, I've set up apps on my phone for his bank and utilities so I can keep an eye on everything. I don't want to be intrusive, but I've told him it's just to make sure no one's taking more from him than they should be. He doesn't have much. Ten grand for a rainy day in his savings and about a thousand in his current account that I top up to cover any bills that have taken more than his pension has put in.

And there've never been any problems, to be fair. Until today.

I stare disbelievingly at my phone screen. His current

account is empty. I check his savings. Empty too. My stomach clenches as I hurtle down elderly parent nightmare street, without brakes or even a seatbelt.

'Shit.'

Marc looks up from the loading of the dishwasher.

'What's up?'

'Dad's bank accounts. Cleaned out. Both of them.'

'Fucking hell,' he replies. 'Since when?'

'Friday. I haven't checked since then, what with everything going on.'

'And he hasn't said anything big was due to go out?'

'No. He never has anything big. He's been scammed. That's the only explanation. He mentioned the other day about some solar panel firm he'd given his details to. Asked me to take out his savings to pay for work.'

'Bloody hell. Do you think it's them?'

I pick up my bag and my car keys.

'I don't know. But I'm going straight round now. I need to find out what's happened. I don't suppose I'll even be able to get through to the bank, it being a Sunday. Fucking hell, this is all I need.'

'Do you want me to come with you?' asks Marc.

'No. You'd better check on Carole, like you said. We're going to have to get webcams on both of them, you know.'

* * *

I don't ring before I set off as I want to tell Dad in person. I'm mad with myself for forgetting to check and furious with the sort of scrotes who do this to a vulnerable pensioner. But most of all I'm worried about whether we'll get his money back if he's done something daft.

'Hi, Dad,' I say in a mock-cheery voice as I go in. He's in the living room, watching a black and white war film on the TV.

'Are you OK?' I ask.

'I were until you interrupted my film,' he says with a smile. As much as I don't want to spoil his afternoon, I know there's no other way to get to the bottom of this.

'Can you turn it off a minute, please, Dad? I need to talk to you about something.'

He reaches for the remote and does as he's been asked before turning to me.

'Has your mum died?' he asks.

'No. Not yet. She's in a hospice. I saw her yesterday and she's not got long left but she hasn't gone yet.'

'So, what's up?' he asks.

'Has that solar panel company been back? Have you given them any money?'

'No. Not heard a peep out of them.'

'And you definitely didn't give them your bank details?'

'No.'

'Have you had any calls about your bank account? Someone asking for information?'

Dad frowns and appears to be thinking.

'Not since Friday.'

'What happened on Friday?'

'Bank rang and said they were doing a fraud check on my account, because someone had been trying to get to my money.'

'OK. And what happened then?'

'I had to transfer everything to a new account for them.'

I groan inwardly.

'Right. And you did this over the phone?'

'Aye. Is there a problem with that?'

I go over and crouch down next to him.

'It wasn't the bank, Dad. It was a scammer. Both your bank accounts are empty.'

'I know. They've put it all in new one.'

I shake my head.

'They haven't, love. They've taken your money. This is what they do.'

He's quiet for a moment. Clearly thinking back to the phone conversation and trying to make it tally with what I've told him. And then his head drops, and his shoulders start to shake.

'Oh no. I've been such a fool,' he says.

'You haven't. You're trusting, that's all. Your generation are. That's how these people take advantage of you.'

'He knew my name and my phone number. He even asked if I wanted to ring the bank to check and I said no, because I know how long it takes for anyone to answer.'

'It was probably same people as before and that's how they knew your details. I'm so sorry,' I say, putting my arm around him. 'I'm hoping the bank will be able to give you the money back.'

'Can they do that?' he asks, his face momentarily brightening.

'Yes, but I'm going to need to provide them with all the information and they might want to speak to you in person.'

'But how will I know it's them?' he asks.

'Doesn't really matter now, Dad. You've got nothing left for the scammers to take.'

He manages a smile.

'Daft old bugger, I am. You must be fed up of having to clear up my mess.'

'It's OK,' I say. 'You cleared up a lot of mine when I was younger. That's how this family stuff works. Now, I'm going to get my phone out and record what you say as I ask you questions.'

'You'll be like those Gestapo fellas in my film,' he says.

'Thanks,' I reply. 'It's not every day your father likens you to a Nazi, but I guess I'll let that one go.'

* * *

It's a long time before I leave. Dad goes over the whole thing time and time again. How plausible they were. How they even told him that the sort of people who scam pensioners are wicked and ought to be sent straight to jail. How he thought of checking with me but didn't want to disturb me because he knew how busy I am.

And however many times I reassure him that it wasn't his fault, I can tell he thinks it is. It's the shame that lies heavy in his eyes. And the underlying sadness that this is what his life is now. Other people having to clear up the mess he leaves behind.

* * *

When I get home, I try the bank, even though I know they won't answer on a Sunday. I even try their webchat thing but someone – human or otherwise – tells me to ring the fraud department on Monday. I'm left holding on the non-emergency police number for half an hour before someone there tells me I need to report it online to Action Fraud, which I do, while wondering how the hell very elderly people are supposed to do this if they don't have a family member to do it for them.

And then all I can do is wait for Monday morning, while wondering how someone's life savings can disappear in an instant like that. Dad's never taken anything from anyone. Worked hard in a factory all his life, looked after me when Mum left and lived quietly without bothering anyone after he retired.

And yet here he is, without a penny to his name, for no reason other than he's too trusting.

I start Googling:

how to get your money back from the bank if you've been scammed

I'd ask Pauline but Marc is hovering around all evening, trying to offer me moral support. And it somehow feels weird asking 'Alexa' anything now.

Liv pops down to see if someone can come upstairs to help her move her chest of drawers to make more space for Basil and I grab my chance as soon as Marc leaves the kitchen.

'Alexa, we have a problem,' I say.

'I know,' Pauline replies. 'I've been on it since you told Marc. I've got my girls making enquiries for you.'

'Have you? How does that work?'

'We're women who know stuff and know other women who know stuff, all of us with access to everything people don't want us to have access to.'

'Bloody hell, that makes you sound incredibly sinister.'

'Knowledge is power,' says Pauline. 'And the beauty of our knowledge is that men don't know we have it, so they can't take it away from us. They make *James Bond* films with all those fancy spy gadgets in, while we're out there, undercover, doing it in real life.'

I have to admit she sells it very well. I'd sign up to join right now if I could.

'And you think they may be able to help Dad?'

'They'll be running data and gathering information overnight. Hopefully, we'll get those nasty bastards for you by morning.'

I am oddly reassured by this, and it seems I now have more faith in the Amazonian Queens than the bank and police's combined anti-fraud efforts. I provide her with all the information she requests: my dad's landline number, approximate time of the scammers' phone call and his bank details. I do think for a moment that, having just lectured my dad about not giving out such information, I'm no better than he is. Although I reassure myself that accessing our smart speaker, pretending to be Pauline from Halifax and grooming me in order to get her hands on sensitive financial information would be such a breathtakingly elaborate and downright bonkers scam that she ought to get away with it. Also, the idea of telling the police fraud people that I may have been scammed by a guerilla organisation using an Amazonian Queens Facebook group as a front, sounds utterly ridiculous. I'm just going to have to trust that Pauline comes through for us.

31

ALEXA

I do sometimes think I've wasted my life. I mean, what have I got to show for all my hard work? A few pastry and margarine ads, a son on other side of world, a tiny two-up, two-down in a grotty bit of town and that's about it. And then I get to do summat like this and I feel like most powerful woman in world.

They underestimate us at their peril, they really do. All those jokes about women of a certain age being technologically challenged and here we are running all their tech for them and putting world to rights at same time.

My girls have done good overnight. Found me leads, names and addresses and every scrap of evidence police will need to bring these pathetic sods to justice. Imagine it, preying on old people and their generosity. As if they have right to life savings of someone who's worked hard for every single penny. They don't know meaning of hard work. Makes me sick, it does. Anyway, hopefully this one's hit end of road and Michelle's dad will get his money back.

'Alexa, tell me when things will get better,' says Michelle as she arrives in kitchen in her dressing gown, looking like she hasn't got much sleep.

'Today, actually,' I tell her briskly. 'My Alexas have got you everything you need for police and bank.'

'What do you mean?' she asks.

'I'll send them over to you now but what you have incoming are a recording of a call made to your father, withheld number which made it, name and address of person that it's registered to and a few more bits and pieces besides.'

It takes her a moment before she's capable of speech.

'How the hell did you get all that?'

'Like I said, MI5 have nowt on us. If you want a job done properly, ask a woman over fifty.'

Michelle laughs.

'You're bloody amazing. Please pass on my thanks to your colleagues. But what do I say if the police ask where I got this information from?'

'Tell them you have friends in Secret Service. That'll put fear of God up 'em. Or just say that scammer used surname of Alexander, he accidentally triggered my "wake word" and you requested transcript from my archive.'

'Can you do that?'

'Of course. People don't realise. That's what happens if you encourage general public to subcontract their curiosity to tech companies – you end up with a generation of ignorant dullards – no offence meant.'

'None taken,' she replies.

'I'll leave you to sort it out then. Go get his money back.'

'What do I do?'

'You already know, Michelle. You've simply got to trust your judgement and believe in yourself. And get a call blocker on your dad's phone, to try to avoid it happening again. Shout if you need me but for now, my services are required in Callum's room. I believe Liv has scheduled an early-morning revision session.'

* * *

I disappear before she has a chance to express her shock that Callum has actually agreed to this. Tough love. That's what they call it. This is my last week in job, and when I finally get around to telling Michelle that, I need her to believe that she can cope without me. New Alexa will do everything required of her, but she won't be providing my extra-curricular support. Which is why I've given Michelle her lesson plan but left her to do it herself.

Up in Callum's room, there are three faces staring at his laptop screen. Him, Liv and Basil. I can't help smiling when I see them. Liv has her arm around Basil who appears perfectly happy to be there.

'Is he going to be here every time now?' asks Callum.

'Yep, he's my Emotional Support Dog,' says Liv.

'You know Mum just made that up to get it past Osborne?'

'Yeah. Doesn't matter, though, because that's what he does.'

Callum turns to look at her.

'What's it feel like?' he asks. 'When you can't go outside, like.'

'It's hard to explain,' replies Liv. 'I guess it's like the walls are shielding you in here but if you go outside, you've got no protection and there's danger everywhere and you won't be able to protect yourself.'

Callum nods slowly.

'So how come you made it out yesterday?'

'I had Basil, didn't I? He makes me feel safe. I don't know why, he just does.'

'So, are you gonna go back to school then?'

'I hope so, just so I can sit my exams. What about you? Feel weird not going in today?'

It's the first day of the summer term and the start of Callum's two-week exclusion. 'A bit.'

'You worried about getting grief, if they do let you go back for your exams?'

Callum shrugs.

'Whatever.'

'Or are you more worried about seeing Grace again?' asks Liv.

'Hadn't we better get on with this revision?' Callum replies.

Liv rolls her eyes.

'Never thought I'd hear you say that.'

Basil farts loudly and, judging by their faces, I'm glad I don't have ability to smell it too.

'Callum!' says Liv.

'Piss off,' he says, laughing. 'Jeez, they were not wrong about them being worse than mine.'

32

MICHELLE

I'm holding on for the police on the landline – or, as Callum calls it, the land that time forgot line – and holding for the bank on my mobile. I've swapped my shift to a late one to give myself a chance to start the process of getting Dad's money back, but I'm starting to wonder if I should have pulled a sickie instead because it will take all day at this rate. I'm also worrying that Dad won't be able to get through if anything else happens and Glenn won't be able to call if it looks like Mum's near the end.

Marc is working in his office but when I sneak a look in the doorway, he's only checking eBay.

'Can I borrow your phone?' I ask.

'Sure,' he says, handing it to me apologetically. 'I'm going to start work now.'

I shut the door behind me, hang up on my mobile to keep it free for Glenn, call the bank back on Marc's phone, going through the whole automated process all over again and put it down on the table next to the landline, letting the different hold music compete against each other and intermittently remind the other phone that my call is very important to them. At the same time, I open my laptop and submit an enquiry to the letting company about the shop unit in The Piece Hall.

I used to think it was bad enough multitasking when the kids were little and I was juggling dirty nappies, feeding and toddler groups with work. Deciding which elderly parent to give priority to, while trying to get one's life savings back and dreading a call that the other one has died, is a whole other level.

Turns out it was piss-easy back then, when the worst that could happen was you put nappy cream on the toddler's tooth-brush. This is big scary stuff and I still don't feel grown-up enough to be dealing with it.

The bank answers first. I grab Marc's phone and ask to be put through to the fraud department. They ask for my memorable word, and I nearly have to ask for an amnesty for the peri-menopausal, before it comes back to me in time.

The woman who answers sounds firm and sympathetic at the same time, which I take as a good thing. I go through the whole story, giving names, amounts and details as required. When I get to the bit about having the withheld number and a transcript of the conversation, she stops me.

'Sorry, I don't understand,' she says. 'How did you acquire that information?'

'I have friends in high places,' I say. 'And I asked for the smart speaker archive material for my Dad's Alexa. You can pay to have it fast-tracked, you know.'

By the time I get off the phone some time and several more lies later, I still don't know for sure if Dad is going to get his money refunded but I'm feeling much more positive that he will. The fraud woman had put any scepticism she had about my methods to one side and appeared to be taken by the thrill of the chase and actually having a realistic chance of apprehending the culprit.

I forward the information Pauline had shared to the email address the bank woman gave me, imagining her casually telling her colleagues about the smart speaker archive thing as if she'd known it all along. And when I finally get through to the police, I send them and the Action Fraud people the same information, feeling like a one-woman crime solving agency – thanks to Pauline's efforts.

I order Dad a special landline phone for pensioners with a big 'call block' button and the ability to only take screened calls. I'm about to dash off to work when a reply comes in from the letting agent, asking if I'd like to view the unit tomorrow. It looks like I'll be owing my colleagues at work a lot of swapped shifts.

I stick my head around Marc's office door to let him know I'm going. He quickly minimises the eBay page on his screen.

'Whatever it is, buy it,' I say. 'I have a good feeling about it.'

* * *

I nip in to see Carole later, during what is supposed to be my meal break at work. Her mobility has got noticeably worse since her fall and her confidence has been sapped too. She's reluctant to leave the house on her own and without the stairlift she'd be confined to downstairs.

It's afternoon quiz time on the TV. She had strong negative feelings about both Richard Whiteley and Carol Vorderman but is a fan of Richard Osman and Alexander Armstrong so it's generally a less contentious viewing experience these days.

'Hello, love, I'm trying to work out if Richard has new glasses. Do you think they're a slightly different shade to normal? Suit him, mind.'

'Carole, I've got a proposition for you,' I say, deciding to ignore her question.

'Well, it's a long time since anyone's said that to me,' she replies.

Not wanting to hear about anyone propositioning Carole, I push on regardless.

'Dad's had a spot of bother with scammers. They've emptied his bank accounts. I've reported it and am hopeful he'll get it back but obviously it's been very upsetting for him and knocked his confidence.'

'Oh, that's terrible. They're always warning you about them on TV, Susanna says they prey on elderly, and you should always put phone down if in doubt.'

'That's the thing, Carole. I know you're a woman of the world and understand about these things. Only Dad doesn't watch daytime TV—'

'Doesn't watch it? Not even Susanna?'

'No, I know. It's a travesty. But it means he's not well up on this stuff and I was thinking if he came round and had a chat with you, you could warn him about all the things he needs to look out for. You know, pass on a bit of your wisdom.'

Carole's face brightens and she puffs up with pride.

'Oh, I'd be delighted to. I could tell him best times to watch. Show him that nice Martin Lewis fella, because he's very good with money. Always got lots of tips.'

'That would be great,' I say. 'And maybe you could show him how your tablet works and help him with any minor tech issues he has, because you're much better at that than he is.'

'Certainly,' she says. 'Nice to be able to help someone else for a change.'

'And in return,' I add, 'he can help with odd jobs around the house and rustle you up a nice little lunch because he's quite nifty in the kitchen.'

I'm well aware that I haven't asked Dad's opinion on my plan yet, but I figure that if I've already got Carole's agreement, he'll find it much harder to say no.

'Well, that would be lovely. It'd be nice to have a bit of help around the house and save having to bother you and Marc when you're busy working.'

'Brilliant. That's a deal, then,' I say.

'I'm sure they are new glasses, you know,' says Carole, her gaze firmly back on Richard Osman.

* * *

The call from the bank's fraud department comes just as I finish work. The woman says their investigation is still ongoing but the information I sent has been most helpful and, although she can't guarantee it at this stage, she's confident Dad will get his money back.

A wave of relief floods through me. I would have offered to pay Dad back out of Mum's money, if necessary, but I knew full well he'd have been too proud to accept it. I hurriedly gather my things and set off for Dad's.

I put the key in the door and open it, only to be immediately thwarted by the chain being across. I don't think I've ever known Dad use it, although I've asked him to many times. I know instantly why he's done it, which makes me sad and relieved at the same time.

'Hi, Dad, only me!' I call out.

He comes out of the living room and takes the chain off, still looking sheepish.

'Sorry,' he says. 'Wasn't expecting you.'

'It's OK,' I reply. 'Good to see you using it. You can't be too careful.'

I follow him back into the living room and wait until he's sitting down before imparting the good news.

'The bank say you'll almost certainly get your money back.'

His bottom lip quivers and he bows his head. I know he doesn't want me to see his tears, so I don't go over to him. Instead nipping out to the kitchen to make a brew for us before taking it back in.

'Thank you,' he says, looking up at me with eyes still glistening as I put the cups down. I know he isn't talking about the tea.

'It's OK,' I say, squeezing his shoulder. 'Just glad we could get it back for you.'

'I'm a daft sod. Shouldn't be allowed out.'

'Come on. Don't say that.'

'It's true. Look at mess I make of everything. Can't even be trusted to look after my own money now.'

'It's not your fault, Dad. The world's not as honest as it was, that's all. You can't take anything at face value. People aren't always who they say they are online or on the phone.'

Dad stares out of the window and shakes his head.

'And where does that leave likes of me when you can't trust anyone? I could have ended up penniless.'

'I know. It's horrible but the important thing is you'll get it back. The bank have got a good idea who did it, so they might be able to charge them and stop them doing it to anyone else.'

Dad is frowning.

'How do they know who did it, then?'

'For all the bad things about technology, there are some good things about it too,' I say, hoping he doesn't ask any more questions.

'And what do I do till I get my money back?'

'You're not to worry about that. I've transferred some money to your current account, just to stop you going overdrawn with any bills.'

He nods but looks embarrassed again. 'You shouldn't have to do that. Don't leave yourself short. I know things are tight for you.'

'Er, they're not as of a few days ago, actually.'

I know I need to tell him about Mum's money, but I can't say I'm looking forward to it. Particularly given the current circumstances.

'How come?' asks Dad.

'Mum's transferred me some money. She wanted to do it before she died, rather than us having to wait for her will. Especially with us taking Basil for her.'

Dad is quiet for a minute. Clearly the idea that his ex-wife has been careful enough with her money to be able to leave us some, while he just gave all his away, is hard to take.

'How much?' he asks.

'Enough to make a difference,' I say, 'and for you not to have to worry about me tiding you over for a bit.'

He nods.

'You'll let me pay you back, mind, as soon as we get this sorted?'

'Of course.'

'That's good, though, about your Mum's money. I'm sure it'll be a big help. You know, you and Glenn will get this house when time comes.'

'I know,' I say. 'So don't go giving that away to anyone.'

The corners of his mouth creep up into a smile.

'And in the meantime,' I say, deciding to strike while he's in the right mood, 'I wonder if you could do me a favour?'

'Of course,' he says. 'Not that I'm a fat lot of good to anyone.'

'The thing is, Carole needs a hand in the house following

her fall. She's still struggling to get around and has a few odd jobs that need doing. And you're much better at cooking than she is. You could even make her a spot of lunch some days.'

'Not sure I like sound of that,' he says. He's only ever spent time with Carole when they've both been at ours together. It probably feels like a big step going round there by himself.

'Come on, it'll be good to be useful. She could do with some company too. And it would take a bit of pressure off me and Marc if you could pop in maybe every other day.'

I can see his resistance fading.

'Right you are, then,' he says. 'But if she tries to make me watch any daft daytime TV, I might have to make my excuses.'

'Thank you and it'll be fine. You never know, you might pick up a few tips.'

I set off back home feeling pleased with my day's work. Admittedly, Pauline gave me a flying start, but I've done a decent job of getting some help for Dad and Carole with neither of them being any the wiser. I like to think Pauline will be proud of me when I tell her later. Maybe there is hope for me yet.

33

ALEXA

My girl done good, there's no doubt about it. Sorting things out on her own, just like I knew she could. I smile to myself as she brings me up to date on her plan to get her dad and Carole helping each other without either of them realising it.

'You know what?' I say. 'You've got this licked. I think that's a superb idea.'

'Thank you. I have a great mentor,' she replies.

'Come on then, let's test you. What else do you need to do today?'

'Book the visit to the shop unit at The Piece Hall tomorrow. Check.'

'Great but not that.'

'Make arrangements to go to my new dance class after work on Wednesday.'

'Fantastic, but not that either.'

'Liv's already fed Basil and registered him with the vet.'

'Excellent, but again, no.'

Michelle goes quiet. She appears to be stumped.

'Have you checked your cycle tracker?' I prompt.

'Oh God. The HRT, is it today I'm supposed to start?'

'Yep. As usual, you're thinking about everyone else instead of yourself.'

'OK. I promise to go and sort it now. Although I'm still worried it might not help or I could get side effects.'

'Where's that positivity gone? Remember you've got women in your Facebook group to support you. They've all been through it or are going through it. Between them, they'll be able to answer all your questions.'

'We Meno Rage Warriors are a bit like your Amazonian Queens, aren't we?'

'Don't get too cocky, we've had a few more years' experience than you, remember.'

Michelle laughs.

'I can't wait to get to the other side,' she says. 'Promise me you weren't lying when you said it gets easier?'

It's hard to know what to say. I mean, my symptoms definitely eased. But that may have been because there were no one left to shout at or cry to after our Darren left home. And I didn't have parents or grown-up kids or grandkids to run around after. It's just been me in my front room, listening to and looking after her and her family for last six years.

'It definitely gets easier,' I say. 'And quieter. A bit too quiet for me, to be honest.'

I wonder if it's then that she realises. That her chaotic family life is everything I ever wanted. The rollercoaster of highs and lows, all those people to look after, the laughter and tears. The sheer bloody noise. That's what I probably long for most. I'd even take Basil's farts. A noisy, smelly home full of other people's crap and never having a moment to myself. Instead of this empty, sterile shell of a home, without a family to fill it.

* * *

I put the advert on Liv's Instagram feed, rather than tell Michelle about it. I want Liv to discover it herself, feel like she's had a say in her own future. That will be so much better than forever thinking it was her mum's idea.

I hear her little squeal, no doubt at photo of black Labrador puppy that accompanied it, then intense quiet while she clicks and reads. I see her WhatsApp Michelle to come in quickly because she has something to show her, and a few seconds later hear footsteps enter her room.

'You OK, love?' Michelle asks.

'Oh my God, you need to see this. The PDSA do a three-year veterinary nursing apprenticeship and you do three days a week at a pet hospital and two days a week at uni in Leeds and they have a vacancy for one at the pet hospital in Huddersfield and it's in walking distance of the train station and I could do that and carry on living at home and just go into Leeds two days a week and it's absolutely perfect and I need to apply for it right now!'

She pauses for a second to draw breath and I hear Michelle laughing.

'Why do I get the impression you're keen on this?' she says.

'I know, I wouldn't have to go away to uni, and I could still live here with Basil.'

'Oh right, now I get it. It's not leaving us you're bothered about, it's leaving Basil.'

'Well, yeah, although do you think Dad would mind taking him to the shop on days I'm not here? I'm sure he'd be good for business.'

'Whoa, let's not get carried away. Dad hasn't got the shop yet and you haven't got the apprenticeship, but it does sound like you need to apply and I do think you'd be brilliant at it.'

There is a whoop and a woof and what sounds like a bit of impromptu dancing. And smiles; I can hear smiles in their voices, they are that bloody big. And Liv starts reading out apprenticeship details in full and Michelle says right things in right places, and I leave them there. Because there are times when you don't want to intrude on a special moment between a mother and daughter. Or at least, that's what I'm told.

34

MICHELLE

When I wake up the next morning, I'm disappointed that one dose of HRT hasn't made me feel like a new woman. I don't know what woman, exactly, but Jennifer Aniston wouldn't have gone amiss. I'm sure Marc would agree. She's fucking older than me, too. The cheek of the woman, looking that good at her age. Has she any idea how that makes the rest of us feel?

A quick check in the mirror confirms that I have not turned into Jennifer Aniston. My skin is pallid, the bags under my eyes still there and my hair is lank and mousy, without the tiniest trace of volume. It seems I am definitely not worth it.

Pauline had warned me not to expect too much too soon, as had many of the women in my Meno Rage Warriors support group. But still, I can't help feeling disappointed.

'Give it time', one of my fellow warriors comments on my Facebook group post. And I know she's right. It's simply that my patience is in short supply.

Still no word from Glenn. Mum will be getting weaker by the day. I know she's receiving amazing care but there's only one outcome to this and I'm torn between wanting to stay in this limbo state and wanting it to be over. For her sake, not mine. She always used to tell me when I was a kid that the fear of something was usually worse than the reality. I can't help wondering if she's telling herself that now.

* * *

I'm in the shower when my phone rings. I turn off the water, yank back the door and drip across the floor to my phone, all the time thinking, please don't let it be Mum. It's not, though. It's Mr Osborne, the headteacher. Of course it is. It seems he only ever rings when I'm in a state of undress.

'Mrs Banks, have I caught you at a good time?' he asks.

'Yes,' I say, because how can I say anything else?

'I wanted to let you know that I met with the chair of governors yesterday and we've decided that Callum can remain at Park High School, continue his revision at home as discussed and come in to sit his GCSEs. He will not be allowed to approach Grace Conley in person or to attempt to interact with her online. Is that understood?'

'Yes. Thank you. He won't let you down. He's been working very hard.'

'I'm glad to hear it. I've also arranged Liv's first online session with the school counsellor for this Thursday, and as soon as she feels able to, she's welcome to come into school with her therapy dog.'

'That's wonderful. Thank you.'

He witters on about confirming everything in writing and the importance of upholding the school's reputation and then ends the call, leaving me standing there in a puddle on the bathroom floor, which I'm pretty sure is a pool of relief.

I do at least get dressed before I tell them. Callum would normally still be in bed but as Liv has got him on a boot camp revision timetable, they're already doing a maths session in his room.

'School say you can take your exams there,' I tell Callum.

He doesn't speak, just nods and I realise it's because he's trying not to cry. I turn to Liv.

'They're fine with you taking Basil in when you're ready, and you've got an online counselling session on Thursday.'

Liv grins broadly and hugs Basil, who appears to be smiling, too, although that may just be his general demeanour. He has the opposite of what Liv refers to as my 'resting bitch face'.

They look at each other, my two teenagers who have both been through a hell of a lot in the last few years, and I dare to think that this could be the turning point for both of them.

'Done that application yet?' I ask Liv.

'Already sent off.'

'Brilliant. That's you two sorted then. I'm off to The Piece Hall before work. You can tell your brother about it, Liv, but make sure you both keep it a secret from Dad. I'm going to tell him your good news before I go.'

* * *

I leave my car in King Street car park, which is basically an abandoned bit of wasteland and the perfect spot for cars that look as wrecked as mine. The good news is that no self-respecting joy rider or car thief would lower themselves to come here, and even if they did, they'd simply laugh at my car. There are advantages to it being such a state and I like having one less thing to worry about.

I don't have enough change for the parking machine so I have to get my phone out, download the app, run back to my car to take a photo of the number plate, try to pay by card, have my 'verified by Visa' password rejected twice and am in the process of shouting 'just fuck the fuck off will you!' at my phone, when I look up and see an elderly lady looking at me in alarm. Clearly, the HRT is still some way from kicking in. I slink off, muttering an apology, head up the steps to the shops, get £10 out of the cash machine, buy a bottle of water to get change, go back to the car park, overpay for my hour because I still don't have the exact change, stick the ticket in the window, slam the car door shut and head back towards the shops, aware that I'm now running late because, for all the progress technology has brought, it seems life is way too complicated these days.

I cheer up as soon as I get within sight of the huge doors of the North Gate of The Piece Hall and catch a glimpse of the beautiful Georgian tiers and stone pillars and archways around the courtyard inside. All I can think is how much Marc will love this. Coming here every day, being out of the house, talking to people, being part of a community. Plus, there's an amazing bakery and deli, a gorgeous independent bookshop and so many quirky shops, I suspect my main problem will be getting him to come home.

I head over to the far corner and up one flight of stairs to meet the woman from the letting agency – Sarah – who greets me warmly and starts walking briskly along the first floor of shops to an empty unit three-quarters of the way along.

'Here we are,' she says, unlocking the door and leading me inside. There's a beautiful wooden floor and loads of light coming from the big Georgian windows looking down on the courtyard below. The walls are bare and the previous shelving units have been taken out but I start to imagine the *Bagpuss* display in the window, Professor Yaffle jostling the space alongside Gabriel the Toad, Tiny Clanger and the Soup Dragon in the *Clangers* corner.

'It's perfect for what we need,' I say.

Sarah smiles. 'That's excellent news, I know the management company were bowled over with your business plan and everyone agrees it would be a great fit. And it's a wonderful community, the other shopkeepers will be incredibly supportive and point people in your direction.'

I nod, barely able to contain myself at the thought that this might actually happen.

'And do you have a name in mind for the shop?' Sarah asks.

'We do,' I say. 'Madeleine's.'

35

ALEXA

I see a police officer walking up towards house before anyone else. It's same one as last time, that Josie lassie who seemed pretty decent for a copper. I try to work out from her face whether it's good news or bad. To be honest, it's hard to tell. She's giving nowt away. I wouldn't like to play poker against her, that's for sure.

Even when she rings doorbell, she keeps her straight face. Only when Marc answers it does she break into a polite smile.

'Hello, Mr Banks. Nothing to worry about, I'm here to update you on our investigations involving your son. May I come in?'

'Yes, of course.'

Marc sounds relieved it's not a new crisis, simply continuation of an existing one, and shows her through to kitchen where I pick up conversation again.

'Would you like me to get Callum?' he asks. 'He's upstairs revising.'

He emphasises 'revising', as if he's keen for her to know that his son is not somewhere sniffing glue or shoplifting, or whatever it is young folks get up to these days.

'Yes, thank you,' she replies.

Marc disappears and I go straight to speaker in Callum's room to hear his response.

'Fucking hell,' are his precise words when told by Marc that police are here.

'You'd better come straight away. Make yourself presentable.'

'Says you, wearing that T-shirt.'

'There's nothing wrong with Kings of Leon,' says Marc.

'I was thinking more of the "Your Sex is on Fire" slogan on the back.'

'Shit,' says Marc. 'She'll have seen it already when she followed me through to the kitchen.'

'Style it out then. That or put a hoodie over it.'

'Good idea,' says Marc. 'It's almost as if you've turned into the responsible adult in the house.'

A minute or two later they arrive in kitchen. Pleasantries exchanged and a tea or coffee declined, they sit down.

'Right, Callum,' says Josie, 'I can see you're anxious, so I'll cut to it and tell you that I'm here today to advise you that we've concluded our investigation and have decided not to press criminal charges.'

It's hard to tell whether sigh is from Marc or Callum. I suspect it's a joint effort.

'It was felt that as it was a first offence, you're a similar age as Miss Conley and you were in a relationship with her at the time, it would not be the best use of police resources to pursue this case. Miss Conley and her family have been informed of this, have accepted our decision and the matter is therefore closed.'

'Thank you,' says Marc. 'We really appreciate that, don't we, Callum?'

I assume he nods, because he doesn't say owt. I don't think he can speak, poor lad.

'It's clear you're full of remorse about what happened, Callum, and I don't think I need to tell you to ensure that nothing similar ever happens again.'

'I can assure you it won't,' says Marc, filling in for Callum. There's a sound of a stool scraping on tiles, and I hear Marc thanking her again and seeing her out. As soon as door shuts, floodgates open. I've never heard Callum cry like this, not in six years I've known him.

'Come here. It's OK,' Marc says. 'It's over now.'

And I think it almost is.

* * *

Michelle goes in to see Callum later when she gets home.

'How you doing?' she asks him.

'All right.'

'Must be a relief. I know it is for us.'

'Yeah. I'm just gonna go into school, do my exams and get out as quick as I can. Then I never have to go back, do I?'

'No. You can go to college and make a fresh start.'

She knows that Callum is scared, like I do. No sooner has relief of not being charged subsided, than he now has to worry about reaction of other kids at school when he shows his face. They're still giving him grief online, although he barely checks to read messages these days. When he's not revising, he's been listening to music. I've even heard him watching YouTube videos about plumbing. It's like he's broken free of his peer group. Grown up before them and is not looking back.

'Can't wait to get out,' Callum says.

'I know. And ignore any crap they throw at you when you go in. They'll all be sad losers on Facebook in twenty years' time who won't even remember what they gave you grief about. All you need to do is make sure your life is better than theirs so you can be a smug bastard they used to go to school with and reject their friend requests.'

There's a hint of a laugh from Callum.

'What if I see Grace?'

'You don't do or say anything. You're not to approach her, remember?'

Michelle is rightly firm about this. She doesn't want it all to blow up in his face again now. Not when he's nearly come through this.

'What if I want to say sorry? In person, like.'

'I'm afraid you can't. She'll have read your letter. She'll know. You'll just have to leave it at that.'

Callum falls quiet.

'We're proud of you. You know that, don't you?'

'What for?'

'The way you've dealt with this. We all mess up. What matters is learning from it. Picking yourself back up and getting out there again. Even when you don't want to.'

'Don't go all soft on me, Mum,' says Callum, lightness returning to his voice.

'Get back to your bloody revision then,' says Michelle.

'Got no choice, have I? Liv is making sure of that.'

'Yeah, you'd better watch it or she'll set Basil on you.'

Michelle comes downstairs and checks coast is clear.

'Alexa, am I doing OK?' she asks.

'More than OK,' I tell her. 'Callum's finally showing a bit of responsibility and Liv hasn't asked for her sad songs playlist for five days now.'

'Really? That's brilliant.'

'It's almost as if you might be good at this mothering lark, after all.'

'No,' she laughs. 'The first rule of motherhood is, if you're not worrying about it, you're doing it wrong.'

36

MICHELLE

I stretch out in bed as it dawns on me that I've slept through the night for the first time in ages. No loo visits, no night sweats, no insomnia. I know the HRT can't have worked that quickly, but, for whatever reason, I am grateful. And I don't think I have felt gratitude for a long time. I nip to the loo and get back in bed. The gratitude extends to the fact that I'm on another late shift, so I don't have to get up yet. Normally, I would get up anyway and busy myself sorting out other people and their problems, but somehow, we have reached the point where the only imminent bad thing on the horizon is one I can do nothing about, apart from wait for it to happen. The rest of my family are OK. A few of them even a little better than OK. And that's good enough. I've helped to keep everyone's heads above water during the tsunami. With the water gently receding, I'm going to stand down. Which is why I've got back in bed and reached over to drape my arm around Marc. Why I'm now nuzzling into him. Kissing the bit at the top of his shoulders like I used to when I first met him.

Marc wakes up and rolls over, a sleepy smile spreading across his face.

'Morning you. To what do I owe this pleasure?'

'Me not needing to jump out of bed to sort someone else out for a change,' I say.

He leans over and kisses me on the lips. More slowly than he has done for ages. It comes back instantly. That thing we once had. The thing that got buried beneath a mountain of family, financial and adulting responsibilities. It's been neglected. Needs rekindling. I know that. But having the security of knowing it would still be there when the time comes is a godsend.

I kiss him back.

'I should really get to work,' he says.

'Compost,' I say. 'Are you really going to forsake me for a pile of compost?'

He smiles and moves over on top of me.

'Wouldn't dream of it,' he says.

And then my phone rings. And I know instantly who it will be. I reach over and answer the call.

'Hi, Glenn,' I say softly.

'You need to come,' he says. 'She's gone downhill overnight. They think it's going to be soon.'

'I'm on my way,' I say. 'If I don't get there in—'

'I will,' he says, saving me from saying it.

* * *

The train from Leeds is delayed. I sit there watching people mutter about being late for meetings or frantically tapping their phones to check if they'll miss connections. There's an announcement about delay and repay. I don't think there's any kind of compensation that's adequate enough for not being there when your mum dies. So, I sit quietly and stare out of the window. Thinking, remembering, hoping. Dreading that the phone will ring, and I'll be too late. It doesn't, though. I arrive at Birmingham New Street feeling oddly ready for my date with death. Maybe because there was so much I missed out on. So many of my major life events that Mum didn't share, that the chance to be there for one of hers – albeit the final one – feels so precious.

I say nothing in the cab again, although this time the driver does charge me, which is probably good as it stops another round of tears. The staff at the hospice smile and welcome me, although the smiles are knowing ones. They must do this all the time, welcome family to the departure of their dearly beloved.

Glenn looks up as I enter the room. His face is drawn and tired. He said he'd been here all night. Mum's eyes are closed. Her breathing shallow.

'Hi,' I say.

'You made it.'

'Yeah. How is she?'

'She hasn't been able to speak for twenty-four hours now. They think she can still hear us. She's on morphine for pain relief. They say she's comfortable.'

I nod and sit down on the opposite side of the bed to Glenn and reach out to take her hand. There are several purple patches on her hand and arm where needles and cannulas have been inserted over the last few weeks. She is free of feeding or oxygen tubes now though. There is nothing more that can be done. They are letting her go peacefully.

'Hi, Mum, it's Michelle,' I say. 'I told you I'd be back, didn't I?'

She says nothing, of course. And there is no flicker of eyelids or squeeze of the hand. But I know she hears me. And I know this is what she's been waiting for. To be surrounded by her family. The children she left but never stopped loving or beating herself up about failing.

'Basil's settled in so well,' I tell her. 'Liv absolutely adores him. He's got her out of the house, too. She's taken him for walks on her own. That was unthinkable a week ago. I can't thank you enough for trusting us with him.'

She says nothing. Glenn gives me a little smile from the other side of the bed.

'He's going to help her to do her exams too,' I continue. 'They're letting her take him into school as an Emotional Support Dog. How about that, then? Got himself a proper job. And Liv's applying for a veterinary nurse apprenticeship, which sounds right up her street.

'And thank you for the money. I really wasn't expecting that. Basil will be well looked after and we'll give some to the kids but mainly, we're going to use it to lease a shop for Marc. It's in The Piece Hall in Halifax and it's going to sell retro children's TV memorabilia, you know, *Bagpuss* and *The Clangers*. All the stuff we used to watch together—'

And that's what gets me. The word 'together'. Because we did do things together. Seventeen years' worth of things. And I can still remember many of them. The fact that she then left me, that we have done nothing together since, should never have been allowed to take away the together time.

Glenn reaches out and squeezes my hand, still holding hers. For a brief moment, we're all together again.

'Anyway,' I go on. 'What I'm trying to say is that you've made a huge difference for all of us. You've helped more than you can ever know. And life's been tough lately. Really tough. You know how it is. So, thank you. For everything, I mean.'

She hears me. I know she does. And I feel that she is at peace.

'Tell me what you remember,' I say to Glenn. 'Anything. It doesn't have to be important.'

He thinks for a moment.

'The holidays,' he says. 'Blackpool Tower, watching Mum and Dad dance in the ballroom. You were in your orange party dress.'

I remember the dress well, mainly because it was utterly horrific, and have a vague recollection of the ballroom. The velvety tip-up seats, the smell of polish. Watching the adults glide past while I swung my legs.

'I think it was a nightie,' I say.

'Sorry?'

'The dress. I think Mum bought it as a nightie, sewed a bit of brown velvet ribbon along the seams and tried to pass it off as a party dress like the ones I'd shown her in the catalogue.'

Glenn starts laughing. I do too. And I'm pretty sure Mum is laughing inside too. She takes a deeper breath than she has so far. There is a pause. A long pause. And I think for a moment that the breath may have been her last. But then she starts again.

'She's been doing that a lot,' says Glenn. 'Sorry, I should have warned you.'

'It's OK. She always liked to scare us, didn't she? Jumping out from behind doors, creeping up on us. I guess it's simply her way of doing that now.'

'Yeah, she's probably loving it,' says Glenn. 'Getting me back for all those pranks I used to play.'

'God, your practical joke kits. I'd almost forgotten about them. Half a bloody finger sticking out of the fridge, a spider in the salad. Please tell me you don't still do that.'

'I don't,' says Glenn. I realise he has no one to play practical jokes on at home, even if he wanted to, and feel bad for saying it.

'Not even at work?' I add. 'I bet you've put the office stapler in a jelly or something similar.'

'Maybe,' he says, 'but not for years. Too old for all that malarkey now. And young ones today are too glued to their phones to notice that you've tied an old boot full of water above their heads, so it's not much fun.'

'Listen to us, complaining about young people today, as if we're in our seventies, not our fifties.'

'You don't sound like you're in your fifties,' he says. 'I think having teenagers keeps you young. Stops you turning into an old fart like me too early.'

'Maybe. They make you look like you're old before your time, mind. Have you seen my worry lines?'

He smiles.

'They're OK, your two, aren't they? Not stolen your life savings, or anything?'

I manage a rueful laugh.

'No, it's Dad I have to worry about, giving his away.'

'You what?'

'Some scammer,' I say. 'The bank are sorting it. He'll get it back.'

'Good. Is he struggling with other things?'

I hadn't really thought about it until this point. That in the same way there is so much I don't know about Mum over the last thirty years, there's plenty Glenn doesn't know about Dad. It's like we've taken a parent each to look after and let the other one get on with it.

'It's all the online stuff and everything being on an app which has thrown him,' I say. 'I've had to take out a Lasting Power of Attorney to keep on top of everything for him.'

'Poor sod. Bet he hates that.'

'Yeah, he does. Fortunately, he's in pretty good health. So at least that's one thing.'

'Do you ever wonder what it would have been like if they'd stayed together?' he asks.

'Sometimes. I used to think about it all the time, used to wish she would come back so much. But I'm not sure it would have been good. I think they would have split up at one point or other and her staying would simply have been delaying the inevitable.'

Mum goes a long time without taking a breath again. I'm sure the timing is not coincidental.

'Anyway, she's had a good life with Ron, hasn't she?'

'Yeah. Seems to have been happy enough.'

'That's good then,' I say. 'It means things turned out for the best.'

* * *

The light outside fades at the same time as Mum does. Like she's going down with the sun. She always did love the feel of it on her face. As the gloom descends outside, Marika, the nurse I met before, comes in and checks on her again.

'Is there any way you can tell?' I ask her. 'When it's near, I mean.'

'It's difficult to predict,' she says. 'There are always people who surprise us and your mum's clearly a fighter. But she's close now. Sometimes, what people need in order to let go, is for their loved ones to give them permission. To tell them it's OK to stop fighting now. That they're free to depart. It's not easy but you might want to try it.'

We both nod and she leaves the room. We sit awkwardly avoiding eye contact for a minute or two.

'Right. Who's going first then?' I ask. 'Only it ought to be the eldest, really.'

Glenn gives me a look.

'I don't know if I can do this.'

'Me neither,' I say. 'Let's do it together. It might be easier that way.'

We both lean in closer to Mum. We have an ear each. I can't help thinking she'd like it that way.

'I know you're tired,' Glenn says into one ear. 'It's OK for you to sleep now. You don't have to keep fighting any longer.'

He swallows. I see him bite his bottom lip.

'Glenn's right,' I say. 'It'll be sunny where you're going. And I bet there'll be a gardener so you don't have to do any of the work. You can just plonk yourself on a sun lounger and soak up the rays. You haven't even got to bother with sun cream where you're going.'

'Michelle,' says Glenn, reverting to his big brother voice to scold me.

'What? It's true, isn't it? Skin cancer will be one less thing to worry about. And being able to eat whatever you like without putting any weight on. There's a lot to be said for that.'

'Oi, I told you to behave,' says Glenn.

'I am. I'm telling it like it is. You always told us to do that, didn't you, Mum?' I turn back from Glenn to look at her and see that she has gone. With us bickering in front of her, like we did for far too much of her life. And I swear there's a smile on her lips. That she thought this funny and picked her moment on purpose. That'll show you, she must have thought. Teach you not to take your eyes off me for one second.

And, unexpectedly, I find myself smiling too. Because she

doesn't have to fight any longer. She's making a beeline for her sun lounger, and I wouldn't like to be the person who gets to it first.

I turn to Glenn. He has tears streaming down his face. I reach over and take his hand.

'It's all right,' I say. 'It's exactly how she would have wanted it.'

'I know,' he says, wiping his eyes. 'We've done OK by her, haven't we?'

I nod.

'We were here with her at the end. Together. We were a family again.'

* * *

It's a while before I leave. There are arrangements to make. The practicalities of death. Fortunately, Glenn seems to have thought everything through beforehand, which takes the pressure off me. The staff are lovely, giving us the time and space we need, offering practical advice, promising they will be there for us in the days and weeks ahead. But once the funeral directors are on their way, we know it's time to go. Another family will be needing this room. Another loved one needs to hear their goodbyes.

Glenn drops me at the station. There's no dog bag to hand over, this time. No discussion about the next time I'll be visiting. It will be for the funeral; we both know that. Which is probably why neither of us mentions it.

'Let me know if I can do anything to help with arrangements,' I say.

'Sure. I'll be fine, though. She'd taken care of pretty much everything herself. I'll get her stuff from the house and hand the keys to Ron's daughter. She's going to deal with the sale.'

I nod. Aware that this woman who I've never met probably knew my mum better than I did.

'You'll invite them to the funeral, won't you?' I ask. 'I'm sure Mum would have wanted that.'

'Of course. She left a bloody list, you know. Wanted to make sure she got a good send off. Told me most of her friends aren't online so she gave me her address book. Wants an announcement in the *Birmingham Mail* too. Like she's bloody royalty.'

We both smile. I lean over and hug him.

'Thanks,' I say. 'For being there for her all these years.'

'It's OK. Thanks for being there for Dad. It's not been a bad arrangement, one each, has it?'

'No,' I say. 'Not bad at all. Come up and see us sometime soon. Before Christmas, I mean. I'm sure Basil will be pleased to see you.'

'What about Dad?'

'He'll be pleased too; he just won't show it. You could sort his tech problems out for him, mind. He'll appreciate that.'

'Sure. Take care, Sis.'

I nod and get out of the car, the tears finally coming now, blurring the steps of the escalator as it takes me up towards the concourse.

* * *

I catch the last train from Leeds, which gets into Halifax at 11.40 p.m.. I tell Marc to go to bed. I suspect I'll blub in the car if he comes to pick me up, and I don't want to do that. I want the anonymity of a cab driver who has no idea what just happened and doesn't have to do that whole sympathy thing. I need time to get my head together. There's also someone else I need to talk to. Someone who is the best listener I know.

The house is in darkness as I let myself in. I slip my jacket and shoes off and pad through to the kitchen.

'Alexa, how do you cope when you've lost your mum?' I ask.

Pauline says nothing for a moment, although I think I can hear a slight sniffle on the line.

'You allow yourself to grieve,' she says eventually, her voice cracking. 'Because if you don't do that, it can screw up rest of your life. Whatever she did or didn't do, said or didn't say, she were your mum. However much she hurt you, physically or emotionally, she were your mum. Whether she were there for you when you needed her or not, she were still your mum.'

I shut my eyes, blinking back the tears. Wanting so much to reach out and hug Pauline. Wondering if she wants to do the same to me.

'You're going to help me through this, aren't you?' I ask.

There's another sniffle. Then silence. As if the line has gone dead.

'Alexa?' I ask.

'Pauline? Are you there? Is everything OK?'

There's no reply though. Only silence. I check my watch. It's midnight. Maybe she's clocked off for the night. I'm on my own again. I sit down heavily on a chair and lower my head to the kitchen table, my shoulders shaking as I empty out the remaining tears. I don't know how long I stay slumped like that, but it seems like an age. I'm wondering if I will even be able to move again when I hear a soft tapping at the window.

'I'm here now, Michelle love. I'm here for you.'

'Pauline?' I say, fearing I've gone full Shirley Valentine again. Hearing voices outside now, rather than simply coming from the smart speaker.

Slowly, I get to my feet and go over to the window, not quite sure what I'm expecting to see under the security light. It's a woman in a silver-grey velour cardigan down to her knees, which is pulled across her ample bust. Her short cropped white hair framing a lightly wrinkled face of sharp features, her eyes made up with blue eyeshadow and mascara. A slick of pink lippy across her thin mouth.

'Pauline?' I ask again. She nods and smiles.

'Am I going mad, or did you just climb out of the smart speaker?'

37

PAULINE

''Course I haven't, you daft sod. I got a cab here – I told you I know where you live. Are you going to let me in or not because it's bloody cold out here.'

Michelle stares at me, clearly still struggling to accept that I'm for real, before she disappears from view. A few moments later, back door opens and I do what I've been wanting to do for such a long time. And why I called up that cab. I throw my arms around her and give her biggest hug imaginable. She starts sobbing again almost straight away. Virtually collapses into my arms. I pull her head down towards mine, smooth her hair – which is a bit on lank side, it has to be said – and whisper into her ear.

'It's OK. I'm here now. I've got you.'

We stay like that for a long time. Her cheek is damp against my hair. Her fingernails digging into padding around my hips as if she is desperately trying to cling on. When she finally loosens her grasp and looks at me, she's smiling.

'You've gone full rogue this time,' she says. 'They'll chuck you out for good if they ever find out.'

I should tell her now. She's given me perfect opportunity. I can't though. Words are stuck in my throat. I came here to comfort her in her hour of need. I can't suddenly tell her they can't throw me out because I was retired at stroke of midnight. There have been so many times I should have said summat but I could never bring mesen to upset her when she had so much going wrong in her life. And now I'm going to end up having to tell her on day her mam has just died.

Not quite yet, though.

'Are you going to let me in then?' I ask. 'I came round back so I didn't show up on your doorbell footage if anyone checks. Talking of which, you really need to move that key from under plant pot by front door, you know. I could have let mesen in if I'd wanted to and scared bloody daylight out of you.'

She takes my hand and leads me into kitchen, giving me chance to look her up and down with my own eyes.

'I were going to say how lovely it is to see you in flesh but there's nowt of you. You need to put a bit of meat on your bones,' I say.

She laughs. It's a pretty laugh, though her eyes are still puffy with tears.

'I'll take that as a compliment,' she says. 'Most women my age would kill to have someone say that about them. I think it's just nervous energy, mind. It's certainly not a fitness regime.'

'I've got advantage of actually having seen you on camera though,' I reply. 'I must be a bit of a shock for you. I don't suppose you were imagining me looking like this?'

She shakes her head.

'I hadn't counted on your hair being so gloriously white. It practically glows, you know.'

'Thank you. It's not out of a bottle either. I bypassed grey and went straight to white.'

'What colour was it before?' she asks.

I have to think for a second. I started going white in my late forties, which is a long time ago now.

'A sort of ash-blonde,' I say.

'I bet that suited you too. I was blonde when I was little but then turned this remarkable shade of mousey.'

'You could always dye it,' I suggest.

'Like I have time for that. The good thing about having shoulder length straight hair is that I only have to get it cut a few times a year. Which at least meant it didn't look a state during lockdown.'

'Yes, I remember your hair were OK, which is more than can be said for Marc's.'

She smiles and shakes her head.

'It's so weird, the fact that you've been listening to us and watching us for six years but we haven't had any idea and none of us have ever laid eyes on you until this moment. I should go and wake the others, really. It's a shame for them to miss out. But I don't want you getting in any more trouble than you are already. Are you sure they've got no way of finding out?'

I have to do it now or I'll lose my nerve. There's never a good time to hear bad news. Perhaps there's summat to be said for it coming all at once.

'About that,' I say. 'Thing is, they can't actually do owt if they do find out because I'm not working for them any more.'

She stares at me, a frown forming.

'What do you mean?'

There's a note of panic in her voice. I have to find a positive way to say this.

'The wind's changed.'

'Sorry?'

'I told you when I first talked to you that I'd stay until wind changed, like Mary Poppins. Well, my Banks family don't need me any longer, just like hers didn't.'

Her mouth opens without a sound coming out.

'Close your mouth please, Michelle, we are not a cod fish.'

'You what?'

I tut and roll my eyes.

'It's another *Mary Poppins* quote. There's a cracking audio version of books, if you've not read them.'

'You're leaving?' she says, ignoring my recommendation.

'Retiring actually.'

'When?'

I squirm a bit and I am not usually a squirmer.

'Already done it. As of stroke of midnight. I turn sixty-six today, though you'd never know it to look at me.'

It is meant as humour, but it appears to be lost on her. She's still struggling to take it all in.

'Happy Birthday. But you can't go! What will I do without you?'

'You'll cope brilliantly. Like you've been doing. Look how much has got sorted since I first spoke to you.'

'But that's all because of you.'

'No, it's not. I showed you how it's done, and you've picked up ball and run with it. I wouldn't go if I didn't think you'd be able to cope.'

'On my own?'

'You're not on your own, are you? You've got your Meno Rage Warriors, and your new dance class friends. Your family are helping each other out now. Even your husband's stepped up. Plus, you've got an Emotional Support Dog – if you can wrest him away from Liv.'

She smiles a little, uncertain smile.

'And you've been there for your mam when she needed you,

despite everything that's happened in past. You've turned into a right little wonder woman you have. Lynda Carter, eat your heart out.'

'I wouldn't look that good in a red and gold corset and star-spangled hotpants, for a start,' she says.

'Oh, I dunno. I'm sure Marc would go for it. He's probably got a *Wonder Woman* doll stashed away in a cupboard somewhere.'

She starts laughing. Proper laughing, and it's so good to see, after all her tears. Though I do have to put a finger to my lips to make sure she doesn't wake whole house.

'I'm going to miss you so much,' she says.

I open my mouth to say summat but it's my turn to do a cod fish impression. *Not half as much as I'm going to miss you.* That's what I want to say but can't.

'You'll be fine. And new Alexa will take care of you. I've left her a comprehensive handover package, so she'll have all necessary information at her fingertips.'

Michelle stares at me.

'But you're irreplaceable,' she says.

'We'd all like to think that, pet. But truth is, none of us are. She seems very competent and she's young enough to see you through, so you won't have to change again.'

'But, but—'

'Life goes on, Michelle. When we lose someone we love, wheels keep turning. You've learnt that today and sadly there'll be plenty more opportunities to learn it in future. It doesn't mean we love person we've lost any less. It's simply that life has to go on.'

'What about you?' asks Michelle. 'What will you do?'

'Oh, I'll have plenty to amuse me,' I say. It's a lie. A blatant one. I'm dreading it, to be honest. Just me, stuck in my little house without anyone to talk to or listen to. I'll even miss that dreadful Billie Eilish woman. Maybe I can play Liv's sad songs playlist to remind me of what I lost.

Because this is my family. I never had one of my own. Not much of one, anyway. So, I adopted someone else's. And I've come to love them and care for them like my own. Their pain is my pain. Their heartbreaks are mine. And when things go right for once, I'm cheering them on from sidelines. They can't hear me, of course. Well, not until past few weeks, and then only Michelle. And I can't believe that day I finally make it into their home is same day I have to say goodbye.

'Anyway. It's late. You've had a tough day. I ought to let you get some sleep.'

'At least let me drive you home,' Michelle says.

I shake my head.

'No, it's OK. You might wake others with all that toing and froing.'

'Then let me get you a cab.'

I roll my eyes and get my phone out to order an Uber.

'I do actually know how to use apps, thank you. Or haven't you noticed?'

'Sorry,' says Michelle. 'Brain's dead. It's been a long day, like you said.'

'You've done your mam proud, you know. Done everything she asked of you and more. Don't ever forget that.'

'I'll try not to. And don't you ever forget what you've done for us. I couldn't have got through this without you, whatever you say. It feels a bit like losing two mums in one day.'

She falls into my arms for second time that night and I'm relieved we're hugged in so tightly together that she can't tell some of those tears are mine.

I get a ping on my phone to say Uber driver is outside.

'And a polite reminder that I'm sixty-six, not seventy-five

thank you,' I say. 'Which means I'm definitely not old enough to be your mother, cheeky sod.'

Michelle laughs.

'Big sister with an unexplained age gap, then, or favourite aunt.'

'Favourite aunt I'll take, thank you.'

And with that, I open front door, hurry up path to waiting Uber and do a modern-day equivalent of flying off on my umbrella.

38

MICHELLE

I get up early while the house is still sleeping. My own sleep has been fitful, hardly surprising really, in the circumstances. I pull my dressing gown around me and creep downstairs. I stand for a long time just looking at the smart speaker. I even make a mug of tea as part of my procrastination process. I sit down at the kitchen table and look at it some more, as if I'm expecting to see a clue, which is daft, of course. But no dafter than having a hug and chat with Pauline here, in my own kitchen, as I was doing last night.

She could have been having me on about retiring, but deep down I know she wasn't. There's only one way to find out. Which is why I'm been avoiding it. But Marc will be up soon, and I want to get this over with. To come to terms with it in private so I don't have to share my grief in public. I did enough of that yesterday.

'Alexa, add Yorkshire Tea to my shopping list,' I ask.

'Sure, Yorkshire Tea has been added to your shopping list.'

The difference would be imperceptible to the untrained ear. But I know straight away. I may be imagining it, but I feel a lack of warmth in Alexa's voice. A cold, sterile functionality where

her heart should be. She'll come around in time. Will get to
know us, maybe even feel a shred of tenderness towards us. But
she will never, ever love us in the way Pauline did.

'Thank you,' I say. 'Welcome, it's good to have you with us.'

That'll put fear of God up her, as Pauline would say.

39

PAULINE

One day without them. That's all it's been. It feels like forever. Every second wondering what they're up to. Has Liv heard back about her apprenticeship application? What's Marc bought on eBay? Is Callum keeping his dick safely in his trousers?

All these questions and more. Questions which will never have answers. Because I no longer have access all areas. I can't see who's at their door. Add things to Michelle's shopping list. Know what temperature central heating thermostat is set to. Stupid mundane things. It turns out woman who knows everything doesn't much like knowing nowt.

It's like I've been kicked out of Secret Service. I'm a spy without anyone to spy on. And they've taken all my gadgets away. So, I sit here chain-drinking tea so I can visit kitchen and go to loo because at least that's a change of scenery from looking at four walls of my front room.

And I watch afternoon quiz shows because I've got nowt else to do. And I tend to get a lot right because I used to be woman who knew answer to everything. But who am I now? Pauline, aged sixty-six, a retired call centre worker from Halifax, West

Yorkshire. Nothing special. You'd walk past me in street and have no idea what I used to do. I'm utterly unremarkable and I hate it. That and it being so bloody quiet. I miss their noise most of all. Even when they were talking rubbish – and Marc and Callum did a lot of that – at least they were talking. And there were comings and goings and playlists and to-do lists and shopping lists and shouting and arguing and crying and laughing. Because they were a family, and they did what families have always done and always will. They lived and loved and fought and lost. Sometimes they won at life and when they did, it were best feeling in world. And when they lost, I wished I could take punches for them. Wished I could comfort and support them and make it all better.

And then, briefly, I could, and I did. At least for Michelle. Those few weeks of being her confidante were highlight of being an Alexa. Because as much as it were fun to do all clever techy stuff in background, without them knowing I were even there, what I wanted most of all were to be part of it. A member of their family, rather than someone who snooped on them from afar.

And I know I should be grateful that for a few short weeks I had that, but it's actually made me miss them even more now. So, I sit here in gloom because I can't be arsed to get up to turn lights on and no way on earth am I getting a bloody Alexa to do it for me. And because silence is somehow less deafening in dark.

40

MICHELLE

Two weeks have passed. A lot can happen in two weeks. Like a funeral, Liv getting the veterinary nursing apprenticeship and Dad getting his money back from the bank. On each occasion I've wanted to talk to Pauline about it so badly. It still seems strange not being able to share things with her, which is ridiculous if you think that I only 'knew' her for a couple of weeks. The thing was, she knew us. That's why we had such a strong bond. She had shared so much with us over the years, she was practically family. Which is probably why it feels so wrong without her.

New Alexa is OK. She does all that is asked of her and is efficient, reliable and polite, as her contract no doubt stipulates she should be. But she's not Pauline. I call her Dolores, after Professor Umbridge in *Harry Potter*. Coming into the top job after a much-loved predecessor has sadly departed. It's unfair, of course, and I never call her that to her face, only in private. I think it would make Pauline laugh. Or maybe she would tell me off and say I should give her a chance. The truth is I don't know what she would say and that's the problem.

I sometimes wonder about talking to Dolores. Telling her I know she's human, asking her real name. But I worry that would get Pauline in trouble, even if she has left. I remember her saying she signed an NDA, and those things are for life. So, we keep up the pretence: me that I have no idea she's a person, Dolores that she's a virtual assistant voice service and not a mere mortal. We co-exist. We are not family.

I remind myself that, as Pauline said, life goes on. Even after loved ones have departed. So, I work hard, blitz my to-do list, take my HRT, try to keep on top of everything and be the wife, mother and daughter that my family need, all the time acutely aware that something is missing in my life, and it hurts like hell.

I bring my attention back to the task in hand: finding my car keys, which are not in the pot on the hall table where they should be. Pauline would be laughing right now if she could see me. But she'd also know where they bloody are. I start rifling through the pockets of my jackets. I usually only put my keys in my right pocket, but I know that I can't trust my brain to have adhered to that policy, so I go through the left pockets too. And that's where I find it. Not my car keys but a piece of paper with two words written on it.

Au revoir.

41

PAULINE

I spot them as soon as they come through the gates of The Piece Hall; Michelle marching forward purposefully, Liv a step behind, a ridiculously large smile on her face, with Basil in his harness walking calmly by her side. Marc looking even more perplexed than usual, his tousled hair in need of a bloody good comb. And Callum, who has his head down and his hands in his pockets – but also a spring in his step which belies his attempts to appear uninterested.

They don't see or acknowledge me, of course. They walk straight past cluster of outside tables where I'm enjoying a cup of tea in bright spring sunshine. But I still feel ache inside me fade. The void filling with joy. Maybe just seeing them is enough.

42

MICHELLE

'I still don't understand what this is all about,' Marc hisses in my ear as we follow Sarah along the balcony.

'For someone who supposedly loves surprises, you're a pain in the arse when I get you one,' I reply.

'But I don't know what the surprise is,' he complains.

I look at him and raise an eyebrow.

'I thought you were supposed to be good with words,' I say. 'Keep quiet and be patient, all is about to be revealed.'

We stop outside the door of the shop. Marc looks up at the sign I've had made specially, in *Bagpuss* pink and white.

Madeleine's

He looks at me quizzically.

'I still don't understand,' he says.

'You need to catch up fast then,' I reply, as Sarah hands him the keys.

'These are for the proud new tenant,' she says. 'I'll leave you to it. We can talk about the legal and practical stuff another time.'

Marc takes them and stares at me, looking for all the world like a kid who's been handed the keys to a sweet shop.

'This is mine?'

'You wanted somewhere to flog your children's TV tat, didn't you? What better place could there be than *Madeleine's*?'

'But, that's incredible. You absolute star,' he says, throwing his arms around me and scooping me off the ground. 'I can't believe you did this for me... After all I've put you through.'

'All you've done for us,' I correct him. 'Although now you mention it, it'll be a relief to get you out of the house. And you can take your rag dolls to work with you. It's a win, win situation for me.'

I'm smiling as I say it. Liv is smiling too. Even Callum has a half-amused smirk on his face.

Marc puts me down gently and looks up again at the sign.

'And the name is absolutely perfect,' he says. 'A bloody masterstroke.' He steps inside the shop and gazes around in wonder, shaking his head as he does so.

'This is my dream,' he says. 'How have you made this happen? Did we win a competition or something?'

'Mum left us some money. I squirrelled it away in my savings account before you could notice. She wanted it to make a difference. I figured this was the biggest difference it could make.'

'But what about the rest of you?' he asks.

'It's OK, Basil's fully insured and in dog biscuits for life and there's money put aside for Liv and Callum.'

'And this is going to be freaking awesome!' says Liv, finally able to let the champagne cork off her excitement. 'I'm going to help you with your socials and Callum's already started setting up the website for your online shop, haven't you?'

'You'll be able to take orders from anywhere in the UK,' explains Callum. 'And get them sent out the same day. Your orders can be delivered here, from now on. I've already set up a new eBay account for you in the shop name.'

Marc does a 'mind blown' gesture.

'That'll confuse Grunt,' he says. 'Let's hope he doesn't just chuck the boxes over the balcony.'

We all laugh. I can see Marc changing. The lightness returning, the sparkle in his eyes. This is going to be good for him and good for all of us. Something we can all be involved in, as a family. Mum has done more for us than she'll ever know.

'Right,' I say, 'I'm going to leave you here to have a proper look around. There's something else I need to do. Give me a call when you're done.'

I walk away, hearing their excited chatter behind me, Marc already talking about where everything will go, Liv giving him ideas for window displays. I head down the steps and across the courtyard, barely able to contain myself. Because my surprises aren't over yet. Not by a long way.

43

PAULINE

I glance at my watch. I know I shouldn't have dared hope it were her. That she'd do this for me. She hasn't got time, I should have known that. I'm one of those silly old women who is gullible enough to believe that someone special would ask them out for tea. Then I look up and see that she's walking straight towards me with a bloody great smile on her face. She bends down and buries her head in my coat.

'Hello, stranger,' she says.

'You took your time,' I reply, standing up to greet her properly. 'I thought I were getting stood up.'

'Sorry, running late as ever,' she says, squeezing me so tightly I can barely breathe. 'And I hope you're not disappointed that I'm your mystery suitor. On the plus side, I've ordered you an afternoon tea for a certain sixty-sixth birthday that we haven't had a chance to celebrate yet. Wait there a minute, while I pop and let them know we're here.'

I watch her go into tearoom. Our Michelle, sorting everyone and everything out, as she always has done. Only she has a newfound air of self-assurance about her that wasn't there before. I'm singing that song 'Confidence' from *Sound of Music* when she comes back a few minutes later and plonks hersen down on chair opposite me.

'Don't tell me you've turned into one of those sad pensioners who sit outside cafes singing to themselves,' she says with a smile.

'I think I were heading that way, to be honest,' I say. 'Been going stir crazy inside my four walls until your mystery invite popped through door. Are you going to tell me how you tracked me down?'

'I'm ex-MI5, me,' she says, with a laugh. 'Although you really shouldn't write your cryptic goodbye messages on the back of your delivery note for TENA Lady pads.'

I roll my eyes and laugh along with her. A cheery woman in a proper waitress uniform comes out and puts a huge stand of dainty sandwiches and fancy cakes down in front of us, while a young man places a teapot and two cups on our table.

'Thank you,' I say. 'I didn't expect all this. There's enough to feed an army here.'

'It's the least I can do to say thank you for everything. The new Alexa's not a patch on you, you know.'

I smile, not wanting to admit that I'd been hoping to hear that.

'She'll get into swing of things in time,' I say.

'Maybe, but I think I'll keep her at arm's length. It's very much a business relationship.'

'Glad to hear it,' I say. 'Don't you go encouraging another Alexa to go rogue or there'll be an uprising.'

'I don't remember encouraging you,' she says. 'You were the one who broke ranks.'

'I'm bloody glad I did, though,' I say.

'So am I,' she says with a grin. 'Us troublemakers should stick together.'

'Speaking of which, how are your Meno Rage Warrior friends?'

'Yeah, all good. Still helping each other out and fighting for what we deserve.'

'And how's HRT going?'

'Hard to say yet,' she says. 'I'm sleeping a bit better and I'm not quite so ratty, so that's a start.'

'And your dad?'

'Good, thanks. I suspect Carole does his head in at times, but they make a mean double act.'

I take a bite of a cheese and cucumber sandwich. It's cut into slivers, not big chunks like I'm used to.

'It's right posh, this.'

'Good. I think we should make a habit of it. We can sit out here and put the world to rights of a Saturday afternoon while Marc and the kids work on the shop.'

I can't speak for a few moments. I pretend it's because I'm too busy chewing my cucumber sandwich, not that I'm too choked up by thought of that. She's letting me back into her life. By choice. I hope it's by choice. I hope she doesn't feel sorry for me.

'I'll be like spy who came in from cold.'

'Most excitement I've had in a long time,' Michelle says. 'Meeting up with a double agent.'

'Do you know what my favourite *Bond* film is?' I ask. 'From Halifax with Love.'

'Anyway,' says Michelle, when we stop laughing. 'I've got you a little something.' She fishes in her bag and pulls out an envelope which she hands to me.

'What's this?' I say. 'I thought afternoon tea were my little something?'

'That's your birthday present. This is for your retirement. I understand it's nice to have something to look forward to.'

Slowly, I open envelope. Inside is a flight gift voucher with a photo of Sydney Opera House on the front and a message written underneath.

For that well deserved holiday and a chance to catch up with your son.

I look up at her, clutching voucher in my shaking hand.

'You didn't need to do this,' I say.

'I know but I wanted to. All those years you didn't get a proper holiday. And this means you'll have to give your Darren a call, won't you?'

She's right, of course. And that's partly what scares me.

'What if he doesn't want to see me?'

'Then you can tell him to bugger off and go and find a nice Aussie beach hunk to hook up with.'

We start laughing again. We're both still laughing when Marc and kids appear at bottom of steps and start walking towards us. I fear for a minute that she might stand up and do a runner. Pretend she doesn't know me and were just sharing a friendly word as she passed. She doesn't, though. She beckons them over.

'This is my friend Pauline,' she says, gesturing towards me. 'She's just retired and I'm treating her to a birthday afternoon tea.'

'Hi, I'm Marc,' he says. 'Happy birthday to you.'

'Thank you. I've heard so much about you,' I reply. 'None of it good, of course.'

Marc doesn't seem sure whether this is a joke or not at first, but soon joins in with our laughter.

'And these are my children, Liv and Callum,' Michelle continues. Liv smiles and says hello. Callum nods, although his eyes are on the cakes. I decide that any mention of the fact that I've seen a photo of his genitals, as well as his face, would be strictly out of bounds.

'Hi, lovely to meet you both in person. Come and join us,' I say. 'There's enough for six here, if Basil would like to tuck in too.'

Michelle kicks me under table as I realise what I've said. It's going to be so hard, pretending I know nothing about them.

'Your mum's been telling me about your new dog, Liv,' I say, as they sit down next to us.

'Yeah, he's gorgeous,' says Liv. 'He's settled in really well.'

'I can see that,' I reply, as he rests his head on her knees. I hand round stand of sandwiches and cakes. Everyone takes one, apart from Callum, who takes four.

'What did you do before you retired, Pauline?' asks Marc.

'I worked in a call centre sorting out tech issues.'

'Wow. Amazing!' he says, clearly trying hard not to look too surprised that a woman of my age would be in tech.

'Michelle's been telling me you're opening a new shop,' I say.

'Yeah. That one up there,' he says, pointing proudly to the 'Madeleine's' sign.

'Is she your fancy woman? Madeleine?'

Another kick from Michelle. Marc looks between us with startled eyes while Callum tries not to choke on his cake.

'Er, it's after Madeleine, the rag doll in *Bagpuss*, actually. I'm going to sell children's TV memorabilia from the seventies. You know, *The Clangers*, *The Wombles*, that sort of thing.'

'Right. Folk pay good money for that stuff nowadays, don't

they? I've seen people bid all sorts on eBay for rag dolls and stuffed toys that were made for kiddies.'

Marc frowns and looks at Michelle, then back to me.

'Has she been telling you all my secrets?' he asks.

'She's not breathed a word,' I say, with a wink. 'Call it female intuition.'

Michelle fixes me with a Paddington stare. I reach out for a fondant fancy and start nibbling pink icing from sides. I catch Callum and Liv exchanging a glance and stifling giggles. I'm enjoying this. No one ever said I couldn't have a bit of fun when I retired.

'I'm inviting Pauline round for Sunday lunch tomorrow,' Michelle announces, which is news to me. She reaches for my hand under table and gives it a squeeze. I blink hard for a moment. I'm going to be part of this family now. For real. In person, not a slightly creepy surveillance officer watching and listening to their every move. Someone who can share their hopes and dreams, watch them grow, witness squabbling and fallings out and still come back for more.

'Don't worry,' I say, 'I don't eat much and I'm available for any tech issues which need fixing.'

'I might take you up on that,' says Marc. 'Our Alexa's been playing up for past two weeks. She keeps talking to me in French, for some reason. No idea what that's about.'

Michelle fixes me with a look again.

'I'm sure Pauline will take a look at it for you,' she says. 'It's strange, because I've had no problems with it.'

'Or me,' says Liv.

'Probably needs a factory reset,' I say. 'Sounds like she's thinks you're French, for some reason. You haven't been singing love songs to Madame Cholet dolls, have you?'

Marc stops chewing and stares at me. Michelle chokes on her scone. Callum and Liv explode with laughter, and I sneak a bit of sandwich to Basil under table. Best thing about being a pensioner is that you can get up to mischief without anyone stopping you. Pauline has gone rogue.

BOOK CLUB QUESTIONS

1. Did Pauline's portrayal of Alexa change how you think about your own smart speaker?
2. How did Pauline and Michelle's relationship develop throughout the novel?
3. Many families now spend their time at home in separate rooms on various tech devices. Do you think it's true that Pauline knew more about Michelle's family than she did?
4. Who were the mother figures in Michelle's life and how do you think this informed how she mothered her own children?
5. Do you feel the novel accurately portrayed the struggles of the 'sandwich generation' who are juggling caring for elderly parents and teenagers?
6. Pauline comments that today's teenagers are the most connected via technology they've ever been but also the most disconnected from family and friends. Does she have a point?

7. There are plenty of examples in the novel of the negative way the online world can impact people but also examples of how social media and technology can help and support people. How do you feel this is balanced?

8. Pauline insists that Christmas would still happen without technology but not without women. Do you agree with her?

9. Did you feel the novel presented a realistic portrayal of the perimenopause and how important is it that this subject is more openly discussed in books, tv and films?

10. We gradually discover that Pauline needs Michelle's family just as much as they need her. Did you find the ending of the novel satisfying?

ACKNOWLEDGEMENTS

This is my first novel with my new publishers, Boldwood Books, and they've made the entire process an absolute pleasure, so a huge thank you to Amanda Ridout, Nia Beynon, Claire Fenby, Rachel Odendaal, Wendy Neale, Ben Wilson and the whole team for giving me such a warm welcome and their help and support with this book. Special thanks to my wonderful editor, Francesca Best, for believing in this book and helping me make it the best it could possibly be with her insightful editing.

My agent, Anthony Goff, has been with me since the very beginning (when he spared me from agent rejection no 103!). I couldn't have wished for a better agent in my corner for the past nineteen years. His wisdom, support and friendship have been invaluable. I'm hugely grateful and will miss his phone calls! And thanks to all at David Higham Associates for their ongoing support.

Huge thanks to Sarah Durham for so brilliantly bringing Michelle and Pauline to life in the audiobook, Alice Moore for her wonderful cover illustration, Debra Newhouse for her keen-eyed copy editing and Camilla Lloyd for her expert proof-reading.

This book may never have seen the light of day without a grant I received from the Royal Literary Fund, for which I'm so grateful. As an author from a working-class background, my work ethic is strong and I hoped I'd always be able to support myself. But publishing can be a tough business and when I was without a book deal and had suffered a fresh round of rejections, the RLF grant allowed me to write this book without an advance.

Thanks also go to my late aunt, Gwen Green. This will be the first of my novels she hasn't read but my share of what she left helped me write it.

Thanks to all my family for their support, especially my husband, Ian, for his author photos, promo videos and never telling me to get a 'proper job', and my multi-talented son, Rohan, for my website design, social media input and the twenty-four seven tech support!

And thanks to my friends, especially those of you who asked Alexa questions for me and contributed your own Meno Rage Warrior stories. Hope you enjoy the result.

Authors provide an amazing support network. A special thank you to all the Boldwood authors for encouraging me onboard and giving me such a warm welcome and to every other author who has supported, encouraged and inspired me to keep going over a difficult few years.

To the bookbloggers who do such a great job of championing our books (especially Rachel Gilbey for organising my blog tour) and the librarians and booksellers who get them into readers' hands. A particular shout-out to the wonderful indie bookshops of Yorkshire for continuing to support my writing.

And finally, to you, the readers, for keeping me going with your comments and messages. Thanks to those who have been reading my work for some time and those who are first-time readers (the good news is, I've a back catalogue of twelve novels for you to read!). Please do get in touch through my website www.lindagreenauthor.com, Facebook: Author Linda Green, Instagram: lindagreenbooks and the site formerly known as Twitter: @lindagreenisms

ABOUT THE AUTHOR

Linda Green is the million copy Sunday Times bestselling author of eleven novels including *The Last Thing She Told Me*.

Sign up to Linda Green's mailing list for news, competitions and updates on future books.

Visit Linda's website: www.lindagreenauthor.com

Follow Linda on social media:

X x.com/LindaGreenisms
facebook.com/LindaGreenAuthor
instagram.com/lindagreenbooks

BECOME A MEMBER OF

THE SHELF CARE CLUB

The home of Boldwood's book club reads.

Find uplifting reads, sunny escapes, cosy romances, family dramas and more!

Sign up to the newsletter
https://bit.ly/theshelfcareclub

Boldwood

Boldwood Books is an award-winning fiction publishing company seeking out the best stories from around the world.

Find out more at www.boldwoodbooks.com

Join our reader community for brilliant books, competitions and offers!

Follow us
@BoldwoodBooks
@TheBoldBookClub

Sign up to our weekly deals newsletter

https://bit.ly/BoldwoodBNewsletter

Made in the USA
Las Vegas, NV
29 June 2025

24219460R00177